PRAISE FOR *TRUSTING ALL I WANT*

Tim Sansone's book *Trusting All I Want* is a triumphant symphony of storytelling! His engaging tale is a smart, sexy, and tender adventure that immediately hooks readers into a compelling, emotional, and psychological journey. It creatively unfolds an intimate portrait of several engaging, relatable characters, with a sizzling connection of twists and turns that leave the reader wanting more page after page.

I especially appreciate that Tim's story touches on several important universal themes, including love vs. desire, self-awareness, exercising good judgment and self-control over our emotions, integrity in being authentic and true to ourselves vs. "society's definition of what's proper and who we can associate with," and the need to be less self-focused and more empathetic to understand another person's perspective. The genuine dialogue Tim expertly crafts throughout his story flows easily and naturally, bringing his characters brilliantly and authentically to life. I highly recommend this deliciously entertaining, "must-read" book!

Marlene Elizabeth, M.Ed.
Founder and Author of MONEYWINGS™
Certified Money Coach®

Trusting All I Want is a powerful and engaging glimpse into the complexity of relationships in the modern world. In his debut novel, Timothy C. Sansone explores love, desire, and unmet expectations, capturing the challenges that lovers (or would-be lovers) have in trying to get what they want from another person.

In my work, I see men and women suffering from an inability to understand each other, and Tim gives us direct access into the inner emotional lives of his characters that is both fun and insightful. The captivating story reads like a thriller in which I found myself engulfed and carried away. Enjoy!

Kimi Avary
Relationship Navigation Specialist
Bestselling Author, *Incredible Life* and *The Grandmother Legacies*

Tim Sansone puts you smack in the middle of an oft-misunderstood contemporary world in his debut novel, *Trusting All I Want*. He uses tight dialogue, intriguing relationship struggles, and masterful insight to pull you deeper into the lives of Lana, a sophisticated but struggling young Chicagoan, and Tom, a burgeoning law partner. If you ever lived through your 20s, are going through them now, or are about to, this book will offer a "fly on the wall" view of what it means to find yourself. It's more than the generational struggle among millennials, GenXers, and boomers. It's a treatise on what everyone faces as we progress through life's many phases. Entertaining and enlightening, this a great read.

Jeanne E. Alford
Author, *Three Magic Questions to Instantly Improve Communications*
Co-Author, *Bloom Where You Are Planted and Shine*
Co-Author, *Step Forward and Shine*

Trusting All I Want is a fast-paced, deep-dive "tell all" into the relational frolics and pitfalls of what Attachment Theory calls "avoidant attachment." Every chapter offers a profound, daring glimpse into the psyche of leading avoidant characters like Lana Delacroix and Tom Edwards. Resistance, distance and drama ensue as the plot unfolds and the four main characters struggle to understand their moves and countermoves with each other. Intriguing subplots reveal why so many relationships fail today, rather than thrive into the love everyone deserves. All the traps of a "me-first" mentality are exposed until one bold character dares to offer something hitherto unseen by everyone: an emphasis on "us." The denouement teasingly shows how lasting love can be invited into our lives. If you want to read a fast-paced, attachment psycho-drama that just might help you understand avoidant versus secure attachment styles, read this wonderful novel.

Gary D. Salyer, Ph.D.
Author, *Safe to Love Again: How to Release the Pain of Past Relationships and Create the Love You Deserve*

Trusting All I Want is a well-written novel, with three-dimensional characters who capture you and draw you in as the story unfolds. Lana, Tom, Jill, and Rudy come to life as you read each page of the opening chapters. I started reading this book and just could not put it down—in fact, I finished it in one sitting! I love the storyline and how Tim develops his plot with expertly crafted dialogue. It is the perfect read on a rainy day, or to curl up with by a fireplace, or just to open up and dive into when it's "me-time."

Teresa Hawley Howard
International Bestselling Author and Publisher
WOM Enterprises
teresa@takeactionwithteresa.com

Trusting All I Want

A NOVEL

Timothy C. Sansone

Trusting All I Want
Timothy C. Sansone
Women's Success Novels, LLC

Published by Women's Success Novels, LLC, St. Louis, Missouri

Cover and Interior Design: Davis Creative, DavisCreative.com

Library of Congress Cataloging-in-Publication Data

Names: Sansone, Timothy C., author.
Title: Trusting all I want : a novel / Timothy C. Sansone.
Description: St. Louis, MO : Women's Success Novels, LLC, [2019] | Series:
    [Trusting ... Being ... Doing]
Identifiers: ISBN 9781733594707 (paperback) | ISBN 9781733594714 (hardback)
    | ISBN 9781733594721 (ebook)
Subjects: LCSH: Women college students--Illinois--Chicago--Fiction. | Asian
    American women--Illinois--Chicago--Fiction. | Self-actualization (Psychology)
    in women--Fiction. | City and town life--Illinois--Chicago--Fiction. | Chicago
    (Ill.)--Fiction. | BISAC: FICTION / Women. | FICTION / Asian American. |
    FICTION / City Life.
Classification: LCC PS3619.A56746 T78 2019 (print) | LCC PS3619.A56746
    (ebook) | DDC 813/.6--dc23

Library of Congress Control Number: 2019900379

2019

to my wife
Xiaohong Sherrie Zeng

Acknowledgments

The story of Lana, Tom, Jill, and Rudy, and the world they inhabit, exist only through the generosity of dozens of family members, friends, and colleagues who inspired, encouraged, and advised me along the way.

I have striven to list below, in alphabetical order by first name, everyone who contributed to the effort in some way over the last four and a half years. I know I may have forgotten to list some of you, and I ask that you accept my apology if I did.

If there is anything I learned during this process, it's that writing and producing a novel will work best when you have a great team and a large group of supporters behind you. I am blessed to have both. To you who gave of your time, experience, or expertise in making this book possible, please accept my warmest gratitude.

Tim Sansone,
From a train bound for St. Louis from Chicago,
January 17, 2019

Abby Militzer
Angela LaRocca Hochman
Aprille Trupiano
Carrie Burggraf
Cathy Davis
Elizabeth Amy Gerard
Elizabeth Niven
Gabriella Lock Cesarone
Heather Crider
Jack Girardi
Jamie Bracewell

continued

Jasmine Chen
Jim Canada
Jim Mosquera
John Gilbert
John Sandberg
Joseph Muller
Josh Hickey
Julia Gray
Kevin Reder
Kyle Haubrich
Lakeshia Ekeigwe
Lisa York
Liz Kroll
Marilyn Crosby Wang
Maura Fox
Najah Fennoy
Nancy Mills
Rebecca Hall Gruyter
Rebecca Rezaei
Rickelle Pimentel
Roberta Moore
Samantha Rhoden
Sara Kuanfung
Scott Crosby
Sonja Shin
Stella Xiuhui Yang
Stephanie Niu
Steve Murphy
Steve Turner
Stuart Hartzell
Susan Storey
Teresa Hawley-Howard
Terry McHugh
Xueqing Linda Ji
Yi Sun

Table of Contents

FOREWORD

PART ONE: DISCLOSURE   1

  1: Lana   3

  2: Jill   15

  3: Tom   21

  4: Nothing Wrong   29

  5: Rudy   35

  6: The Invitation   41

  7: Lana's Haven   51

  8: Public Display   59

  9: Chaz   65

  10: The Garden   77

  11: Repercussions   87

PART TWO: SEARCH   93

  12: Cousin   95

  13: Gameplan   105

  14: Grandma   119

  15: Hyde Park   127

  16: Appeal   133

  17: Invalid Hypothetical   147

  18: The Beach   155

  19: About My Father   167

  20: All I Want   173

  21: Both Sides   181

  22: Trial   193

PART THREE: DISCOVERY   **201**

   23: The Maze   203

   24: Barbara   209

   25: The Salad   215

   26: Trust   225

   27: The Meeting   243

   28: Getting Tight   255

   29: Traveling Alone   261

   30: Desire and Love   269

   31: The E-Mail   279

   32: Ones That Give   285

   33: Pats on the Back   291

   34: Commencement   295

About the Author   309

Suggested Questions for Book Clubs   311

Foreword

There is something special about connecting with someone the first time you meet. It could be the way the person smiles, laughs, or makes you do the same, for a moment forgetting about the problems of the day. I am not talking about manufactured merriment that rings hollow; rather, the lingering feeling is one of veritable contentment. The first time I spoke with Tim, I likened it to connecting with a kindred spirit I could relate to on multiple levels, transcending gender and race.

I was excited when I learned about this book and am deeply honored to share it with all of you. *Trusting All I Want* explores the complexities of multigenerational relationships and our perception of love, security, and acceptance. In today's society, we highly value privacy, yet we want transparency and partners who exhibit vulnerability and compassion. We want space, but we don't want a distant partner. We want love on our terms, with our needs at times encroaching upon our partner's desires to such an extent that things become irreconcilable based on the strongly entrenched ideas, beliefs, and opinions of each partner.

Tim deftly explores the complexities of relationships and behavioral nuances that all of us can relate to and experience in our own lives. I consider this a "water-cooler" book, the kind that you gather around the office water cooler and talk about with engaged colleagues to discuss how the story unfolds, debating the actions of each character.

As a Global Personal and Business Transformation Strategist, International Bestselling Author, TV/Radio Host, Empowerment Leader, and Speaker I am always seeking ways to help people live their best lives as their authentic selves. When we live authentically without the burden of societal expectations or personal fears, we can explore what makes us truly happy and how we can attain lasting fulfillment. I love how Tim masterfully takes readers on a journey that makes them critically examine their long-held beliefs with the scrutiny of a master jeweler looking for defects in a polished gem.

I know you will be enthralled by this book and come to love the characters, because each of them speaks to something innate in all of us. I hope his book will encourage you to bring another perspective to your relationships and the people you encounter in the future.

I know you will enjoy Tim's masterful storytelling, relate to the characters, and feel encouraged to think about your own journey and its impact on others. I invite you to enjoy *Trusting All I Want* by my friend Tim Sansone.

Adrian Jefferson Chofor,
Global Personal and Business Transformation Strategist

Author, *Aspire to Your Greatness!*
CEO, Aspire2Inspire Transformational Practice
www.adrianjeffersonchofor.com
connect@adrianjeffersonchofor.com

PART ONE:

DISCLOSURE

$$\boxed{1}$$

Lana

Pulsing flashes of light reflected sharply off the front grille of her convertible, demanding that she return to her side of the pavement. But double parkers had blocked half the street, and she was almost there.

Horn replaced high beams, yet Lana Delacroix did not stop or slow. *In a game of chicken, she who controls her nerves wins*, she knew.

And she always won.

This latest win came just in time, too: As the approaching SUV swerved to avoid her, Lana saw to her right, at the end of the block, her intended destination: The Southside Ballroom.

It greeted her with bells and clanging mechanical sounds as she walked inside, her soul whirring with a matching level of energy.

"I'm signing you up for our pinball tournament," a clipboard-toting server told her.

"No thanks," Lana replied, pushing past him while dusting powdery snow off her black full pleated scuba skirt. She spotted one of the guy-friends in her collection and reached for a casual embrace.

"Glad you made it. Wasn't sure if the forecast would keep you away," he said.

"Rudy would have cried if I didn't show up."

He chuckled with a hint of apprehension and carefully turned over a brim-high craft brew: "Here, this is for you. I'll be back to talk at you later."

The guy was useful; having the frame of a bodybuilder didn't hurt, though she preferred to simply absorb his energy and optimism. The occasional free beer was nice, too.

Taking a few steps toward the adjoining room of buzzing and chiming, she noticed the complimentary buffet Rudy had promised her. A local startup he worked for was celebrating its pre-launch party. As she looked over the offerings, an amplified voice sprang from tall speakers standing in two corners of the room.

"Tom and Rudy, you're at *Terminator 2*," the server with the clipboard announced, shuffling his hands in a circular motion like a stage manager, inviting the performers to move beyond the curtains.

Two men approached a machine whose backglass featured the stylized face of Arnold Schwarzenegger, half synthetic skin and half metal.

Lana recognized the shorter of the two players: her former boyfriend, the eternally helpful Rudy Santana.

The other man—Tom presumably—firmly placed a hand on the machine and with his other sharply pressed a button twice. A steel ball appeared, ready to be launched. Grabbing the gun that substituted for a plunger, he propelled the ball into the playfield.

Flippers, bumpers, lights, kick-out holes, and sounds absorbed his attention; his assurance, purposeful style, and out-of-place polish drew in hers.

The guy had to be in his midthirties at least, she surmised. Probably 5'10" and a lean 170. No wedding ring. *Too bad*, she thought, preferring a challenge tonight. But the hipster-friendly dive bar/pin-ball arcade wasn't exactly a place for older, married types.

Then again, the slicked-back dark hair atop a mostly pale baby face, the navy-blue Brooks Brothers blazer over a white dress shirt, and the light brown Italian trousers held up by a flashy belt weren't exactly what you'd see around this place, either. The only thing unkempt about this guy was the Viking-red goatee he'd let grow for a few days.

Lana walked up behind him, approaching from his right side. She leaned in slightly, looking over his shoulder and causing his head to turn just enough to make out her shape—without causing him to lose track of the ball.

"I'm Lana."

"Tom," he responded, without looking in her direction. The ball remained in play.

"Are we having fun tonight?"

"Haven't played one of these in ages," he replied.

He can do better than that, she thought.

"What do you like to do…Tom, was it? Sorry, I forget names easily, unless someone really impresses me."

"Well, Lana," he began, adding a dry pause and ignoring her dig, "I like to meet inspiring people."

"Am I inspiring?"

"Who knows…I guess we'll see."

That's more like it, she thought.

He leaned toward the machine and kept the ball under his control a bit longer. Eventually it left the playfield, at which point he stepped aside, signaling for Rudy to take his turn.

Lana kept her place near the table. Tom turned to face her and saw a smile he thought was amiable enough.

"You're staring," she said.

"Hardly. In what dictionary is a half-second glance called a stare?"

Oh you're good, she thought. *But I can see right through you.*

Lana said something inaudible in reply; the music from the bar was louder now. Tom noticed it was a little after 11:00 p.m. He touched the back of his right ear lobe with a cupped hand, holding it there as he shrugged his shoulders.

She moved closer, gently pressing the right side of her petite chest against the right side of his, holding it there, and placing her mouth right behind the ear he'd just released.

"You were staring. Admit it," she insisted.

He spoke louder so his voice would carry better. "Let's be precise. I took a gander at your face. Where I'm supposed to look."

Yeah, no need to look when you can feel, she thought.

Satisfied with herself, Lana placed a couple of inches between them. "Let me ask you something."

He again touched his ear. He'd obviously heard her that time but was up for another unsubtle move being made upon him. "Huh?"

She was enjoying the game. Granting his unstated wish, she again pulled her shoulders back, stood erect, and pressed her side into him. "How old do you think I am?"

Slowly lowering his head, he eyed her lean, model-height frame. Above her black skirt was a sleeveless gray shirt atop a white camisole. She had finely trimmed eyebrows that thickened at her temples; her eyes hinted of Eurasian heritage yet were green. He knew she was college age, probably nearing the end of her days on campus.

"Seventeen. Shouldn't you be home with Mommy and Daddy?"

"Ha. I'm twenty-one actually. I finish college next fall."

"A college girl, huh? You do seem kind of smart."

You have no idea, she thought.

"Kind of, huh?" she replied, crossing her arms.

"Need more data," he countered.

And you want it, she knew.

Lana pushed his shoulder. He stiffened, assuming an unflinching stance.

You liked that, she thought.

"*Lana*," Rudy said with a slight tone of derision while looking in her direction. "You're up, Tom."

Tom was somewhat enjoying the banter and paid a bit less attention to the pinball game. After a couple of minutes he let the ball pass one of the flippers and stepped away from the machine.

Her guy-friend who'd given her the beer reappeared, observing, "You've met someone."

"I have," Lana replied. "Kurt, this is Tom."

"Be careful with this one," Kurt advised, placing a hand on Tom's shoulder.

"Yeah, what do you think might happen if you hang around *me*, Tom?" she asked.

"I'm sure I'd find myself in trouble soon enough."

"That's because you want to fuck me."

Tom leaned down slightly to whisper something in her ear. "I wouldn't be so sure."

She made a fist and landed the bottom of it on his shoulder. She then pulled him a few feet away from the table, toward a corner of the room.

"Oh, I'm not only sure, I'm right," she said. "After all, I figured you out in ten seconds."

"Really? Then you know what I'm going to do next."

"What's that?"

"Get you in my car."

She paused. A smile slowly crept onto her face. "Let me tell Rudy I need to run an errand, and I'll grab my coat. I'll meet you at the front door."

* * *

The streets of Chicago by then were slippery but passable. The first snow of the season coated the city with a thick, powdery reminder of youthful wonder at a perfect time: Christmas was just days away.

As Lana and Tom exited the bar, a strong gust swept down upon them, making the falling snow seem to hover momentarily before being propelled directly into their warm faces. The powder turned wet almost upon impact with their skin. Tom instinctively snatched hold of his scarf.

"Close your eyes for a moment," he told Lana.

She looked at him in deadpanned silence, one eyebrow raised. Two or three seconds passed before she shrugged her shoulders and shook her head, allowing her eyelids to close. Tom applied one end of his scarf to her eyes, nose, and mouth, followed by her cheeks, chin, and forehead.

"That one got you good," he observed, grabbing the other end of the scarf to wipe his own face.

"You planned that, right? That we'd walk out and then boom— Tom to the rescue. But if I had the scarf and you didn't, what do you think would have happened?"

"That's easy: You'd have wiped your own face."

Damn right, she thought.

"Of course. Now where's this car of yours?"

A delivery truck puttered along the street, temporarily delaying their crossing. After the truck passed, Lana spotted an S550 opportunely parked less than a hundred feet away.

She was impressed.

The lines separating the hood from the grille revealed the sharp contrast created by the temporary white blanket of snow and the permanent black sheen beneath it.

"This you?" she asked, pointing directly at the car and grabbing his left arm as she carefully stepped into the street.

"Of course it is," Tom replied.

"Yeah, it's a little out of place…as are you."

"Hmmm," he muttered, looking at his left arm. "Very quaint of you to fasten yourself to me like that."

"Oh, I'm just making sure that if I fall down I'm taking you with me."

Tom chuckled and started to open the passenger door for her; she placed a hand on his chest, directing him away from the vehicle and showing herself inside. She closed the door behind her. Tom nodded his head in amusement and walked around the front end to open the other door, half expecting to find her in the driver's seat.

"I see you've relented," he remarked, seeing her still sitting as a passenger. He situated himself behind the wheel and felt the cold leather seat enveloping him.

"Don't get your hopes up," she said. Lana didn't expect anything to happen. *But occasionally they will fool you*, she thought. *Better to make a few things clear early.*

"Fierce and pretentious—a deadly combination," he commented.

"Does being able to take care of myself make me fierce?" she asked, crossing her arms and rocking herself as she could not hide the chill.

"Oh, you want some heat?" Tom asked.

Avoiding my question, she thought, waiting a few moments then looking at him impatiently.

"You need help getting her started?" she wondered.

Tom chuckled then fired up the engine, turned on both seat warmers, put the car into gear, and pulled into the snowy street. The stoplight at the approaching corner turned to yellow then red as Tom easily brought the sedan to a safe stop.

"So."

"So," Lana mimicked.

"You from around here, Lana?"

"No, St. Louis originally. And I didn't get an answer to my question."

"Right. But *can* you take care of yourself?" he asked.

"Would I be in here with you if I couldn't?"

"But you said—"

"—I said don't get your hopes up," she replied.

"Yeah, and back there at the bar you *also* said I want…"

He paused.

Aww, he can't say it, she thought.

"You *do*," she insisted.

"Do *what*?"

"Don't play dumb, Tom. I know what you want. And *I'm* the one who's pretentious? Tell me, which is more frustrating to you: what I know or what I *said*?"

"Wow. You are really something."

"Of course I am," she said. "Would I be in here if I weren't? I appreciate the invitation, by the way."

Another pause.

"The light is green now," she noted.

He looked over at her then turned on the satellite radio. A songstress began to recount the tale of a starlet singing in a garden for a man whose soul was both sweet and blood red, as the starlet wondered whether anyone else could put up with her—and her ways.

"And where are *you* originally from, Tom?"

"We'll get to me later. You have family down in St. Louis?"

"My grandmother, yes."

"And you live here now…on the one hand a college girl, but on the other, probably living with your parents, right? They're waiting for you back home somewhere west or north of here?"

"It's kind of—"

"—a long story? But one you've told *all* the boys, no doubt. I'm listening."

"Ha. You can stop with the weak digs."

Say one thing for him, she thought, *the guy can keep up with me… for the most part.* And Lana *did* want to let him in on some things. With many guys, though, learning those things inevitably led them to make wildly wrong assumptions about her.

Now looking directly at Tom, Lana was not ready to open herself to the drawing of more assumptions—not now, anyway. Moving her eyes away from his face and down toward the steering wheel, she noticed the ring on his right hand. Set in the ring's center was a large blue stone featuring a woman's arm holding a scale.

"You're a lawyer," she noted, not realizing he'd just stopped along a street not far from where they had started half an hour earlier.

"You don't miss anything."

She smiled to herself.

"So Lana, before I let you go, tell me something interesting about you that I otherwise wouldn't know."

"OK. So my grandfather was from Vietnam. He came here in his twenties after the French left, before the U.S. came in."

"Mmmm, yes. There was *something* about the way you looked when I first saw you."

"You mean it wasn't my charm and charisma? Wait, don't answer that. Anyway, so you get off on Asian chicks. Good to know, and good for you. And hey, I'm glad twenty-five percent is still plenty for you. Now do I get to hear where you're from, Tom?"

"*Are* you enough for me? Much less *plenty*? I doubt it. Maybe grow up a little more first, then we'll talk. But to answer your question, I'm from Bellwood."

"Wow, I'll pretend you didn't say that. And Bellwood, huh? Just a small-town boy."

"Livin' in a lonely world."

"I like that," she said.

"You can thank Mr. Steve Perry."

"Don't Stop Believin'?"

"That's right."

"So you were a little out of place in Bellwood too, weren't you?"

"Our family figured we helped contribute to its diversity," Tom said with a chuckle.

Lana smiled at Tom for a moment, then said, "We should get back."

"Step ahead of you. We're actually just a few hundred feet away. See that building ahead?"

Tom felt his cellphone vibrating. "Let me get this real quick."

He swept two fingers across the front of his phone, which he held in front of him in his right palm. A voice spoke through the earpiece grill, loudly enough for Lana to make out the words while staring at the floorboard.

"Want to come over?" the voice asked.

"Hadn't thought about it. You do have me at a good time," he responded.

"Really? That's encouraging."

"Yeah, I went for a little drive in the snow. I'm somewhere on the South Side," he said.

"It's a little cold. I could use some companionship," the voice responded.

"Grab an extra blanket and a good book then."

There was a long pause on the phone. "What?"

"Just playing," he said. "I'll drop by. Probably in the next hour."

"OK, well, be careful."

"Yep. Later, Jill."

Tom pressed a red button on the screen and looked over to Lana. "Shall we go back inside?"

Lana did not immediately answer. She felt the soft seat beneath her, tilted her head back a bit, and looked through the top of the windshield. Soft, heavy flakes fell from the sky, painting stars on the glass.

A fan of cars, particularly ones of this make, Lana took a moment to admire the sweeping design of the dashboard. Placing the tip of a forefinger just below her lower lip, she peered through the passenger window and grinned.

"In a hurry to hook up with Jill?"

"Out!" Tom ordered, pointing toward the opposite door.

2

Jill

The arch above the glass door and the lamps on either side could have greeted a churchgoer. Instead they greeted Tom, who strode into the lobby and removed his wet scarf. The three-block walk to the Gold Coast high-rise was coldly invigorating and a small relief following several days of intense preparation for an upcoming *Daubert* hearing in federal court.

The elevator doors opened. Down the hallway to his left was Jill, who stood on a dark wooden Zurigo chair outside the door to her apartment. Her modest, white-polka-dotted-on-red dress covered her shoulders and ended just below her knees. At thirty-six she looked at least ten years younger, and had a petite figure that was unusually curvy for an Asian woman. Her long black hair, neatly parted down the middle, contrasted with the silky white dots on her dress. She wore little makeup because she had little need for it. Her full, unadorned eyebrows matched the fullness of her lips and figure.

"Need a little help with that, Ms. Nguyen?" Tom inquired, as he extended his hand to ease her return to the carpeted floor.

With her other hand she thrust a wreath into his chest.

"Yes. See that nail there?"

"You drive that yourself?" he asked.

"It's painted the same color as the door trim."

"Ah, so that would be a 'no.' Anyway, I think I can manage hanging this for you."

Jill shifted her hips to the right, propelling her around Tom and the chair and through the door, which slowly closed behind her.

"Oh, so you got what you wanted and now you're done with me? I see how it is. Well fine, I'm keeping the chair then," he announced, as he centered the holiday wreath and leaned back to admire his handiwork.

The door cracked open, revealing Jill's face.

"Oh, that's right, you were wanting to come in."

"*You* were wanting *me* to come in. Although, if you've changed your mind, I'll look into other options for the evening."

Jill opened the door completely, placed an arm against the wall, and leaned toward it.

"I don't think so. Get in here."

"With or without the chair?"

Jill tried hard to conceal a slight grin.

* * *

He'd known Jill since becoming a partner two years ago at a large law firm located in Chicago's West Loop. There he'd managed to find his place. He had his quirks and wasn't ashamed to admit the fact.

But in the profession of law—and especially in the domain known as "BigLaw"—rules, precedents, conventions, and expectations were less forgiving of rough edges.

Indeed, a dozen years earlier, "Tom, you're an oddball" was the matter-of-fact statement the head of litigation at Tom's previous firm had made shortly before unceremoniously transferring him from a suburban branch office to the firm's Chicago headquarters. Less than a year after that transfer, Tom was in her office again, summoned to be told his services were no longer needed.

"I just bought a house," he muttered. "I realize that's not the firm's problem, it's mine, but—"

"—We'll pay you through the end of February, Tom. Good luck to you," she replied, interrupting what she didn't need—or want—to hear.

Fortunately that setback happened in the early 2000s, when employment in the law business was still easily had. In Tom's case, he soon had a temporary position performing document review at the largest law firm in Chicago. That job soon led to permanent employment at his current firm in mid-2002, when it was still mid-sized.

Everything had worked out perfectly on the surface, regardless of what his old firm may have thought of him. Even so, less than a month after starting at his new position, Tom crashed emotionally. The fact he'd been fired had caught up to him, despite the fact he had a new, fulltime, well-paying job.

For the first time in over a decade—the first time since leaving the Air Force Academy in 1992—Tom was reminded that overcommitting to an employer or a career had its pitfalls.

In addition, for the first time in over a decade he recognized he needed professional help.

What he was feeling was unfamiliar, though. For the first time, he understood what depression felt like. It was a feeling he feared, and to preclude its return he'd spend the next decade undercommitting.

* * *

"Am I ever going to make an honest man out of you, Mr. Edwards?" Jill asked, touching Tom's nose with the tip of her finger as she turned over to his side of the queen-size bed.

"Sorry, what?" he replied, surreptitiously looking for the alarm clock.

"Lifelong bachelors have a lower life expectancy, are in poorer health, and have less verve later in life," she asserted, lifting her smartphone off her nightstand. "So says this story I read yesterday on Flipboard."

"So what you're saying is, they just need to lock in a good woman."

"Exactly."

"Well, I've already done that and am finding life to be pretty good, actually," he responded, propping himself up on one elbow.

"Who says you've got me locked in?" she demanded to know, throwing one of her extra pillows at him. He deftly dodged it, ducking beneath the sheets.

"Well, there's this: After two years, you're still with me. You haven't run off yet. Must be doing *something* right."

"You have your uses."

"And besides, who says I'm not an honest man already?"

"It's just an expression."

"No, really. I mean, how did the notion come to be that tying the knot creates honesty? There is nothing inherently dishonest about being single while male."

"Being married to a good woman makes you a better man."

"*Does* it now? I would say being *with* a good woman, being *close* to a good woman—those things can make a man better."

"Without a commitment, how long will that last? When you have those things, why not make them permanent?"

"This is where we look at things in a different light. If something is going well, why not just go with the flow?"

"There's something about forever that's more appealing."

"Forever is uncompromising, Jill. Putting everything into something—or someone—may never be enough."

Jill sat up, placing a pillow behind her as she stared out the window. The snow still fell. She wondered how many inches she would see at Oak Street Beach if she were to walk past this morning. *Go with the flow*, he'd said. But how many years was she supposed to wait?

"There are some things that aren't forever, Tom, which every good woman knows. Time takes things away from women sooner than it does men."

"True. Which is why it can be helpful to live in the present, appreciating what we have. And like they say, good things happen to people who—"

"—I appreciate what I have," Jill interjected. "A commitment would make me appreciate you more."

"We can talk about 'more' later. And are we really that different, Jill? So far, you're a lifelong bachelorette. To be fair, you could be asked some of the same questions I've been asked."

"I'm picky. I don't settle. Knowing how to pick them is vital to a woman's sanity."

"Men need to be good at it too."

"Yeah. So do you doubt yourself?" she asked, leaning back and bracing herself with her hands.

"What do you mean?" Tom wondered, as the sheets fell away from her neck. Unconsciously, he took hold of them, pulling them in his direction.

"I mean, you picked me. You're supposed to be good at this, right? Two years and you're doing alright for yourself, wouldn't you say?"

She waved a hand in front of Tom's face. He didn't move for several seconds.

"You're staring," she said.

"Yes, at that lovely pendant."

"Ha," Jill responded, pulling the sheets away from Tom and back against her neck.

3

Tom

"**I**'m *two minutes away.*"

Tom saw the text message pop up on his phone. Sitting at a table at the Wigwam in the Union League Club, he had the *Wall Street Journal* open to a story about Typhoon Haiyan in the Philippines. He wore a gray patterned sport coat over a lightly starched white dress shirt and black single-pleat wool dress pants.

Lana arrived, smiling and giving Tom a hug as he stood to greet her. A week earlier, they'd exchanged contact information outside the Southside Ballroom. She had suggested keeping in touch; as for Tom, he remained quite curious about this confounding, exotic creature who seemed entirely too clever and assured for her own good—or his.

In other words, he knew better…and yet…

"Hungry?" he asked her.

"I kind of am, actually."

"Do you eat red meat?"

"I love it," she replied.

"Good," he said, turning toward the nearby server. "Rob, I'll have the steak appetizer."

"Medium rare, Mr. Edwards?"

"Yes, thanks." Turning toward Lana, he said, "I'm not terribly hungry. The steak comes chopped into small slices, so we can share."

"Anything for the lady?" Rob inquired.

"I'll go with a cabernet," said Lana.

Tom refolded the newspaper. "Find your way here OK?" he asked.

"Your directions were adequate."

This was Lana's first time at the Union League Club; she said she liked to try new things. Tom hadn't offered to pick her up from her apartment, preferring to have her come to him on his territory.

"We didn't talk much about you last time. Tell me more about Tom," she said.

"I don't know enough about you yet. Tell me more about Lana."

"Well, I know you joked about 'Mommy and Daddy' last time. But I didn't tell you anything about my parents, did I?"

"No. Let me guess: daddy issues?"

Lana opened her mouth wide and stared at him incredulously. He had a slight grin and had tilted his head a bit to his left, looking like a confused dog.

"Actually, I've never met my father. I don't know who he is. Happy?"

Tom immediately raised a hand in front of his chest and briefly dropped his head. "Look, I'm sorry. I, uh…"

When he looked back up, she gave him a serious stare. Satisfied to see his reaction, she then let out a loud laugh, covered her mouth, and pointed at him.

"Wow, went kind of lame on me there. Get a grip. I'm a big girl."

Tom could only chuckle. "Well *alrighty* then! How about Mom? Must have been a strong personality, I'm sure."

"Wait. Let me tell the story. Save your questions for the end, please."

"Objection, Your Honor. Calls for a narrative."

She gave him a brief look. "Is that a real objection?"

"It is, actually. But I'll withdraw it. Go ahead."

A few moments passed as she gathered her thoughts. "As I was growing up, especially after four or five, my grandparents were a big part of my life. They became my legal guardians when I was in eighth grade."

"Why is that?" Tom asked.

"Nancy—my mother—had paranoid schizophrenia. It got worse as I got older."

"*Man.* Why do I feel like the other shoe hasn't dropped yet?"

"Hey, you're kind of rude," she said. "Has anyone ever told you that?"

"Yes, and plenty more. Anyway, about your mom and her condition. Can't that be treated with therapy and medication?"

"It can. She was stubborn, though, and would stop taking the medicine. Sometimes she'd go to therapy, but less and less over time. Eventually she stopped altogether."

"OK, now you said your grandparents eventually got custody. Family law is not my specialty, but I know it takes a lot to strip someone of parental rights. What happened?" he asked.

"Her paranoia turned her against me. She became abusive."

Tom said nothing, but was clearly interested.

Lana noticed and added, "Not physically, but emotionally. I haven't seen her since she left the psychiatric unit at a hospital in St. Louis."

"How old were you then?"

"I was thirteen," she replied. "I actually had to testify against her at the involuntary commitment hearing."

Dumbfounded, Tom took a moment to consider what he'd just heard as Lana went on to explain how she'd moved forward from that point without her birth parents. She'd known one who was no longer in her life; she sensed and believed in the existence of the other—one she'd never known.

She knew there was a profound difference between not having a father and not knowing one's father. She felt she had a father: someone who was part of her, albeit unconnected. She had made finding him a large part of what she described as her journey. She wanted to know where she came from and who that part of her was.

Having faith in her father's existence was easier and more "rationally idealistic" (as she put it) than many might have thought.

Credit for having this faith went largely to her grandparents. Their wholehearted acceptance of Lana into their lives and into their home presaged a time and place where her father, she hoped, would do the same.

"Again, I'd like to know more about you," Lana said.

"What do you want to know?"

"Tell me something you don't tell most people."

Tom leaned back, crossing his arms. He sensed that hers was a well-trodden story she'd told many times. It was comfortable, like an old pair of jeans, and he believed it. But was the interest shown by the young woman real? She was now attempting to turn the tables, inviting him to make himself vulnerable for the promise of human connection.

"OK, here's one: Being a lawyer wasn't my first choice."

"What was your original plan?" she asked.

"Air Force pilot."

"Why did you change your mind?"

"Actually, my mind was the problem," he said.

Lana appreciated Tom's candor. At the surface, he looked every bit the well-put-together fellow, the successful professional. She knew well, however, that these things revealed little of substance. To know someone—to know oneself—required jumping into the deep end and plumbing the bottom.

"Your mind, huh? Some kind of mental break?" she asked.

"Maybe."

"How old were you at the time?"

"Almost your age; I was twenty," he answered.

"You were in college."

"That's right, at the Air Force Academy, actually."

"What was that like?" she asked.

"What, having to leave the Academy?"

"No, the break. What do you remember about it?"

"I didn't say I had one. But I do remember a lot. Vividly."

"Lots of people have experiences like you did, Tom. They just didn't talk about it as much before as they do now. Tell me about yours."

He uncrossed his arms and looked past Lana at a television that was tuned to a cable news show.

"I'm interested to know because it relates to what I'm studying. I'm double-majoring in psychology and finance at UIC. In my psych classes, we've discussed that many people have a serious episode in their late teens or early twenties."

Her interest in such details didn't surprise Tom. Unlike Lana, most other people had little personal experience with or around mental illness, and for various reasons perhaps preferred to remain ignorant.

Understanding came easier when a family member, co-worker, or friend had a condition or sought treatment.

"Well, I was dating a fellow cadet at the time; we'd known each other for almost two years. She was born in Vietnam, actually, and came over when she was six."

"Got it—another Asian chick. Let me guess: your first?"

"First one I dated? Yes," he replied.

"So was she with you when you experienced whatever 'it' was?"

"For part of it, yeah. I remember looking up into the sky at night. We were sitting next to each other on the grass, and I saw the stars moving around in space."

"Hallucinating?" she asked.

"Perhaps. And later, the next day or something, I remember saying things to an officer, an Air Force captain who was kind of in my chain of command—saying things that didn't make sense. The captain ended up taking me to the hospital. After I got there, I remember saying I wanted to see some of the patients and visit their rooms, to help them."

"Grandiosity, some hyper-religiosity perhaps," Lana commented.

"You know your psychology. Anyway, they shipped me off, first to one place for about a week and then another for three more. Ended up getting elected president of the ward during my last week there, which I'm still kind of proud of. Leader of the nutcases."

"Being king of a tiny world is still being a king," she remarked, nodding. "Did your girlfriend keep in touch with you during that time? What was her name?"

"Grace Ann. And yes, she called a few times. It wasn't meant to be, though—being with her and being at the Academy. After I got back from the hospital, a medical board determined I was unfit for commissioning. I appealed the decision all the way up to the Secretary of the Air Force but lost at every stage. My first loss of an appeal, and I wasn't even a lawyer yet." He chuckled.

Lana smiled. "It's good that you can laugh about it, looking back."

"Yeah. Things have worked out fine. I probably wouldn't have become a 'BigLaw' attorney if I'd stayed at the Academy."

"Maybe you'd have been shot down somewhere," she observed.

"Exactly. I've often thought about that."

"Interesting," she said, taking another sip of wine and poking at the last piece of steak.

Tom looked at the time on his phone: 9:41 p.m.—a couple of hours had gone by.

"Well, I should get going. I have to meet some friends," Lana announced.

"Merry Christmas to you," he offered, standing up after she started to gather her things.

"Thanks. Send me a text sometime, Tom," she said, reaching for and receiving a quick embrace.

"Better yet, send me one first," he countered. "Then I'll think about whether I should reply."

4

Nothing Wrong

"Where were you?" asked Jill, as Tom took off his black wool coat and placed it on a chair in the kitchen.

"I had dinner with my friend Lana."

What went unmentioned was that it was actually his second dinner with her in the last two weeks: first the fancy club that was his favorite hangout, then several days later the craft brewery she loved to frequent.

Jill remained silent. Though Tom had mentioned having met Lana back in mid-December, her name hadn't come up since then.

Tom apparently wasn't going to volunteer any further information. He took a seat at her kitchen table.

"Friend, huh? Did you need to wear *that*?"

Tom had on a black shirt and olive-colored Italian dress jeans, along with black dress shoes and the black belt he normally wore at work.

"I wanted to look nice. Nothing wrong with that," he responded.

"Tell you what. Let me turn the table. How would you feel if I went out for dinner with one of my young male colleagues at the office?"

"That would be fine. You wouldn't find anything interesting in him."

Hands now on her hips, Jill turned and took a couple of steps away from him.

"And hey, I actually invited Lana over to my place for New Year's Eve," he continued. "She wanted to come, but has to visit her aunt. I thought I'd introduce you."

"Wait. I thought just you and I are getting together that night. When did you invite her?"

"On my way over here."

"Oh, were you hoping for a threesome?" she asked.

Tom cocked his head slightly to the left and placed a fist under his chin, as if pondering the possibility.

"Hmmm. No, I prefer them one at a time."

"Go ahead, make jokes all you want," she replied.

"You went there first, Jill. I was just playing along."

"Is that what you're doing, Tom, playing? Is this all fun for you?"

He stood up and casually walked toward the chair where he'd placed his coat.

"Say, you still want that frozen custard? It's getting late, and I'd really like to have a taste. They close at midnight."

"I've lost my appetite for sweet stuff," she said.

"Oh, but it'll do a body good."

Tom grabbed her upper arms and nestled his head against hers, as she continued to face the opposite direction.

"Temporarily," Jill commented.

She pulled away and looked at the city lights seeping through the white inner curtain of her living room window. Even from the eighteenth floor, the sound of cars and urban life easily made its way to the top of her building.

"Am I not giving you enough space, Tom?"

"Jill, I feel like you're reading into things. Sometimes a dinner is just a dinner. Sometimes when you meet someone, you take an interest in the person as a person. If they happen to be female and you're a man, you can still take a genuine interest."

"What if they're female, young, attractive, and single?" Jill asked.

"Wait, the only thing I've ever mentioned to you about Lana is having met her. So female, yes."

"Be honest, Tom."

"It's true. I've not mentioned any other features."

"It's not what you said or didn't say. Come on, you weren't born yesterday, and neither was I. Women have a sixth sense about these things. You know that. And I know you. She's all four."

Jill turned around and walked toward him, placing her hand against his cheek. He seemed both impressed and befuddled, letting out a laugh that hinted of frustration.

"OK, but that shouldn't disqualify her," he said.

"From what?"

"From—"

Tom chuckled and now had hands on hips.

"Look, choosing who I associate with is kind of a big deal for me," he noted. "Let's talk about this more tomorrow. Right now, I'd like you to join me for that frozen custard you invited me over here for."

"Is that all you came over here for?"

* * *

The following morning, Tom closed the front door to Jill's apartment and joined her in the elevator. They said nothing to each other on the ride down, though Tom winked at her once. She answered back by slightly arching an eyebrow.

In little time they were on the sidewalk in front of the building, ready for another run together.

"So," Jill uttered as they reached the nearby intersection.

"So," was Tom's guarded response.

Jill laughed. Unsurprisingly, Tom knew her quite well; she was more prepared to talk now regarding what there was supposedly nothing wrong about. And being very familiar with her unusual childhood, he cut her some slack when it came to her insecurities.

During the two-mile run, Tom referred to Lana's "interesting backstory" (as he put it) and told of her quest to find her father. He provided the pertinent details that he felt explained his budding friendship with Lana.

"She probably has a lot of friends," Jill commented.

"Making friends is not a problem for Lana."

"Are any of them men twice her age?"

He admired Jill's directness and analyzed the question dispassionately as he focused on the pavement ahead of him.

"I never asked her," he replied. "I didn't see it as relevant. Anyway, right now she's focused on school and would really like to find her father."

"Do you think she'll find him?"

"Yes, at some point," he answered. "She seems like someone who can make things happen."

"Oh, *no doubt*," she said, marveling at how the male brain seemed unable to recognize certain things that were painfully obvious. "So, are you sort of filling in for now, Tom?"

He looked over to Jill for a moment and back to the street ahead of him as it rose slightly in grade. He chuckled, half wondering whether Jill had secretly taken a trial advocacy course or some side lessons on the art of cross-examination. She was turning the tables on him, taking on the role of a seasoned courtroom attorney who could make a witness squirm in his seat.

He pled his case. "Objection, Your Honor. Argumentative. And she's badgering the witness."

Jill didn't miss a beat. "I'll withdraw the question."

"Nicely done," Tom acknowledged. "And because I'm feeling generous today, I will answer it anyway."

He took a few more strides then stopped, ostensibly seeking to gather his thoughts. Jill turned around and shot him a scrutinizing stare.

"Look," he began, "I'm sure Lana appreciates an older man's perspective. But don't get me wrong: She's very much her own person. She doesn't want to change who she is. She's the only person she's had her entire life. For her, it's nice to have guidance, but she values independence and freedom."

"So it sounds like you have no chance with her anyway."

"Oh, I have every chance, but I'm still working on someone else. And it's a never-ending struggle."

5

Rudy

A palette of garish lights reflected off the hood of the rented Ford Mustang, which Lana disliked and had not selected. To her the car was mediocre performance wrapped in pretty packaging.

She watched in awe from the passenger seat as a roller coaster mounted onto the side of a nearby hotel went through two inversions. Meanwhile, across the Strip the jade and gold opulence of the MGM Grand rose into the sky.

"We should go for a ride," Lana declared, pointing in the direction of the New York–New York. Steering her phone sideways with both hands, she snapped a shot of the city ahead and immediately posted it on Instagram for everyone to see. Not wanting to leave out Tom (*probably not on Instagram*, she thought), she copied and pasted the image into a text message to him that read, *"Guess where I am?"*

As Lana tapped on her phone, Rudy glanced over to the screen. "Who's Tom?"

"Oh, it's Tom Edwards. You met him at the pre-launch party at the Southside Ballroom."

"Oh yeah, the guy who's old enough to be your dad."

"Ouch. Anyway, he's a nice guy. We're just friends. Just like you and me, Rudy, except I know you a lot better."

He laughed without mirth. "With the age gap, though, I guess some people would see it as maybe a little creepy," he remarked, as he reached for and squeezed her thigh.

"Rudy, you're getting grabby," she said, returning his hand to the steering wheel. "I didn't come here for that; you still haven't gotten that through either of your heads."

"There's always hope."

"Yeah, 'hope springs eternal,' right?"

"In the human breast," Rudy replied, finishing the line from Alexander Pope as he feigned another move toward her and copped a feel of nothing but air.

He prized Lana, at times physically more than in other ways. She understood Rudy quite well, and showed him enough regard to foster a feeling that what he wanted could be had. They had dated for a year or so after she broke up with a classmate at UIC. But back then and still now, there was a boundary she rarely let him cross, frustrating him to no end. He figured she was asexual; she never hinted otherwise. They remained close, though she was right: They were "just friends" now. As she often had to remind him, however, her regard for him had not changed. She wanted him to remain a part of her life.

Rudy fancied himself the "Asian Sensation," and was the founder's right-hand man at the startup where he worked. He could design, code, troubleshoot, and execute with efficiency. After a successful crowdsourcing campaign, the startup had the funds to create a promising gaming application. Rudy was essential to the enterprise and liked being needed. Lana was all too aware of that fact, and more.

"As human beings, we have a thirst for affection, don't we Rudy?"

"Trick question, right Lana?"

Ignoring his sarcasm, she continued. "Many of us demand a high level of affection to feel satisfied."

"By 'us' you don't mean yourself, obviously."

"I don't know. I just find satisfaction elsewhere."

"Then what drives you? We all have needs," he said.

"I'm driven by freedom. It's exciting to have so many opportunities right now. I definitely feel more real and alive than I did last year, and I want to keep becoming more alive."

For Lana, the notion of having someone to need, to depend on, seemed agreeable in principle. At the same time, she recognized her inability to obtain balance. *But that is what I am striving for*, she often thought. She believed she was still finding herself, and didn't want a commitment to someone to prevent her from reaching her destination.

She didn't think of *herself* as a destination, though, like some hidden treasure on a map. She was creating herself, not fixed in place or boxed into a little pigeonhole. Plenty of people she'd worked or been with tried to see her (and themselves) that way; they liked to identify, classify, assume. From her point of view, this mindset, though perhaps slightly better than stereotyping, involved the same small way of thinking and largely remained at the surface.

To Lana, surface-level thinking left little room for the journey of finding oneself. Surface-level thinking left little room for dreamers like her who throw themselves onto a canvas and grab hold of the palette. Approaching life this way was an experience of the mind, heart, soul, and body and minimized any interest in what others wanted for her, of her, or from her. There was not only independence in this process but also self-acceptance.

"Your quest for freedom has a party of one," Rudy opined, offering a variation of an argument he'd made many times before.

"First of all, there's nothing wrong with searching, especially at our age."

Rudy had on his best poker face. He did not want to give Lana any indication of agreement with her point.

"Also, I know I'm not much of a romantic—"

"You think?" Rudy interjected, unable to resist the invitation.

"—but I appreciate how well you understand me. And it's amazing how much we share in common."

Rudy's eyes tightened; Lana caught the tell, sensed the opening, and concluded her point, placing as many chips on the table as she was able: "I love knowing you."

Lana was not one to use the word "love" cavalierly in connection with another person. Rudy knew this fact, but also knew—and even worse, felt—she wasn't all-in.

"Loving knowing someone is much different than loving someone, Lana."

"How so?"

"Loving knowing someone is about what you get out of the experience of having someone in your life. It's inherently self-centered."

"That's not necessarily a bad thing."

"Not a bad thing…not bad to be self-centered? OK. Wow. I wish you could hear yourself, how others hear that."

"Rudy, you know as well as anyone I couldn't care less what anyone else thinks, especially when it comes to how I feel about you."

"Well, think on this, Lana: You said you're *amazed* at how much we share, but you're just talking about the pieces of me you see in yourself. You look at me, seeing those things, and are attracted to your own reflection."

"I get it, Rudy. You're calling me a narcissist. But really you're saying you don't accept me. You talk about loving knowing someone, treating it as inferior to loving someone."

"It is inferior."

"No, the problem as you see it is that it's not on your terms."

Rudy found himself where he'd been many times before with Lana: running into a wall.

For Lana, breaking up with Rudy last year had taken much strength and courage. She still considered him her best friend. The easier route would have been to put on a façade and become the girl he wanted her to be. But she would have been lying to herself, and to others, about the true nature of their relationship. She cared about him enough to know he deserved much better than what she could give him. Rudy deserved someone who wanted him equally.

"We're so different," Rudy said with resignation.

"But we're not. We are much more similar than we are different."

"It's *where* we're different though…*how* we're different, Lana… there's a chasm there."

"Rudy, we're too young to be miserable. There are so many adventures to take, people to meet, things to see, and experiences to be shared to be upset about what we don't have. We're sharing those experiences now, together, here, these few days together, away from the rest of the world. Let's appreciate that."

"I try to. When I'm with you like we are now, just the two of us for several days on end, I sometimes say to myself, 'How lucky a man I am to be able to spend this time with such a wonderful, attractive, smart woman.' I treasure this time together, Lana. I treasure that you want to be with me. I have your attention; I know you enjoy this time too. I know all of that."

"It's true, Rudy. I love being here with you. I treasure this time too."

"I also think to myself how anyone seeing us together in the casino or at the bar or driving around on the Strip can *see* that we're close. 'Look at that beautiful couple,' they say to themselves. They *assume* we're a couple, that we're *in love*. But it's a mirage, Lana."

"You look at it as all or nothing, Rudy. I don't see it that way. Having most of what you want is still having a lot."

"I wish I could see things that way, Lana."

"Tell you what…let's agree to disagree, at least for now. We've got one more day here. We should make the most of it."

Rudy was silent, spent. The conversation had sucked out some of his spirit…as it always did.

Lana placed a hand on his shoulder. Her touch awakened him, as it always did.

"Rudy, there used to be something unique and adventurous about us. That's what Las Vegas symbolizes. That's why we came here. I want to go on an adventure. Will you do that for me, for us?"

Rudy felt as though he wanted to remain angry, or needed to. Part of him felt manipulated, even teased. He hated that feeling. Nevertheless, he remained in Lana's orbit, holding out for what he really wanted.

6

The Invitation

"*Are you coming?*" read Lana's text message. She stood near a corner of East Chicago Avenue in Streeterville, not far from the Museum of Contemporary Art. A week earlier, she and Tom had agreed to meet there to see a new exhibition after grabbing something to eat at Puck's Café.

The late January chill and allied winds pierced Lana's black trench-coat she'd tied tightly around her waist. A fine chiffon leopard scarf blended well with her dark brown hair that fell several inches below her shoulders. Ankle-high black boots rounded out her ensemble.

She turned back her head, looked at the bright winter sky, and walked back to the café, figuring Tom must have thought they were to meet at 11:00 a.m. rather than 10:30. She'd have another coffee, see what her friends were up to on Facebook, and prepare something scornful to say to him when he finally arrived.

Lana enjoyed having Tom's attention. She saw in him an earnest-ness she craved—it was, in fact, what she'd first seen in him at the pinball arcade.

Their conversations were deep, wide-ranging, and open. He showed interest in her mind and—like any other guy—her body, but mostly met her eyes when they talked. His gaze occasionally shifted, like when she'd invited him to guess her age back at the arcade.

He showed genuine interest in her, spoke to her with candor, and did not act as though his age placed her far below him. She recognized, esteemed, and on occasion sought after the wisdom his age conferred. Nonetheless, he was modest about his ability to offer advice, preferring instead to suggest multiple options and brainstorm the pros and cons with her.

This approach was refreshing. She had no difficulty gaining or having the attention of other men, and could count many friends who were guys. In fact, all of them were, including her best friend, Rudy. She could hold her own with fellow millennials as well as GenXers and boomers in any setting.

But she hadn't run into an older type like Tom before. The much older ones—his peers and elders, basically—nearly always focused on her physical attributes, or at least more so on those attributes than on anything else about her. Inevitably, they saw her age as a novelty and could not or would not hide their underlying pretension and condescension. She had no use for their patronizing sense of superiority or their clichéd fantasies.

And when compared to her own peers, Tom was refined, comfortable in his own skin, and able to hold his own in any situation, just like she could.

The guy had his uses.

Lana felt her phone vibrate. *Must be Tom telling me he's running late*, she thought. She set the phone on the table to read the text.

"Hey, not going to make it. Just got off a long call with a client. They want me to take over a case from another law firm. Going to trial in two weeks in New York. I'll check in with you after this trial ends."

"*We'll see*," Lana replied.

* * *

At that moment, Tom reached for his favorite steel mug, which an assistant had just filled with fresh coffee. The brew's intense heat and bitter taste stung his tongue and upper lip, and he quickly returned the mug to his desk. Soon, he knew, he'd be looking at pleadings, discovery, research memoranda, and other documents deposited for his review—all to get up to speed on the new case he'd just been handed.

This case had sparked Tom's passion for a challenge: a chance not only to save the day for the client, but also to open the next chapter in his career *and* life. Fueled by the intensity of this new assignment, Tom knew he needed to find a way to maintain his elevated state of mind.

He wanted to see Lana again, but felt conflicted. He certainly had a valid excuse for standing her up. But he also knew seeing her now would cause him to lose focus at a time he simply could not afford this luxury.

What Lana didn't know is what he feared, what he hid from view—from everyone—and what he least needed: to feel the sting of loss or rejection, whether in the courtroom or in his relationships. Underneath the outward signs of fulfillment and bravado was a desperate need for respect, acceptance, and acknowledgment, along with reassurance and healthy companionship.

And he sensed that getting the kind of companionship he wanted… he needed…would require him to step out of his comfort zone.

Which he intended to do very shortly.

* * *

Back at the café, Lana turned to face the light coming through the window next to her table. She looked down at her new outfit for a moment, then turned to spy in the distance a few of the exhibits she'd planned to see with Tom at her side. A solitary tour wouldn't be the same; she'd looked forward to his perspective and his reliably eccentric observations.

The phone vibrated again.

"*In the meantime, while I still have your attention, do two things for me*," Tom texted.

Lana was not pleased. She *never* got stood up. She thought about powering down and giving him a powerful dose of the silent treatment. She started to type a response, then erased it, and finally texted, "*Let's start with one*."

"*Fair enough. Stand up and take a selfie for me.*"

"*You're <not> serious.*"

"*Just do it*," he replied.

"*Motion denied.*"

Lana's rebuff was unexpected.

"*Testy. I'll move on.*"

"*Let's*," she answered.

"*Very well. Now, assuming you haven't deleted any of my older texts in a previous act of fury…*"

Lana couldn't resist the opening.

"*You assume a lot.*"

"*Actually, what I know is you've got 'em all archived & backed up somewhere like it was Fort Knox or something*," he responded.

"*I never knew how much you thought of yourself…until just now.*"

"Here's the truth: Whenever Lana needs that pick-me-up before bed-time after a tough day at school, she grabs her phone and picks a few of Tom's musings, lost in euphoric bliss."

"Only in your twisted dreams," she responded, adding a follow-on text that read, *"Anyway, let's get to it, what am I supposed to be looking for in this archive?"*

"Go to last week, the morning after we last had dinner."

Lana scrolled through the stream of texts, having to press "Load Earlier Messages" twice.

She saw the text in question and immediately, reflexively pressed her hand against her cheek, eyes and mouth wide open. She was reading it for the first time.

"Yeah, I never got an answer, so I knew you never saw it," he texted.

Lana abandoned any pretense of debating him, taken aback by his pluck and nerve. A few seconds later, her phone vibrated again.

"So, in a sense, who's really been stood up?"

She had to hand it to the guy: The invitation was original, unexpected, and brazen, even when measuring the latter facet by *her* standards.

She supposed she could forgive him for not only making her wait, but also opting out of seeing her—even for a quick hello—when he was just a fifteen-minute drive away.

Not that she didn't have other options.

* * *

About an hour later, lost in a late-morning nap, Lana felt something tapping her on the shoulder.

"Hey, can I bother you for a second?" an attractive young man asked.

"Huh, what?" she answered, turning around abruptly after having dozed off. Her trenchcoat and scarf were still draped over the chair next to her, covering her purse.

"Oh, I'm sorry. Were you catching some beauty sleep? Didn't mean to disturb you."

She took a fast look at the guy: collared white dress shirt, lightly starched; medium gray dress slacks atop black wingtips; black wool overcoat draped over his left arm. Maybe twenty-five or twenty-six… twenty-seven tops.

"Dude, it's Saturday. Nice outfit and all, but this isn't the tea and crumpets club," she told him.

"Nice to meet you too. I'm Scott," he said, extending his right hand.

Ignoring his gesture, she extended a fist, waiting for him to curl his fingers for a bump. He chuckled and went along.

"Yeah, let's not give each other colds," she said. "Anyway, what do you want?"

He stared at her face a moment, then noticed her leopard scarf. "Nice scarf. Headed to the zoo later today?" he asked.

"Oh, OK. I see how it is." She looked him up and down again, stopping at the shoes as before, and laughed to herself. "Actually, you kind of remind me of someone I know. I was supposed to meet him here."

"So is he coming?"

"No, he stood me up."

"Too bad for *him*. Mind if I sit down?"

"Why not? I wouldn't mind the company. So what brings you here, Mr. Scott?"

"It's Mr. Mason, actually, but you can call me Scott. I just felt like checking the place out."

"You've never been here before?"

"No."

"Are you a tourist?" she asked.

"No, I'm living right here, in Streeterville."

"For how long?"

"How long do I plan to stay?"

"No, how long you been living with this treasure right in your backyard?"

"Less than a year."

"Got it. Tell me again what you want?"

"I was going to ask if you've been here before," he said a tad too earnestly.

"Wait, what? Did you just come up with that? It's so cheesy. There had to be something else you were planning."

"OK, you got me. I really just wanted to bother you."

"Yeah, well…mission accomplished. Consider me officially bothered."

"You don't seem *too* bothered."

"You haven't bored me yet," she replied. "Do you normally just come up to random women and grab them from behind?"

He smiled. "I didn't grab you."

She stood up, placed both elbows on the table right in front of him, and shot her eyes into his.

"No, but you wanted to. In fact, if you could get away with it, you'd grab right here right now, where the thickness is just right," she said, slapping her right glute, hard.

He pulled his head back and moved his chair a few inches away from her. "Careful, girl. That ego of yours will be your undoing." He gave her a long pause before adding, "But your description is apt, I will say."

"I know," she deadpanned. "It's always been like this. Can't help it." She saw that he was slightly blushing. *So, it's at least in part an act,* she noted to herself. "Hey, I like that you try to go head-to-head with me and still have a certain…sincerity about you," she observed, deciding not to tease him about the receding redness in his face.

He nodded his head and smiled at her again, then looked out the window as if lost in thought.

"Well, it was nice meeting you, but I need to go," she told him as she started to gather her things.

Unable to help himself, he got another good stare in as she began to walk away. "Wait, what's your name?" he blurted out.

"I'm Lana."

Another pause, this one not forced. "Nice. Fits you well," he replied.

"Yeah, how so?"

"It's sophisticated and different."

She slowly walked back to the table. "Well, my last name is Delacroix. What does that do for you?"

"Oh, wow. That's perfect."

"So, more of the same?" she asked.

"Yeah, in a good way, of course."

"Of course!" she replied, adding, "Hey, I'd be up for meeting you again. I'm free next Thursday and Friday after 6:00 p.m. Give me your phone."

He handed it over.

"OK, there. Sent a friend request to myself," she said. "I'll text you later and we'll figure out the details."

"Great."

He watched her walk away. He appreciated the bounce in her step that looked very natural yet somehow…odd. It seemed out of place for a woman of her age—of any age, really. It was the kind of happy-go-lucky stride one would associate with a child who is oblivious to the world around her. It wasn't a strut; there was nothing showy, flashy, or flirty about it. It was cute but not intended to be so.

One thing was for sure: She could make an impression on someone.

7

Lana's Haven

Scampering from one building to the next with two books, a laptop, and a portfolio tucked under one arm, Lana contemplated the presentation she was about to give in her portfolio management class at UIC. *Running late again,* she thought.

She stepped over expansion joints in the sidewalk and sashayed around slow-moving bodies blocking her path. She was a hamster on a wheel; her degree and a hoped-for follow-on job felt like the elusive rewards hanging above her.

Rhetorical questions came at her like arrows: Did she or could she see anything above her on that wheel? Was anything really there?

The world seemed to want her to have life figured out by twenty-five. She didn't even have *herself* figured out. And that was fine to her.

Right now though she just wanted to get to her next class.

She hurried past someone who sat next to her in the front row of her abnormal psychology class, hoping he wouldn't notice her.

"Hey Lana."

Too late, she thought. *Just keep moving.*

"Hey Cory, sorry, gotta run."

"Good times last night."

"Would have been better, actually…we just couldn't get you to leave," Lana taunted.

Nearly four months had passed since Lana, with a dramatic assist from Tom, uncovered his invitation residing on her phone. But the initial surge of energy she'd felt at the prospect disappeared as his trial went on indefinitely. In New York, giving all of himself to the defense of his client, Tom had fallen out of touch. What had been expected to last four weeks turned into five, then six. She'd learned the disappointing result of the trial through Kurt, not Tom. There had been radio silence between them for nearly three months now.

Regardless, in recent weeks Lana had been cutting back on socializing. Her friends and those she cared about no doubt felt they were afterthoughts to her. But she just wanted some time to focus on herself. At the same time, social engagement was what she craved. Shutting off human connections, or even throttling them down, was to act against her nature. She liked targeting human connections as well as she did knowledge. And bullseyes were everywhere.

Like Kurt, people around Lana liked to absorb her energy and optimism. She instinctively sensed this osmosis, seeing it in their faces and their sparks of enthusiasm when they interacted with her. The social influence she had over others intoxicated her; it kept her fueled and vibrant. In fact, it was like a drug. As a result, regulating her access to people felt like cutting herself off completely, which presented its own challenge. But again, she needed focus.

"Ready for your presentation, Ms. Delacroix?" asked her portfolio management professor.

Lana approached the lectern, excited to be the center of attention. She was in her element, but not as well-prepared as she would have preferred. Procrastination was that steady companion she could not ditch.

Taking the lectern, she made her delivery. What she lacked in content she compensated for with relatable insight and a dash of humor. She fed off the nodding heads and thumbs on chins. The instant yet subtle feedback helped her shape and mold her presentation, somewhat on-the-fly, into one more relevant and interesting, less abstract and technical. Eye contact came easily compared to most people, and not only enhanced her poise but also enabled her to spot the various nonverbal signals of deference from her peers.

She wondered whether any earlier version of herself would have recognized the person standing there.

* * *

Lana sat on the commode's lid, secluded in one of the stalls in the restroom. On a hook was her bookbag; in her hands was a sandwich from her bagged lunch. She was in one of her safe havens, a place where she often sat to eat her lunch away from the taunting of the kids in the cafeteria.

To reach the stall, she'd walked past several classmates talking near the sinks. They were looking at themselves and each other with their magazine-quality, long, straight locks. They'd all seen her and immediately stopped chatting.

"It's that weird girl," one of them loudly whispered.

The girls resumed talking after Lana closed the door of the stall.

"You missed my birthday party last weekend," one of the girls noted.

"Sorry I couldn't be there, Evelyn. How did it go?"

"My dad gave me a $100 Famous-Barr gift card."

"Wow. Have you used it yet?"

"Yeah, he took me there on Sunday."

"Cool. What did you buy?"

"I got a really soft white sweater, a black dress, and an aquamarine winter coat. I thought they were out of that color, but he asked the lady at the counter if they had anything in the back and they did. I got the last one!"

"Awesome. I had to watch my little brother this weekend. The kid is such a pain. What about you, Janet? You're kind of quiet. Anything exciting happen over the weekend?"

"Yeah, I went to a sleepover at Holly's house."

"Oh yeah, I heard Rachel say that was a blast."

"It was. There were like twelve of us there. We watched movies and looked at pictures of John and Nathan."

Lana heard giggling and voices trailing off until there was silence; the bathroom was now nearly empty. Hearing the girls praise their fathers, complain about their brothers, and talk about boys and their many friends made Lana feel inadequate and alone.

Finishing her lunch, she exited the stall, threw away a Ziploc bag, and looked in the mirror. Staring at her reflection, she saw a distinctively tall and thin frame that she hated. It made her stand out when she was desperately trying to fit in. She hated her wavy, unruly hair. She spent little effort on it, having no idea how to use the hair products her grandmother occasionally bought for her.

In time the bell rang at Wydown Middle School in Clayton. She would have to walk the gauntlet now, making her way through the long hallway. Not many people knew Lana's name, but she still wasn't invisible enough. She resolved to keep her head down and hide from the world, hoping that by not engaging anyone they would leave her alone. She felt both uninteresting and awkward.

"Hey, Lame–a. How was your lunch?" asked the bully of the week, a portly boy who was half Lana's height but twice her width.

Horizontally challenged, she thought to herself with a private sense of satisfaction. She ignored him, focusing on just getting from her locker to the door at the end of the hall. The boy hoisted his bookbag over his right shoulder and walked past her, aiming to strike the back of her head.

The bookbag reached its target easily, upon which a gaggle of sixth graders began laughing and pointing at her. Lana said nothing, crouching to gather her fallen books. She noticed that what remained of her lunch, intended for an afternoon snack, was missing from her bookbag.

"Looking for something?" asked the boy who'd just hit her.

"Hey, give that back," she demanded, hands on hips, towering over the boy.

"Hmmm, this cookie looks good. The rest is crap," he sneered, throwing a quart-sized Ziploc bag onto the floor. Pieces of a wet, pre-sliced orange were on the dirty, uneven floor, a stream of juice rolling toward the center of the hallway.

The gaggle, which by now included several seventh graders and even a few eighth graders, erupted in horrible laughter.

Lana looked at them, observing their pointing fingers and hands cupped over their mouths. She struggled to maintain her composure. She didn't need this now. She had enough weaknesses, or thought she did, and didn't want to show anyone another one.

"You look even uglier when you cry," opined the chubby kid, strutting off convinced he had the awe and regard of every middle schooler around him.

* * *

"Very nice, Lana, thank you," said the professor, joining the students' applause as Lana closed her laptop and disconnected it from the projector. "We'll hear from Joe next time. Until then, go ahead and read the next chapter of the textbook and be prepared to discuss it in case we have any downtime."

Before leaving her perch, Lana surveyed the lecture hall, randomly looking into several classmates' eyes. She saw something that had to be earned: respect. And it felt refreshing.

A familiar face approached her from the nosebleed seats.

"Hey, that was really awesome. I don't think I've ever seen you in a suit."

"You stalking me now, Cory? You're not even in this class. In fact, are you even enrolled here?"

"I think it's wrong to put a price on knowledge."

"That's an interesting viewpoint. Anyway, I have to go. I have to get to work."

* * *

Lana blew past her manager and sat down in an available cubicle.

"You're late," the manager noted, having followed Lana step-for-step the moment she entered the bank. "By the way, cover that tattoo on your ankle."

Lana had a pair of stockings in her purse—an easy fix.

"How are you today, Lynn?"

"Everyone here except you knows how to follow the rules. Showing up on time and looking presentable are basic requirements for any client-facing job, Lana!"

Several other relationship bankers looked up from their desks. A bright-eyed young woman in the cubicle next to Lana's looked at a male colleague on the opposite side of the lobby and covered her mouth.

"You're right, Lynn. I apologize."

The public chastisement did not bother Lana. Her face still glowed from the reaction of her peers in the lecture hall. And her internship at the bank was near its scheduled end anyway. She'd learned a lot about what she didn't want in a job, and that knowledge was the most valuable thing she'd gained from the experience.

8

Public Display

It was late May and still cold in Chicago, but not piercingly so. Summer and a trip to Oak Street Beach were around the corner; Lana could feel the sand at her feet, her body swimsuit-clad at Lake Michigan, her eyes staring out at the horizon.

Back to reality, Lana thought. Kurt had invited her to an art show he was organizing, curating, marketing, presenting, and directing for an artist-friend of his. Looking at the promotional materials for the event, Lana thought Kurt had overdone things a bit in assigning himself so many credits, but also understood his need and desire to prove his "growth engineering" talents to the world.

The show was at the Union League Club in one of its exhibition galleries. *Ironic*, thought Lana. She'd met Tom for dinner one evening at the club half a year ago, and wasn't sure if she wanted to run into him again, here or anywhere else. Something didn't seem right to her; there was no explanation for what seemed to her a vanishing. She half wondered whether that cable show she occasionally watched, *Disappeared*, would soon produce an episode about Tom.

She knew she'd done nothing to upset him; he certainly had done nothing to upset her. Indeed, she doubted either of them *could* upset the other. They'd gotten to know each other fairly well over a two-month timeframe—remarkably so, actually. There were occasional debates that were really playful banter. Nonetheless, their connection was bereft of fuss or provocation.

Lana looked around the large room and at the grandeur of the event.

Then she saw him, standing on the opposite side, looking pensively at the floor. She decided to observe him for a time. She'd earlier thought something didn't seem right, and now could see her thought proven true with her own eyes. He looked lifeless, disengaged, and pained.

Lana debated whether she should approach him. Part of her still cared about him; another part was simply curious. She purposefully snaked her way around the room, enabling her to advance upon him from his right side.

"Tom?"

Hearing a familiar, distinctive voice, Tom raised his head slowly and looked up.

"Oh, hi Lana."

That's all I get? Lana wondered. She sensed that now, however, was not a time for repartee; Tom seemed to need something else.

She said nothing and just intuitively opened her arms. Tom showed half a smile, paused as if in thought, then rather abruptly grabbed hold of her and simply held her there, not saying a word.

Lana was beyond surprised; she wasn't expecting this outward, public display of affection. He'd never shown this kind of physical warmth toward her before. They released each other at nearly the same moment, moving back a step or two, looking at each other's faces. Several attendees eyeing the art strewn about the place noticed them there in the center of the room and wondered what was transpiring.

"Tom, what happened to you?"

"The trial…it—"

"I heard about the result. I'm sorry."

"Tough one to lose. I wasn't ignoring you…at least, not on purpose."

"You were in the middle of a trial. You needed to be focused and at your best."

"Lana, after I got back to Chicago, things were different."

"How do you mean?"

"I thought…"

Tom didn't or couldn't finish his sentence. He again stared at the floor.

She looked around the room, then back to Tom. The few onlookers had returned their attention elsewhere.

Tom wasn't expecting Lana to be so kindhearted. The scene was not playing out as he'd envisioned it. Appearing on stage with her was a welcome surprise.

Reaching one of her long, slender arms in his direction, she rested a hand on his shoulder and took hold of one of his hands.

"Tom, do you want to talk somewhere where it's quieter?"

There was something about his vulnerability she found both shocking and appealing, even attractive. This wasn't the daring, fearless man she'd met the previous December. And she was fine with that. Like her, he'd let his guard down.

She led him to the Wigwam. She recognized a familiar perch and seated herself there, guiding Tom to a spot opposite her.

"Rob, would you get Mr. Edwards here a Talisker, neat?"

"Certainly, ma'am. May I get you something?"

"No, I'm good," Lana replied.

Tom was intrigued. "How'd you—"

Lana placed a forefinger on his lips.

"You told me it was your favorite single malt."

"When?"

"Doesn't matter. Now tell me something more I don't know about Tom."

Lana's line was familiar, yet welcome and encouraging. He knew Lana deserved an explanation; he would try to give it to her.

The loss of his trial had sapped him emotionally, for the first time since joining his firm. At that point, and certainly by the time of his return to Chicago, he felt the person she'd gotten to know quite well—"Tom 2.0," as some of his friends had started to call him—was a façade.

Powered by a hypomania that conveniently arrived the previous autumn as he was preparing for another high-stakes trial, Tom now felt like an impostor. He knew that absent his euphoric mood, he wouldn't have dared to interact with her the way he had back at the Southside Ballroom.

"Don't dwell on the past, Tom. Like you've said before, some things happen for a reason, and some things just happen."

"You're right, of course."

"Of course."

Tom smiled, appreciating Lana's injection of a little wit. The evening was turning out to be unlike what he had conceived.

"Tell you a secret?" he asked.

"Sure."

"Promise you won't get mad?"

"I'm not going to give you a blank check."

"OK, how about this: Promise you'll keep an open mind?"

"I can manage that," she said.

"The truth is, tonight I saw you on the other side of the room before you saw me. I chose not to approach you."

"Doesn't matter. Just be glad I saw you."

"I am. You are really something."

"I know."

9

Chaz

Lana carried a large, unwieldy bag of Kokuho rice from a small pantry to Rudy's black, ultra-contemporary kitchen table. The anachronistic sack was completely out of place there; the high-backed, sveltely and subtly curved set of four chairs surrounding the table only made the fact more obvious.

Doubtful of her ability to wrestle the bag into position, or to do so without breaking something, Rudy moved toward her. "Let me—"

Instinctively she stretched out an arm to halt his further approach. "—I got this," she said.

Rudy shook his head and grabbed an eight-inch chef knife, deftly flipping its handle around like a gunslinger.

"Thanks but don't need it," she declared. "So what are we making again?"

"Well, *I* thought *I'd* try making this new jambalaya recipe I found at the Food Network site."

Ignoring his emphasis on the first person singular, she tore open the bag.

"As for *us*," Rudy began, "we know what would happen if I let you too close to the stove."

Lana rolled her eyes, quickly turning her head around to peer at her frequent tormenter on the subject of her cooking talents, or lack thereof.

"Right, 'Lana's going to burn something again?'" she scoffed.

"I'm just amazed you managed to place that huge bag on the edge of my table without it falling over on you. Might make more sense to bring it over here, closer to the action?"

"I may not be 'stacked' like you, Rudy, but I have to be careful not to get too close; the testosterone and other hormones may act out again."

"Yours or mine?"

"Don't flatter yourself."

"Get over here," Rudy enjoined with a smile, outstretching one arm while grasping a cooking spoon in the other.

Lana complied in part, coming close enough to peer into the pot on Rudy's stove by propping herself up on her toes, but not close enough to find herself pawed.

"What is *that*?" she asked.

"What is what?"

"That," she said, pointing at the pot.

At just that moment, a surge of bubbles overcame the pot and stove. Seconds later, a smoke alarm went off near the corner of the kitchen.

Lana took two steps back and slightly crouched, holding a hand over her mouth in a weak attempt to hide her hearty laughter.

Rudy flipped two switches above the stove, venting the steam. Lana went for the front door and began moving it back and forth, converting it into a massive fan. Eventually the alarm went quiet again and she closed the door.

"High-five," Lana said, putting up her hand for Rudy to slap. "You thinking pasta?"

Rudy took the debacle in stride. It wasn't the first time his best-laid culinary plans had gone awry.

"Yes. And you can leave the rice. Just grab the mostaccioli from the pantry."

"Gladly," she replied.

She knew exactly where to look for the item. Pasta was a frequent fallback for the pair.

"Lana, I noticed you stopped short again when I invited you to join me at the stove. Haven't you ever heard of 'kiss the chef'?"

"First of all, it wasn't really an invitation. Sounded like an order to me."

Rudy held his tongue, waiting for Lana to proceed with what he figured would be a multi-staged comeback.

"Second, the chef obviously needs to focus more on cooking and less on distractions—however difficult that may be," she remarked, gesturing in the direction of her summer outfit.

Lana wore a peach-and-white, high-low hem, strapless dress, its front cut nearly a foot above her knees, its back touching her calf and ending half the same distance above her ankles. Counterbalancing the getup were a pair of simple, white-bow loafers and a ribbon of finely tattooed icons about her right ankle, each representing one of the five factions from *Divergent*, one of Lana's favorite book series.

"I love this…what we're doing now," Rudy observed, putting down his cooking tools for a moment to face her.

"We make a good cooking team, I must admit," she responded.

"I just wish it really was more like a team, in other ways."

Lana turned away from Rudy and walked into the dining area of the kitchen. She grasped the heavy olive window curtains and pulled them open, affording herself a view of the sprawling city beneath her. The vast expanse of red lights moving away from downtown contrasted with the bright-white uplights mounted on the building below and on the surrounding complexes. She could almost feel the warmth of the uplights as they illuminated her face for the world outside to see.

"Lana, it's really only when we're together like this that I have your attention, and even then—"

"—even then it's not enough—"

"—No, that's not what I was going to say."

"It's what you were thinking though, Rudy."

"No, you are very attentive and responsive in person, Lana. *I* actually get more distracted when we're together than *you* do."

"Yeah, I know," she observed matter-of-factly. "And that's fine."

"But put you back in your apartment or at work or on vacation, and it could be an hour, a day, a week before I hear from you—who knows, right?"

For emphasis and to introduce a related point, Rudy placed his arm in front of him at nose level and parallel to the floor, then dropped it limply at gravity's bidding.

"The drop-off in attentiveness is incredible sometimes," he remarked. "I wonder if I'm dealing with the same person when we're not in the same room."

She fought the urge to roll her eyes. "What, are you saying I don't always instantly respond to your texts? We've talked about this before, Rudy."

"That's just an example—and a good one—of the lack of reciprocation in our relationship."

"I'm not going to be at your beck and call—I couldn't be," she responded.

"The fact that I am always there for you when you need me, and that it just doesn't seem to work the same way on the flip side, is very frustrating," he explained.

"I appreciate what you do for me, Rudy. You are important to me, and you know that. At least I hope you do. I call you my best friend because you are."

"Lana, you're right: I do. But between friends—and certainly with 'best' friends—things aren't supposed to be one-sided. If they are, then one person in the relationship is clearly using the other. And I'm sorry, but with us I *do* feel used and I *do* feel things are one-sided. And always have been."

"It's useless to keep talking about the same issues, the same problems, the same things you feel you deserve—"

"It's not that I *deserve* anything or *feel* I deserve anything, Lana—"

"But it is. You feel you deserve me, to possess me."

Rudy paused in thought, his heart rejecting the point, his mind knowing she had one. "I deserve something."

Lana chuckled and placed a hand on Rudy's thigh, giving it a momentary squeeze. Nearly as quickly she pulled her hand away, and for a moment the waters of dissension settled.

"Anyway, like I was saying, Rudy, talking for hours on end about the same things won't solve anything. I don't mind talking about *doing* things, though."

"Don't get me wrong. Doing things together—that's great, Lana. Those trips to Vegas and New York and other places are nice and fun, but in the end are just escapes. Lots of thrills and excitement, only to return to the status quo."

"The status quo being what?"

Rudy rose from his chair and paced from the dining area toward the kitchen. Lana watched him and remained silent, waiting for a response.

"Don't get me wrong; I like you when you're here with me, a *lot*. I *love*—"

"—Rudy, I know. But you need to accept what you do have. You need to appreciate the amount of time we do spend together."

Rudy stopped pacing for a moment, then turned abruptly in Lana's direction. "And you need to appreciate how much I accept you!" He took a heavy breath. "*Who else* is going to put up with you this way? Sometimes it's maddening."

Lana was astonished but also amused at Rudy's tone.

"A lot of people, actually."

"I don't think so, Lana. Not like me. Other people don't know you like I do. Lana the individual, that person beneath who supposedly only wants acceptance, is *far* from ideal."

"Really. Hmmm. I'm surprised to hear you say that. But go on."

"Fine. I will."

But before he could go on, she said, "Rudy, let's face it: As far as *you're* concerned, what stands between you and me being ideal partners—is me."

"That's right."

Rudy took satisfaction in hearing Lana finish his thought for him. He sat down again on the chair he'd vacated near her: he on one side of the kitchen table, she on the other.

"By the way, what is so 'maddening' about me? Wait; let me make some popcorn."

"Oh. My. God. 'Let me count the ways.'"

"By all means," Lana replied, motioning with her arm as if she were presenting someone on stage.

"Well, like I said, doing things together—that's great and all. Yet it seems like whenever we go out, you get very chatty with whoever's around—for some reason, mostly guys."

"Not sure what I can really do about that. But yes, I'm flirty, it's been said before. What's your point? And where is this going?"

"One point at a time. Be patient."

Lana gave Rudy a good-natured shove to the chest. He liked it and she knew it.

"Anyway, as I was saying…the flirting thing. I think it gives them the wrong impression, Lana. Take that Tom guy, for example, when we were at that pinball bar."

"Tom is a friend."

"I know he is; I don't question that. I didn't bring him up to suggest he wasn't. But you clearly came on to him. You basically came right out and said, 'You want to take me right here, don't you?'"

"That's not what I said. At least, not exactly. Anyway, did I freely engage him in spirited conversation? Yes. But that's no crime. And half a year later, we're still friends. I know how to pick them."

"See, there's the next thing. So competitive. 'Yeah, you're the best, Lana. You sure can pick them.' Is that what you want to hear?"

"But I am. It's a fact; I like to hear it acknowledged."

"And that *ego* of yours!"

"It turns you on."

"Some of the time, but most guys aren't going to know what to do with that…or with you."

"Oh, I'm sure they *think* they know…"

Lana casually stood and stepped toward the same window she'd peered through earlier. At its sill was a catnip plant. She stole a couple of leaves and crushed them between her fingers, crouching low and sprinkling them into a tiny bed where sat Rudy's cat, Chaz. As she proceeded to stroke him slowly and firmly, he purred almost immediately; she raised an eyebrow. *At least someone is having a good time,* she thought.

Rudy was facing the other direction, unable to pace farther forward as the front of his shirt touched the kitchen counter. Gathering his thoughts, he paused a bit longer, then spun rather dramatically to face Lana again.

"Why do you think they think that? I mean, you weren't even *subtle* about it at the pinball bar. Lucky for you Tom's not—"

"—You mean lucky for *you*, right?"

"What?"

Lana smiled at Rudy. "Like I said, I know how to pick them. I may take risks, but not recklessly."

"Whatever. It's just hard for me sometimes. I wish my attention was enough for you."

"You have my attention now."

"*Now*, yes."

"You want all of me; I'm offering most. It's a lot, but never enough I suppose."

"Lana, people like us, who are as close as we are, are in relationships. You and I are in a relationship, something that goes beyond friendship or even being best friends."

"From your perspective, I suppose."

"We are. There is emotional intimacy. There's a depth of under-standing; there's compassion…well, at least—"

"—Go ahead, say it," she muttered.

"At least I feel as though *I'm* compassionate. You tilt to the cold side."

"Ouch. Well that's your opinion. I know I can come off as cold and selfish, but I do care about you. And I've done many things over the years to show that," she noted.

"At one time I had no doubt of that. When you were my girlfriend, I—"

"When I was your girlfriend, I was hurting you. I didn't want to keep hurting you. That was compassion; I did something about it to try to make it stop."

"Yeah, you broke up with me. How magnanimous of you."

"You don't see it as compassionate; I do. But again we're treading old ground. We will never see eye-to-eye on some things, and that's OK. Variety is the spice of life, isn't it?"

"You're right that we don't see eye-to-eye. I agree with you there."

"Why should I pretend to be something I'm not? Maybe someday I will be better at compassion, commitment—whatever else you see as flaws. I don't think it's going to be another person who 'makes' me 'better,' though—who 'gets me' to commit. It's going to happen on my time and in my way. I will choose when, where, and how."

"Try listening to yourself for once, Lana. That pedestal you put yourself on is awful flimsy—you know that better than anyone, and you're the best at pretending not to."

Rudy immediately beat a path toward his bedroom, snatching his laptop from the countertop before abruptly closing the door behind him.

Lana wasn't in a mood to argue; she found herself tired, bored even. Knowing Rudy, he wasn't coming out anytime soon.

Meanwhile, the mostaccioli remained in its bag near the boiling pot of water. Stoically, she gave Chaz a final stroke and pat and walked to the stove, turning off the burner and replacing the lid.

Eyeing her metallic blue Schwinn in the hallway near the front door, she looked around the kitchen and the surrounding area of the apartment for a moment—all of it except the bedroom containing the sequestered Rudy—and decided to leave.

* * *

Hearing the front door close and the soft, fading clicks of bike gears, Rudy felt a sense of bitter satisfaction…Satisfaction at having caused Lana to leave. Satisfaction at having asked for what he wanted, sort of—and certainly more assertively than he had back in Las Vegas. Indeed, he was surprised at how far he'd just taken it.

Intuitively, he knew what was happening—what had been happening for months now. He knew what Lana was doing to him, or perhaps more precisely what he was allowing to happen. He knew she was using him.

In the months leading to their breakup as a couple last fall, he'd wanted more of her—too much, in her view—and was propounding more of himself than she could take, apparently.

Seemingly ever-avoidant, she pulled away, giving even less. But somehow she ended up taking more.

Then she cheated on him once for good measure. With a shirtless, muscled Asian model she'd met at Venice Beach during a solo excursion to the West Coast. A one-day stand.

And then told Rudy about it, as soon as she got back to Chicago. It pained him at his core, like a humiliating physical attack—indeed the ultimate insult, given her apparent asexuality.

Earlier in their relationship, she would find excuses for dodging a pass, and if the topic of defining their relationship came up after she rejected an advance, she would change the subject. Later, she simply turned away without saying anything. And then at the end, she firmly, authoritatively ordered him to back off. She only had to do so once.

Meanwhile, Asian shirtless guy was still right there in her photos on Facebook, lying next to her in the sand at Venice Beach.

It was sick, really…what was still happening, what he was still letting happen to him. It was masochistic. And again, he knew all this. He thought of the self-satisfaction she surely felt in seeing him always there for her, at her beck and call, providing her exactly what she needed.

Narcissistic supply—that's what someone told him it was.

Ding.

The sound meant a new e-mail message had just arrived in his inbox. He forgot about Lana for a moment and popped open his Outlook window.

"*Nguyen, Jill*" appeared in bold.

He didn't recognize the name.

Also in bold was the subject line, "*Chicago Game Design Conference.*" He figured it could be a potential new client or someone just curious about his company and what it had to offer. He opened the message.

Hi, your post showed up in my news feed on Facebook. I work in IT for the City, and I'm really intrigued by game design. I hadn't heard of your company before. Are you a startup? Your website is pretty impressive. Anyway, I was thinking of stopping by the conference and wanted to take you up on your company's free ticket offer if you have any left.

There wasn't really a limit, of course. Handing out tickets for this kind of event was kind of like printing money. But making something seem scarce often could make it more attractive. Rudy hit the reply button and started typing.

Hey Jill, thanks for your message. I've got a ticket to spare. Sending it to you as a PDF (see attached). I'll be at the conference all day and would be happy to demo the game we're currently developing. It's kind of a cross between Sudoku and a crossword, with some Candy Crush thrown in for good measure. Hope to see you there.

10

The Garden

Tom held down the large gray button for a second or two until the garage door began its descent. He exited the black sedan and strode into his house, passing quickly through the laundry room before entering the expansive, modern kitchen with oak cabinets and red granite countertops.

A light, early June breeze passed through a window screen on one end of the kitchen and out another on the opposite end. Tom placed the day's mail on the island near the center of the kitchen. Shortly afterward, the doorbell rang. He walked through one short hallway and then another, and opened the front door.

Standing two steps away from the edge of the porch was Jill, wearing a familiar dress she knew to be Tom's favorite. She held a khaki Coach top handle pouch, its signature red stripe a near-perfect match for the color of her lips.

"Hey there. Wasn't expecting you."

"Was in the area."

"And how is Ms. Nguyen?" he asked, pecking her on the cheek.

"You seem rather chipper tonight. You hungry?"

"Yes, but I have plans."

"Plans?"

"Yeah, I'm meeting Lana."

Jill frowned. "That's a name I haven't heard in a long time. What are you meeting *her* for?"

"We're having dinner actually."

"Dinner? Can't you meet her for lunch?"

"Nah, dinner is better. I haven't seen her for awhile and felt like catching up. Give me a second. You can come in if you like."

Tom left the door open for her and walked to a small mirror to adjust his tie. He then stepped behind a smoky interior window that separated a custom-built whiskey bar and its countertop from the kitchen.

"Just what are you hoping to accomplish with her?" Jill asked, as she closed the door behind her.

"Jill, she's a friend. Nothing more and nothing to hide."

"Tom, you're twice her age. And even if it's just a friendship—"

"—There is no *if.*"

"Really. That's not what the Joneses told me."

Tom rolled his eyes, adjusting a few strands of hair he'd pulled down to form bangs against his forehead.

"And what did the Joneses have to say?"

"Something about an exhibition at the Union League Club. And it wasn't the art, apparently."

"So you *have* heard her name recently."

"Not her name. The Joneses had no idea who the young woman was."

"Jill, I'm really not in the mood to argue with you right now. I need to leave in a few minutes."

Tears had formed in Jill's eyes, but he didn't notice.

"I'm not going to *compete* with her, Tom!" Jill shouted, reaching for the door and slamming it behind her.

So much for transparency, he thought.

Seconds later, he heard the sound of her car starting up…then the screeching tires wailing once, twice, and a third time as Jill entered the main street of the subdivision.

In little time, she came to a crisp stop at the subdivision entrance. Her tight grip on the steering wheel and fierce stare at the driver on the opposite side of the road were a bit disquieting. He had the right of way and his left turn signal on, but in apparent apprehension raised an arm to wave her on. Another screech marked her right turn to exit the subdivision.

She headed east toward the city, pulling a parking permit badge from her purse and clipping it onto the rearview mirror. Visiting her office might take her mind off things, she figured.

For the last year or so, she'd been working at the City of Chicago's Department of Innovation and Technology as a software engineer. Having managed employees for a dozen years at her previous job, she now managed just a single machine.

At least it would listen.

* * *

Lana looked at her watch then re-entered the lobby area of the Chicago Botanic Garden's visitor center.

Waving her hand toward a colleague working at the front desk, she stepped outside, warmed her face in the early evening sun, and walked to her silver Miata in one of the Garden's several parking lots. The top was down, just as she'd left it a few minutes before the start of her shift. Though the convertible had a few dings and scratches, she loved it.

She started the engine then plugged in her phone, allowing it to select a random song. Mezzo-soprano angst burst from the car's sound system at near-full volume, backed by an orchestral, cinematic intensity that heralded the breathy songstress' haunting lyrics.

Energized by the music's power and surrounded by the beauty of the Garden, Lana Delacroix was off to reconnect with a kindred spirit whose dings and scratches had begun to show. And she was fine with that.

* * *

Two white-and-blue police cruisers sped by along North Clark Street, beacons and sirens activated. One of them just missed the curb that formed the edge of a bus stop several feet away from the florescent orange chair Tom occupied at a table set for two. He was in the mood for Middle Eastern fare, and Lana said it was the best in town.

"Anything to drink other than water, sir?" asked a middle-aged server.

"Not right now; thank you," Tom replied. He checked the weather and some unread e-mails.

He had asked a mid-level associate to stay late that evening to work on an appellate brief. Despite the loss of the trial in New York, the client had decided to continue retaining Tom and his firm in seeking post-verdict relief. He hated to lose, but having a client stick with him meant his effort had not gone unappreciated.

After setting down his phone, Tom sensed the approach of some-one from behind. Looking straight ahead and donning a familiar grin, he said, "Trouble at six o'clock."

Lana walked around the table.

"It's great to see you again."

"And very nice to see you," she replied.

The server returned to the table, having noticed her arrival.

"Care to hear our specials this evening?"

"Actually, we know what we want," Lana announced.

"We do?" Tom asked.

"Yes. We'll have the Mediterranean Style Tilapia with lentils and rice and a Tabouli Salad. And please bring an extra plate; we'll be sharing."

"We will?"

"Yes."

"OK," Tom responded, looking at the server. "It's decided then."

"We'll have the salad out right away. Anything else to drink?" the server queried.

Tom and Lana both said "No" at nearly the same time, though Tom probably beat her to the punch by a nose. She shot him an amused smile.

"So, what's new with Lana?"

"Rudy and I aren't talking again."

"You still stringing him along, huh?"

"No. I've known him since my first year at UIC. We've been through a lot together."

Lana looked across the street then down at the sidewalk. As Tom looked at the side of her face, he could tell she was somewhat distraught; she also seemed a bit unsure of herself. It was a side of her he hadn't seen before. He liked it though.

She turned to face him again. "Well, there's nothing more I can do. It's his decision to distance himself from me. His choice…"

Tom sat silently, amused at the mixture of determination and uncertainty evident in her eyes.

"Hey, I like your hair," she noted, changing the subject. "You always dress well."

"Thank you. I think we both have good taste, actually."

Lana grinned, placed one hand atop her other in the center of the table, and pushed herself rearward in her chair, staring at her black fingernails. A long pause ensued.

"So, I have to ask you something," she stated.

"OK. I can't promise an answer."

"You'll answer."

"We'll see. Shoot."

"So last January you send me a text…inviting *me*…to meet *you*… in Europe."

"Right."

"A week goes by; you get no response."

"Right."

"Did it ever occur to you I thought your invitation was rather *forward*—inappropriate even—and that, rather than giving you a response, I just ignored it?"

"No."

"It's not a yes or no question," she said.

"Sounded like one."

"It was rhetorical."

"Okaaay?"

Lana just stared at him. Tom chuckled and looked away.

"Anyway, you answered it. Now you have to explain your answer."

"Explain what? I reject your premise," he said.

"And what's my premise?"

"Your premise is that you had anything…to even think *about*."

"What?"

"You heard me."

"You're very cocky sometimes. Has anyone ever told you that?"

"I've been *told* it takes one to know one."

"Maybe."

"Well, about the invitation. It still stands. I'm ready when you are."

Uncharacteristically, Lana had no response.

"Are you blushing? This is a first," Tom observed.

She laughed and looked across the street again, her eyes tracking left and right and back again as cars moved past the restaurant.

"The big question is whether you will say 'yes' to your adventure."

"Joseph Campbell," she noted.

"Yes, or close enough anyway."

Lana gazed and smiled at Tom, then slowly tilted her head backward, raising her chin an inch or two.

"Would you like to take a walk with me at the Garden tonight?"

"Isn't it going to be closed soon?"

"We can go there after dinner. I can take a guest in the evening. One of the perks of the job," she explained.

"Sure. I've never been to the Garden after hours, at night. Now about my question."

"Here we are," the server declared upon reappearing, placing their selections around the table. "Anything else I can get you?"

"No, thank you," Tom replied.

Lana smiled again at him. "Just come with me to the Garden."

* * *

The chirping of crickets and other nocturnal sounds permeated the darkness, and Tom could see the outlines of trees, ground cover, flowers, and various manmade structures. Walking the Garden's winding pathways in the dark was a unique, surreal experience for him.

"What do you think?" Lana asked.

"Definitely different at night."

"I have a place I want to show you."

Lana led him through one turn in the pathway and then another, an expert navigator in this haven of contentment and tranquility.

Eventually they reached a small nook. Lana took a seat on a stone wall in the Japanese Garden.

Tom paused for a moment, noticing a sudden stillness in the air. Surveying the clear night sky and its many bright stars, he recalled another time and place, over twenty years earlier, when he'd sat next to his Academy girlfriend Grace Ann in a similarly serene, hidden spot. He was not hallucinating, though. The stars were fixed in place; everything was real.

"I have some exciting news, Tom."

"I'm all ears."

She closed her eyes and sharply turned her head toward the ground, gathering herself. "I've got a promising lead in my search for my father."

"What have you found?"

"I went to Social Security to request some records. It took forever for them to get back to me."

"Did you try Vital Records in St. Louis County?"

"I told you before: My birth certificate doesn't show my father's name. Besides, Social Security has a lot more information on people."

"Of course."

"I'm not sure if the person processing my request knew what she was doing. When I went to pick up the records, I got some things I hadn't even asked for."

"Such as?"

"Well, for one thing, some kind of medical record with my information and Nancy's information on it, and a name I didn't recognize. It might be my father's surname; I'm not sure. It's pretty distinctive…I can't even pronounce it."

"What nationality, or can you tell?"

"Not sure, but might be Turkish."

"It does sound promising…very promising, actually. Nice work."

Tom leaned slightly backward and spread his arms. Lana slowly moved toward him, accepting his invitation to share a congratulatory embrace. To his surprise, she then rested her head on his shoulder, saying nothing as a minute went by, then two. She was content, peaceful, totally at ease.

Lana removed her head from his shoulder and sat facing him again. Her face beamed with happiness.

"I haven't told anyone else yet."

Tom felt very happy for her, and was impressed at her resourcefulness. "You definitely have to fill me in on any major developments."

"Of course. You know, if I do find him, I'm still not sure what to say to him. Do you have any wisdom for me?"

"There is no *if*. Knowing you, you will make it happen."

"Thank you. I appreciate your optimism."

"And you know, I would just tell him you've been waiting twenty-two years to meet him and want nothing from him but his time."

"Just like you, when it comes to me, right Tom?"

"What *do* I want?" he asked, looking at the sky for a moment as he placed a finger under his chin.

"Well, there is that certain adventure you mentioned back in January…"

"Well, I—"

Lana abruptly placed a finger on his lips. Just as quickly, she removed it.

"We'll talk about that later. For now I'd just like to lay back and look at the stars, if you'll let me."

She turned and eased herself rearward; the back of her head gently fell into his lap. Her face now looked up at his. Tom placed his hand on her shoulder and turned his head away, gazing straight ahead into the darkness, enabling Lana to fix her eyes on the stars above.

They said nothing to each other, letting the minutes pass.

"We should get back," Lana declared after a time.

"Ready when you are."

11

Repercussions

The ceramic base of the table lamp separated into dozens of pieces upon impact with the stone wall surrounding the huge maple. A pounding rain struck the pieces and the top of the wall, partially burying some of the shatters in the thick, rich soil of the planter bed. Other pieces were now lost in the lilac that separated the wall from the maple's trunk.

A split-second after the moment of impact, Tom awoke as if in a trance, touching the front and rear of an olive La-Z-Boy couch to gain a sense of his surroundings.

Did something just break? he asked himself.

He opened his eyes and looked to his left, using motor memory to reach for an alarm clock that wasn't there. An Xbox One wireless controller was the only device he managed to find. Hiding under the couch, it rested next to what felt like a stale Doritos chip or Frito.

He now realized where he was: the man-cave in his basement, complete with its sixty-four-inch plasma screen, six-speaker ultra-amplified sound system, and various other gaming accoutrements. He'd been sleeping for barely an hour, having gotten home from the Garden around 4:30 a.m.

Another violent sound came from outside his home. This time, Tom thought he'd heard something like plastic being dropped right above him. A thunderclap followed, prompting him to sit up, toss aside a blanket, and rub his eyes and hair.

The thumping of feet signaled someone's descent.

"Did you have fun last night?! *Must* have!"

"What? What are you doing here?" asked Tom.

At the bottom of the staircase stood Jill, her crossed arms holding fast to a black double-breasted trenchcoat that had obviously kept her very dry. "I thought you were just having *dinner*. Apparently you wanted dessert and a nightcap too—well, how did it *taste*?"

Tom fastened his hands to his hips. "Jill, you have the wrong idea. Let's have an adult conversation about this."

"No. You have to make a choice. And be prepared to live with it," she replied, uncrossing her arms to reveal a sleeveless cream blouse and below it a mauve skirt that covered her knees.

"I don't have to do anything. And anyway, I made my choice."

"At one time, maybe. But now you want a girlfriend and a plaything. Well, I'm not going to let you have both."

"Jill, I've never done much more than hug her, in like half a *year*. We've never kissed. I wouldn't call that a plaything, would you?"

She gave him a sardonic harrumph and recrossed her arms, seeming self-satisfied. "Men think it's all about the physical. 'I did not have sex with that woman.'"

Tom faintly grinned at Jill's loose impersonation of the 42nd US president. She didn't think it was funny.

"Well, it's true, Jill. I didn't."

"Maybe, maybe not. The truth is I couldn't care less if you've fucked her."

"So what *is* it then? I've been above-board with you. What's the issue? And, by the way, what were those sounds I heard out front? Sounded like something breaking."

Jill motioned toward the staircase with one arm.

"No. Don't tell me you—"

"I did."

Tom ran up the stairs, into a short hallway, and out the front door. He slapped his forehead with his right hand, looking left and right. His neighbor Richard opened the front door of the house next door and walked onto its front porch.

"Everything OK, Tom?" asked the white-haired Marine and retired CFO who shared Tom's love of the single malts.

"A small dispute, Richard."

"If you say so. Let me know if I can help. You've got a live one there. But you knew that."

"Thanks Richard," Tom replied while staring at the concrete porch at his feet. There he saw the remains of the Xbox One Jill had given him for his birthday.

Upon re-entering the house, Tom saw her standing on the other end of the entry hall, her arms again crossed.

"Jill, you're being highly irrational."

She pounded a fist against the wall. "Go talk to Lana!" she screamed, bolting for the front door. "I'm sure she is more rational!" For Jill, the conversation was clearly over.

Tom wasn't so sure. "You don't realize how wrong you are, Jill. How wrong this is."

Jill swept right past him.

"There is no competition here," he continued. "That's not what she wants!"

Now standing on the front porch, she spun her feet around with frightening speed, took a couple of steps toward him, and jabbed an accusatory finger into his chest.

"And what does *Tom* want? What Tom wants is a side dish with his main course. He wants a beautiful, young trophy he can hold in his arms for all to see in the middle of an art gallery…someone he can spend *hours and hours* with while he ignores me."

"Wait, so what are you saying? Is this about me not instantly responding to your texts when I'm in the middle of a conversation with someone? We've talked about this before, Jill. I'm a grown man. I'm not going to be at your beck and call."

"That's right. Only Lana's. And she beckons and there's that sudden spring in your step, that surge of adrenaline and all those other hormones. And you don't even bother to hide it. And did you ever *think* that maybe she's triggered another hypomanic phase in you, Tom?"

He went silent. She'd hit a nerve, while also raising a valid question (as he was acutely aware).

"After what happened in New York with the case, you weren't yourself. It went on for months. I could see it, but didn't want to say anything. I just tried to support you through it."

"It was a pretty down time for me, I admit," he said, staring at the floor.

"And then you see *her* again, and the next thing you know she's in your *arms* and you're on *cloud nine* for all to see at the Union League!"

"*Really*, Jill. You're being dramatic. I wish you could hear yourself right now. If other people—"

"—Do you think I care what anyone else thinks about how I feel about you, Tom?"

"Apparently not, if you're going to keep acting like this, throwing things out the front door 'for all to see.'"

"This isn't *acting*. This is real life, Tom. Which you haven't been living much of lately. You're off in some fantasy world. Well, go live that fantasy! Go sow some wild oats!"

"Jill, you let me know when you've calmed down, and then we can talk some more. Until then, I'm going to get some work done at the office. You can show yourself out."

Tom said nothing more. He grabbed his phone and an umbrella, then walked out the front door.

As he prepared to enter his car, he looked back at his house of the last dozen years. A rogue wave of uncertainty suddenly crashed upon his psyche: He was in a mess of things; he knew that much.

He refused to believe it was a mess he'd made. In his mind, Jill was relentlessly encroaching upon his space. As he bent down to pick up some of the larger pieces of his broken game console, he felt betrayed…betrayed by his knack for making what (to him) were increasingly reckless disclosures.

PART TWO

SEARCH

12

Cousin

Google search after Google search, hour after hour, had worn her down; around 1:30 p.m. she'd consumed the last item of fresh food in her micro-fridge: a salad she'd prepared at the nearby marketplace on her way home from a morning class.

The empty salad container still sat in the trash can beneath the miniaturized sink in her miniscule Logan Square studio. She'd need to go shopping before heading back to school the next morning. But it was only five in the afternoon; she figured she could slog through another half hour or so of internet research before heading out.

Trying to function as her own private investigator was as challenging as Lana had thought it would be. She was saving at least $1500 but consuming a considerable amount of time she'd normally spend with friends.

Saving was a must, though—and she actually enjoyed doing it. Becoming a ward of the state at fifteen and emancipated at eighteen had both forced and enabled her to learn very quickly the art of managing money. Becoming a finance major was a natural, presumptive choice, and meshed well with her personality, as did her second major, psychology.

Lana didn't need anything from anyone, and rarely even wanted it. And now she was depending on herself again, looking for the key that would unlock the door behind which stood her father, assuming he was even alive.

As far as she could tell from the Social Security records she previously managed to obtain, his last name was Yilmez. Lana turned up little useful information on the internet using that spelling, but quickly found that an alternative spelling, Yilmaz, was fairly common in Turkey. She assumed someone at the Social Security Administration must have made a spelling error.

Though having the surname was unquestionably helpful, she estimated there could be tens of thousands of people in Turkey sharing it, thousands in Europe, and unknown numbers outside Europe. Thus far she'd managed to eliminate as "unlikely candidates" perhaps ten percent of the people bearing the name who were dead, not male, or not old enough to be her father. At this rate, she figured she'd need another hundred hours (at the very least) to narrow the possibilities down to one hundred or fewer "most likely candidates."

What she could really use, as she was painfully aware, was some way to significantly streamline the process. Lana was not shy about taking practical shortcuts; she'd risk a wild goose chase if she had something in hand to place her quarry within range. Indeed for her, there was adventure in such a gambit rather than risk.

As she prepared to close her laptop and head out to shop for a bit, she noticed something peculiar in a list of corporate records she'd pulled up when running her most recent Google search on the name Yilmaz. In particular, one item in the list of available records had a hyperlink; none of the others did. She clicked on the hyperlink, which pulled up a graphical representation of the corporate and family ownership of a series of companies in the Czech Republic. What appeared to be a holding company and a number of subsidiary companies were all owned by Yilmaz family members, all of whom (if she was reliably deducing what she was seeing on the page) originally hailed from Istanbul. Lana thought it was odd that so many Turks from Istanbul with the same last name, and apparently from the same family, would be in the Czech Republic sharing in the ownership of several companies. At the head of the holding company, apparently, was someone named Duygu.

As she explored additional information in what appeared to be a corporate database maintained by the Czech government, Lana noticed one of the Yilmaz family's companies owned two jewelry stores. She ran a search on the jewelry stores' names and discovered that one of them regularly did business with another store in Paris.

Lana's mouth dropped open. Suddenly the family history that her mother Nancy had told Lana's grandparents—one always suspect in Lana's eyes in light of her mother's strained and stretched version of reality—gained a new credibility.

She figured that Facebook was now her best chance, and typed "Yilmaz" in the search field. She found several individuals who listed their hometown as Istanbul. Impulsively, she clicked on the first profile she found: a woman named Gamze living in Uskudar, which Google Maps showed as being just northeast of Istanbul.

To ensure she could get a message through on Facebook Messenger, Lana paid a small fee to send a message directly to Gamze's inbox. Relying on her Google Translate app, Lana began to write words in English that were translated into very elementary Turkish: *"Hello, do you know a Duygu Yilmaz? I was hoping you can help me."*

Many minutes passed; she continued to review webpages she'd found as part of her research. Not getting any response, she wrote more bluntly, *"I want to talk to you. I'm trying to find Duygu Yilmaz."*

This time there was no delay.

"Who are you?"

Lana appreciated the direct question.

"I'd like to help," the person continued. *"Why do you want to find him?"*

"Duygu was a friend of my mother. He met my mother in Paris in 1991."

"Do you have a little more information? How were they friends? Do you know Turkish?"

"I am using a translating application. I only speak English. Duygu met my mother while in Paris. They were together for several months."

"Can't your mother help you?"

"My mother is sick and cannot help. I believe Duygu is my father, from Istanbul."

"I am his niece. He is from Istanbul, true. He lived in Paris, true."

"How old is Duygu?"

"How old do you think he is?"

"I know very little about him. My mother was born in 1964. I think they are close to the same age. I was born in St. Louis on February 2, 1992."

Again there was a long pause. Lana's usual impatience was nowhere to be found—not at a moment like this one.

"I appreciate you answering my questions and trying to help. Do you know if Duygu has an e-mail address?"

"I will talk to Duygu. He is working right now. Give me your number."

She complied, and added her e-mail address.

"I would like to speak with Duygu. Did he know someone named Nancy?"

"I don't know. Can I see your picture?"

"Yes. I have plenty of photos on Facebook," Lana noted, sending Gamze some links. *"Does he have green eyes?"*

"Olive skin and green eyes, yes."

After a minute or two, Gamze added, *"Like you."*

"I looked at your photos too," Lana noted.

"Duygu will call you sometime. I gave him your number."

"I don't think my phone can take international calls."

"Duygu knows foreign languages. He can talk some English."

"Did you call him just now?"

"Yes, my cousin."

Drawing her hand to her face, Lana began to sniffle.

* * *

Jill looked around the convention hall, marveling at the number of small IT and gaming companies that could afford booths at the expo. Though it was the middle of the day, the lights had been dimmed inside the windowless hall so that several laser shows, a myriad of neon and backlit company logos, and dozens of massive monitors could draw in the attention of those present.

If one were looking down from the empty balcony rimming the walls, the scene was like a miniature version of Los Angeles in *Blade Runner*.

Jill presented her smartphone as she approached the registration table. A QR code on the screen served as her virtual ticket to the Chicago Game Design Conference. The "ticket" was courtesy of Rudy, who'd promised her a demo of the game his company was developing.

Jill had never worked for a video game company and had never tried to code anything related to gaming, even as part of a class during college or at a hobby club. But the idea of creating and selling games appealed to her. She saw people like Rudy as the rock stars of her trade.

After donning the lanyard she'd just been handed, she found her way to Rudy's booth.

"Hey Jill, glad you could make it!" Rudy said, greeting her with a firm handshake. Despite the dark hall, he wore equally dark Coke-bottle sunglasses, along with a noticeably wrinkled white dress shirt he'd buttoned straight to the top. His jet-black hair was trimmed very tight at the ears but flowed rather freely on top, artificially made to appear a bit unkempt as it tailed a bit upward at the ends—all doubtlessly aided by gel or some other product. At about 5'5", Rudy was barely an inch or two taller than Jill, but to her that was nothing unusual. She knew lots of family members, particularly back in Vietnam, who came in around the same height.

He got away with the dark sunglasses thanks to his company's booth, which was easily the brightest-lit in the auditorium. Several powerful uplights and other strategically placed fixtures made the space a can't-miss.

"Thanks again for the invitation, Rudy. How did you recognize me?"

"I looked you up on LinkedIn."

"Got it," she replied.

"So let me take you over here for the demo," he said. "We're tentatively calling it Cross-Doku-Crush, but haven't settled on the name yet."

He walked her over to an Apple laptop that was running an application emulator. Half the screen showed the app running; the other half showed a video of someone operating the game on an iPhone.

"Very intuitive," she commented. "It's seamless. I don't need to hear anything to understand what's happening."

"Yep, that's the idea. What you're seeing there is stage one of the game. Want to try it out for yourself? I've got a beta version running on my phone." He handed her an iPhone 5S and pressed a button to bring up the game app. "Go ahead and take it for a test drive. I'm going to say hi to some other visitors over there."

She nodded her head as she started to experiment with the controls. In little time she figured out how to play the game; the interface particularly impressed her.

A few minutes later, after getting about halfway through stage one, she saw a text message appear as an alert on Rudy's phone. She recognized the name.

"*Parking now*," the message read.

Jill immediately walked the phone back to its owner.

"Expecting someone named Lana?" she asked.

"Yes, how did you know?"

"She just texted you," Jill responded, pointing to the alert that remained on his screen.

"Great, I would love to introduce you. She's—"

He paused to choose the right words. "She's a really good friend of mine."

"Can't wait," Jill replied, trying hard not to come off sarcastically.

"Yeah, she's really something. Very smart, outgoing. And into video gaming, just like you. You'll really like her!" he gushed.

Jill nodded her head but turned away, hiding the glower on her face. She doubted Lana was, in fact, into video gaming. But Rudy obviously thought she was.

From the opposite direction, Lana approached wearing black leggings and a loose, light blue crop top.

"Hey, Rudy. Nice outfit," Lana said. "You fit right in."

"Thanks, that's what I was going for," he responded. "I want to introduce you to someone. This is Jill Nguyen."

Lana recognized the name immediately, but needed Rudy to point her out. There were several people congregated around the laptop that was demonstrating Cross-Doku-Crush, none of them particularly standing out from the others.

The two women's eyes met. Jill's eyebrows involuntarily lowered for a split-second. Lana spotted the tell and felt uncharacteristically nervous. A bit belatedly, she extended a cold, soft hand, which Jill took with a sense of satisfaction.

"Nice to meet you in person, Jill."

Rudy seemed surprised. "You've met before?" he asked.

Jill was inclined to unload on Lana—verbally, if not physically— but could tell that Lana and Rudy were close friends.

"We know *of* each other," Jill said after a brief pause. "By way of both knowing Tom Edwards."

Rudy again looked surprised. "Oh," he muttered. "What a small world we live in here in little Chi-Town."

Anticipating Rudy's next question, Jill preempted it with a statement. "I've known Tom for about two and a half years. We've been dating most of that time. He told me he met Lana at your company's pre-launch party last December, but I hadn't met her until today."

Jill turned now to directly face Lana. They stood perhaps two to three feet apart. "It's nice to finally meet you, Lana. Rudy and Tom both tell me you're a very smart and interesting person."

Lana thought the words sounded sincere, and felt much of her confidence coming back to her—the result not of Jill's words, but of Jill's restraint. The woman had grace *and* class, which Lana respected and appreciated.

"You are too kind, Jill. Tom has been generous to me and has treated me like a daughter. I don't know if he told you, but I grew up without a father, and I'm still trying to find him. Tom has been kind of a mentor to me for the last few months."

Lana gauged Jill's reaction to the statement, but couldn't get much of a read.

"You are very lucky to have him, Jill. I want you to know that. He has been a gentleman to me. I hope we can—"

A thunderous boom came from a small stage near the center of the room. A local cover band was starting to play its first set, making it nearly impossible for anyone to carry on a conversation.

Jill leaned in near one of Lana's ears to get the last word. "I know I'm lucky to have him. You're absolutely right: He is a gentleman. And I want you to know something too, Lana: That's not going to change."

Jill stepped back from Lana and walked over to Rudy, extending him as firm a handshake as he'd first given her. "I need to get back to work. I appreciate the demo, Rudy. You've got a great app. Best wishes to you and your company."

A feeling of satisfaction came over Jill as she strode away. Lana was pretty, smart, and clever, though Jill did not join Rudy and Tom in considering her interesting.

13

Gameplan

A rust-colored wooden desk wrapped around Tom on three sides. Stacks of papers of various heights covered much of two of them; a docked laptop and twenty-three-inch monitor occupied most of the other.

Tom leaned backward in his large, black leather chair and peered into the recessed florescent light fixture immediately above him.

Outside the two windows of his office, the lights of the city revealed outlines of structures and the movement of cars and people.

A familiar tone rang from the phone on his desk. Reaching for the handset, Tom looked at the bright color display that showed the caller's name.

"Still here?" Tom asked his friend and managing partner, Roger Steele.

"I thought I might catch you at your desk, and was going to ask you the same question," Roger responded.

"You did. I'm here. So are you. Preparing for the *Polaris* trial, I presume?"

"Right. And how's your trial prep coming along for *Nexfurnace*?"

"Pretty well," said Tom. "I sent the associates home. Going over my direct examination outline for our corporate representative right now."

"So, what's your angle with him?"

Two black dress shoes struck the top of Tom's desk as he again eased himself rearward in his chair.

"It's kind of unique, because Jeffries was actually there demonstrating the furnace when the fire happened. I'm going to have him as the eyes and ears of the jury, describing the blow-by-blow."

"Will you be able to get the temperature into evidence through him?" Roger asked.

"I should be able to."

"Don't underestimate Judge Bolton. She's a stickler."

A few seconds passed.

"Say, how's Jill doing?" Roger asked.

Tom took his feet down, turned to his left, and looked into the mostly clear night sky.

"She's doing OK, all things considered," he said—and wanted to believe.

"Good. At least you won't be out-of-state for this trial. She appreciates having you in town, I'm sure."

Tom remained silent as he tracked a white stretch limousine's slow movement on a nearby street below.

"Tom?"

"Uh, yeah. That's right."

Tom felt his phone vibrate. He opened the magnetic latch on the black leather holster at his belt to view the screen of his iPhone.

"I have a call coming in. I'm going to have to let you go, Roger."

"Sure, don't stay around too late."

Tom pressed a red button on his desk phone then pressed a green one on the other.

"Hey, are you still at work?"

"How'd you guess?" Tom responded.

"You at a good stopping point?"

"Why do you ask?"

"I want to talk with you about something."

"Sure. Give me fifteen minutes to wrap up," Tom said.

"OK, what time should I expect you?"

"12:45?"

"Sounds good."

"Right," Tom replied, hanging up.

* * *

The gray key fob held near a metal latch triggered a long beep and buzzing sound. Tom pulled the handle of the glass door and entered a newly renovated, well-lit parking garage. His car sat not even fifty feet away, the result of having arrived at 6:30 that morning. He fell heavily into the driver's seat and reached under his collar to remove his tie, which he placed on a hook above the window behind him. As always, the interior of his car was nearly immaculate.

A subscriber to the notion that the most efficient number of times to have a thought is once, he hadn't thought twice about heading over to Lana's apartment. After spending the day planning how he'd later approach several lay and expert witnesses in the courtroom, he was ready to place his mind elsewhere. And he still sort of owed her for that unintentional ditching at the Museum of Contemporary Art—notwithstanding the invitation to Europe.

In short time Tom's car disappeared from the garage, the Mercantile Exchange Building, and the downtown area. Skyscrapers faded into smaller structures until living spaces mostly replaced working domains. Gray and glass and stone arranged in neat patterns became brown and brick and wood mixed together eclectically.

He now approached Logan Square, having encountered little traffic this late on a weeknight. Three adjacent parking spots beckoned within half a block of Lana's building. Upon stopping he spotted her leaning against the front wall, one knee bent as she held her phone in front of her, illuminating her pale face.

Tom got out of the car and took half a dozen steps toward the building. He paused, turned his head slightly to the right, and pressed a button on his keyless remote. Satisfied to hear his horn sound briefly, he spotted a long green awning bearing several familiar numbers where it ended at a sidewalk. Lana put her phone in a back pocket of her jeans and walked toward him, meeting him under the awning about halfway between the sidewalk and front door.

"Hey, thanks for coming," she said, placing a hand on each of his shoulders and looking him in the eyes.

"You're staring," he deadpanned.

"Ha. Come upstairs," she replied, releasing one of his shoulders and lightly pulling on the other in the direction of the front door.

He stopped to admire an assortment of yellow, red, and orange perennials planted along both sides of the walkway, just outside the coverage of the awning above him. Well-placed lighting fixtures made the colors remarkably bright at this hour.

Lana watched him blink and gazed at his thick, curly black eyelashes. When he finally turned in her direction, she reached for the front door and held it open for him, then used a key fob to open a second door.

The building's lobby was small but included two wings for the reception of guests. Four steps led to a small elevator.

"Do you think we'll get stuck again?" Lana asked Tom as they entered the elevator.

Tom laughed, recalling the time in late spring he'd aided her move from her old apartment in under four hours flat, with no other helpers. Her relatively small number of belongings, his ability to handle a larger vehicle, and their easygoing rapport had made the experience unexpectedly enjoyable, even if the elevator hadn't cooperated entirely.

"Go on in," Lana said, motioning in the direction of her apartment as the elevator door opened.

Tom opened the door and entered the studio apartment, a testament to the art of minimalist design complemented nicely by Lana's own style.

"Impressive," he commented as she soon followed behind him. "Looks very homey since we moved everything in here."

"Thanks. How do you like the accent wall?"

Reaching the main room of the studio, Tom took in the high-gloss peachy orange sheen and grinned.

"It's so you," he said.

"I know, right? Glad you like it."

Tom took off his navy blue cashmere blazer, draped it over the dark walnut privacy screen next to Lana's bed, and made himself comfortable on a nearby loveseat.

"You wanted to talk with me about something?" he asked.

Lana poured herself a glass of water and sat next to him.

"Yes, I have some good news."

"I'm listening."

"I think I've found my father. At least, I'm pretty sure I have."

Tom spontaneously placed a hand on Lana's closest knee.

"Tell me more," he said.

Lana looked at her knee, then at Tom, and blinked several times. He smiled and slowly removed his hand, tapping her thigh with his forefinger as he did so.

She feigned a smirk and proceeded to describe the payoff from her recent research. Tom listened intently, occasionally chuckling or nodding his head while admiring her resourcefulness and determination. She talked for at least ten minutes straight; as she continued, he kicked off his dress shoes, turned to face her, leaned back, and crossed his legs.

"What do you think?" Lana queried as she showed Tom the last few text messages between her and the woman she believed to be her cousin.

"It's amazing. I'm impressed."

Lana smiled and twirled a tress of her dark brown hair.

Mirroring her smile, Tom shifted forward at the waist and leaned back a bit. "My turn to ask you something."

Lana touched one of her temples and ran her hand through her hair, reposing the bottom of her palm against the top of her ear. She looked at the tips of Tom's toes as outlined by his thick black socks.

"And this is merely a question of intellectual curiosity, you see," he went on.

"Which means it's not, but go ahead."

He looked at her for several seconds, just long enough to test her patience. "Why have you been unattached for so long?"

Lana was amused. "Nobody meets my expectations."

"I think you're holding out. You like to play hard to get, and enjoy having several guys in your orbit."

"I mean, I know any guy would be lucky to have me, but what guy would I be lucky to have?" she said. Reflecting on her query, she added, "It's really isolating being the one who loves less."

Tom instantly pointed a finger toward her and declared, "Ah, but the one who loves less has all the power, or at least more of it."

Lana considered his statement but said nothing.

"And it's not a matter of luck really, is it?" he asked. "Saying one is 'lucky' to have another suggests one doesn't otherwise deserve to have the other."

"I never thought of it that way. Regardless, I don't know a guy who actually 'deserves' me."

Tom took a turn being silent.

"Oh, it's hard to be a narcissist," she continued. "And what you said earlier is true. Until I meet someone who I think 'deserves' me, I will be single."

"Yes. You will also maintain your power," Tom added.

Lana sat upright, resting her hands in her lap.

"But ultimately, two people earn each other," Tom went on. "Anything not based on mutual worth will be unequal, with one placing the other on either a pedestal or footstool."

"Yes. So has Jill earned you?"

Tom smiled. "Well, it's more a question of whether I deserve her. I *am* driving her crazy lately."

"You've been upfront with her."

"I have. But she has this fierceness to her. And she's not used to me standing firm in the face of an objection."

"An objection about me?"

"Yes."

"And you're standing firm," she observed, slightly raising both eyebrows. "Why?"

"Because you've added value to my life, Lana. There's acceptance; you respect my space. I'm a better person after knowing you."

Lana lightly bit her lip and opened her arms. Tom delivered a hearty hug and deftly placed a kiss on her cheek.

"Time for me to head back. Thanks for having me over and sharing the good news," he said.

"Wait, stay here a second, if you don't mind? There's something I've been meaning to show you."

Tom sat back down on the loveseat. Lana whisked herself around the corner to her dresser, which sat in a short secondary hallway within her tiny apartment. Opposite the dresser was a tall, narrow mirror mounted on a closet door. To her left was an open door leading to her bathroom.

She unbuttoned and unzipped her jeans, then wiggled her way out of them.

"Don't come back here!" she warned, turning her head toward the main hallway.

She then reached into an open dresser drawer, selected an undergarment, removed the one she was wearing, and quickly put on the replacement. Her gray camisole came off next, as she turned to face the open hallway. From that position she turned back her head and looked into the mirror. She admired every curve, large or small, accentuated by her tall, lithe frame. She ran her hands through her hair, the waviness giving it volume and character. Her pride in her body and in herself felt right and good.

Satisfied for now, she reached for the closet door handle and soon saw what she was looking for. She pulled two items of clothing off their hangers, threw them on, removed the socks she was still wearing, and sauntered back into the main room.

"Tom?"

Stretched out on the loveseat, his head resting on the end closer to Lana and facing away from her, Tom sat up and turned around.

"Whoa," he said, unintentionally giving a decent impersonation of Keanu Reeves.

Lana wore a simple, sleeveless two-piece dress that nearly matched the peach-orange color of her accent wall. A high-waisted, lightly pleated skirt ended a quarter-foot above her knees. An elegantly cropped top made of the same thick, soft fabric covered the top quarter-foot of her skirt, thus leaving the illusion—at least when she was stationary—that she was wearing a one-piece, slip-on dress.

"Stay there," she commanded, putting out her hand in his direction.

She crept up to the accent wall. Still facing it, she asked, "You like?"

"I do."

"Good," she replied. "I have another question for you."

"Go for it," he said, momentarily distracted by a vibration in his pocket, which he resisted the urge to respond to.

Lana continued to face the wall, slowly pulled off the top part of her dress, and loosened her skirt, which she grabbed hold of at her waist so that it didn't fall.

"Want to give me a massage?"

Not sure if his ears were playing tricks on him, he looked up and shot a glance in her direction. His eyes sensed and immediately targeted the black strap of her bra, still firmly clasped, and then—as Lana's skirt hit the floor—her bikini-style panties adorned with an inch or so of lace, all the same color as her dress. Half of her ample posterior was fully exposed to him.

A few very awkward seconds went by, for both of them. Tom felt as though he were having an out-of-body experience…as though he were looking down at the unfolding scene from the ceiling. He saw himself there, immobile on the loveseat, and thought of Jill again. The vibration undoubtedly had signaled a text from her.

After what seemed like nearly a minute, Lana let out a large sigh of frustration and reached for a pair of green soccer shorts and a white T-shirt she'd left hanging on a chair earlier in the week. She put them on and assumed a prone position on her twin-size bed, spreading her arms wide open.

"Yes, I can do that," he answered in matter-of-fact fashion. He got on top of the bed and placed his knees to either side of her thighs. He then dug deeply into her skin, starting at the shoulders and neck and working his way down.

"Oh, you're *good*," she said, lightly sighing in pleasure several times as he thrust and spun his fingers around her body. He went as far as the waistband of her shorts, avoiding her breasts on the way down and shifting himself rearward to prepare to work below her pelvis.

"I'm going to work your upper thighs now and go down from there," he announced. And he did just that: no more, no less.

This guy is either secretly gay, a big tease, or torn about something, Lana thought. After Tom massaged her feet for several minutes, he let go of her and said nothing. A couple more awkward seconds passed; she again made a loud sigh and turned onto her side, facing the accent wall just a few inches away.

Once more Tom felt like he was having an out-of-body experience. As before, he imagined himself looking down for a moment from the ceiling. He saw Lana lying there on her side with her arms folded and him sitting next to her, motionless, gazing in her direction.

Instinctively, he at that moment reconnected with himself and moved beside Lana into a modified spoon position, resting his head against her upper back and placing his right hand and upper arm around her right shoulder in a tender embrace. And they lay together that way for nearly an hour, Tom unable to fall asleep while Lana easily dozed away, eventually entering a brief dream state.

* * *

As Lana was sleeping, Tom thought of what she'd just placed in front of him. Indeed, the green light she'd given him was still fully lit; he wasn't even sure if Lana was sleeping.

But physical intimacy with Lana beyond an embrace, a brief stolen kiss, or a light touch of a thigh, nose, or arm was not something Tom wanted. He'd already made that decision many months ago, not long after meeting her at the Southside Ballroom. The lawyer in him was again kicking in. He thought of the facts and applied indifferent logic: Lana was twenty-one years younger than he was; he already had a steady relationship with someone much closer to his age (well, a relationship that had been fairly steady—and stable—until recently).

Sure, physical intimacy—an exchange of bodily fluids of some kind—would feel amazing. He hadn't checked his manhood at the door. His cold logic could not override his hormones, unless he willed it to.

But he knew himself well enough to know that once he had a taste of Lana's flesh—if he chose to have it—his desire for her would overtake the platonic, emotional intimacy that made the bond between them what it was.

What's more, he didn't want to repeat the past. While at the Academy, he'd let his relationship with Grace Ann devolve into one based heavily on and around sex—and increasingly less upon the emotional intimacy that had been the foundation of their connection.

Well, to be accurate, both he and Grace Ann had let that happen. They were young: he eighteen, nineteen, and then twenty; she half a year older. But he felt more responsible, because his libido was perhaps as high on one end of the spectrum as Lana's seemed low on the other. Grace Ann's was certainly toward the higher end too…but Tom—well, he took it to another level.

To be sure, Lana was right about one thing: He was torn about something. On the one hand, he didn't want to hurt her feelings, or her ego. He knew she was giving herself to him freely. He knew all too well what the sting of rejection felt like and hated being the one to inflict it, particularly in this situation.

On the other hand, as deeply as he'd allowed himself to dive into the complex, intense connection he had with Lana, he always saw a clear boundary he would not cross—was not willing to cross. He sensed and felt that Jill was the woman who could best fulfill his wants and needs. Yeah, she drove him crazy sometimes—as he'd been doing to her a lot lately—but he couldn't see himself winding up with someone else as a life partner or future spouse.

And anyway, in his eyes, Lana had her issues: She was too distant, too in need of space, and too independent to be someone he could ever date (at least in a traditional sense) or marry. He thought she required a lot of patience and tolerance; he was certain that many men would not put up with her—or the way she related to men generally. But she seemed to have a knack for avoiding the ones who wouldn't or couldn't, and for finding the ones who'd supply her what she needed.

Many employers would not put up with her either, which is why she'd had some difficulty being accepted and successful with several of her previous bosses.

But because Tom didn't have a desire to date Lana in the traditional sense, much less marry or hire her, he didn't take great issue with such aspects of her personality.

To him, the bottom line was that Lana was a cool friend to have at this time in his life. Unlike Rudy, Tom wasn't looking for something more. That was a truth he could hold onto, despite what others—particularly Jill—might think of the relationship.

14

Grandma

The bright rays of the midday June sun reflected sharply off the jade gemstone set in the small gold ring on Lana's hand as she gripped the wheel. Five hours of driving had taken her to the St. Louis suburb of Richmond Heights, where she would soon meet her grandmother at a senior living center.

The drive had given Lana an opportunity to think about the future, including a hoped-for call from Duygu—and forget about the recent past, including Tom's surprisingly mild response to her overtures.

At the moment, she found herself behind a tractor-trailer as it slowly made its way ahead of her along eastbound Clayton Road. In light of the fumes she'd started to smell from the truck's malfunctioning exhaust system, she thought about putting the top back up. But she was close to her destination, and the weather was perfect.

Inexplicably, the truck soon stopped right in front of her, blocking the entrance to the senior center. She tapped the horn twice with the palm of one hand.

The truck's occupant, a middle-aged, heavy-set man, rolled down the window and stuck out his hand, briefly extending a one-finger salute. She blew her horn again, but he merely smiled at her in his side mirror, saying and doing nothing.

"Are you just going to sit there? People need to use this road!" Lana yelled, beginning to attract some attention from drivers passing by as well as those lined up behind her Miata.

The driver opened the door, dismounted, and took a few steps in Lana's direction. "Hey, Trixie, I'm workin' here. Don't get your panties in a bunch. We'll have you on your way to the hair salon in no time."

She poked her head outside the car, where he could clearly see her. "Hey, how can you block half the road like this? There are five lanes here!"

A St. Louis County Police officer, who'd been waiting two cars behind Lana's, got out of his cruiser and walked toward her. "Ma'am, I'll speak with the driver. Where are you headed?"

"I'm trying to visit my grandmother at the senior center, right there," she said in her best calm, measured tone while pointing at her intended destination.

The officer looked over at the building she'd pointed to, then back to her. "Your grandmother has Alzheimer's?"

"Actually, yes, why?"

"Well, I have an uncle who stays there too, and he has Alzheimer's."

Lana considered the situation, looking at the line of cars behind her and again at the tractor-trailer, whose driver was now back at the wheel. "Thank you, officer. I guess I lost my cool a little."

The officer rested a hand on Lana's left shoulder for a second or two, then removed it. "Happens to the best of us, ma'am. Hope you enjoy your visit with your grandmother." He then went to speak with the driver.

Lana dropped her head and let out a heavy sigh. By the time she looked up again and re-gripped the wheel, the truck had begun moving away. Its driver gave her a sarcastic wave.

Ignoring him, she turned into the entrance of the senior center and found a perfect parking spot not far from the front door. After checking in at the front desk, she made her way to her grandmother's room in little time. Upon entering, Lana found her staring through the window, even though its white inner curtain was still closed.

Lana drew the curtain, revealing the clear blue sky, the early afternoon sun, and the outlines of downtown St. Louis and its stainless steel Gateway Arch. She pulled up a chair next to her grandmother, reached into a jeans pocket, and drew out a small toy plane emblazoned with the old logo and detailing of American Airlines. She placed the airplane on the window sill and took a seat next to the woman who, along with Lana's now-deceased grandfather, had raised her for many years as her mother's condition deteriorated.

"No clouds, Grandma. What a beautiful day to fly off somewhere."

Grandma was silent, but turned her head slightly in Lana's direction.

"Whenever a plane leaves the tarmac, the passengers are always a little nervous or excited or just happy the thing is finally getting off the ground. And whether they realize it or not, there are new adventures awaiting them wherever they're headed."

"Oh boy!" Grandma said, showing a smile and looking at Lana's face. The clearly spoken response was immediate and unexpected, sharp even.

Just as quickly, a tear formed in each of Lana's eyes. She had not emotionally connected with her grandmother in quite some time.

Once in awhile she reminds me of herself, Lana thought.

Grandma continued to look at Lana's face. Regardless of the state of Grandma's mental faculties, Lana still saw the warmth and grace she remembered from her childhood.

"Coming here reminds me what is important, Grandma. Thank you."

Grandma reached out and grabbed Lana's right arm, looked her in the eyes, and responded, "Thank you."

It was almost as if her grandmother remembered her—if not in mind, surely somewhere in the spirit or soul.

Grandma released Lana's arm and resumed staring through the window, looking peaceful and almost content.

After a few moments, Lana sat back in her chair and placed her hands in her lap. She looked at the jade ring she wore, a birthday gift Grandma had given her eight years ago. It reminded her of Grandma's strength and support when Nancy's delusional behavior was intensifying.

* * *

Lana sat on a wooden chair in her bedroom and peered through the window. The impatient sentry could continue to wait for Grandma's car to appear on the street, or confront Nancy now.

Rising from her chair, Lana walked briskly to the den. As expected, the door was locked. She knocked three times, then waited.

Several minutes went by. To occupy her time, Lana resumed reading her latest young adult novel, *Wasteland*. She again happily became lost in the world she held in her small and delicate ten-year-old hands. Slight smiles occasionally appeared on her face as she took in the emerging narrative of Lex, Marina, and their friend West.

Eventually, a soft click announced an audience could be had with Nancy. Lana instantly thrust a bookmark between two pages, set the novel on an end table, and opened the door to the den.

"I want to go to Stephanie's house," Lana said in a strong, almost commanding tone after entering the room.

Nancy turned away from the television and scrutinized her daughter. A crumpled forehead signaled only apprehension and disbelief. At thirty-nine, she still looked to be in her late twenties. But her deep brown eyes, once full of life, were dull and haunting. Gaunt and slightly unkempt, the former model appeared a wraith whose outward beauty both persisted and faded with each passing moment.

"Why? Why would you do that to us?"

"Do what? I want to go to her sleepover. She invited me."

"Now is not a good time. I don't know enough about Stephanie's parents. They might be helping them follow us."

Crossing her arms, Lana prepared herself for yet another inane debate. "Mom, why would the FBI be following us? They have better things to do!"

"That's what they want you thinking."

Lana rolled her eyes. "No, they are there to help people. Just like after 9/11."

"They made 9/11 happen! You are so naïve."

"You are so wrong."

"Is this how you treat your elders? Would you talk that way to your grandfather?"

Lana shrugged her shoulders. "Grandpa wouldn't say things that don't make sense."

Nancy turned off the television and stood to face Lana, pointing an accusing finger. "*You* don't make sense! You are a *mistake*! I *never* should have had you!"

Lana winced and took a step backward. Nancy said nothing, waiting for a response. Lana gave none. Instead she looked to her right, propping herself up on her toes to get a good view of the end of the street outside one of the den's windows.

"What are you looking for?" Nancy demanded.

Lana saw only an empty street. Tears formed in her eyes. *I'm cursed*, she said to herself. Thinking of Stephanie and other middle school friends, Lana wondered, *Why is this happening to me?*

The front door of the house then opened and quickly closed. Lana quickly wiped her eyes and ran out of the den and into the living room.

"Grandma!"

"Hello, Sweetie," was the reply from the stately older woman, who accepted a desperate hug from her granddaughter. "Are you OK?"

Lana hesitated. She wanted to respond, but instead looked back toward Nancy, who'd arrived from the den.

"Fighting again with your daughter?" Grandma inquired.

"She doesn't listen. She's stubborn and she needs to learn how to obey," Nancy declared.

"Maybe sometimes you need to listen to her. She has a lot to say," Grandma observed.

"Yes, a lot to say but a lot more to learn. Maybe those who have a lot to learn should focus on doing that, before they open their mouths and say silly things."

"And what has she said this time?"

With a harrumph and crossed arms, Nancy took a couple of steps back toward the den. "She wants a sleepover. But it's too danger—"

"—She should have one," Grandma asserted, interrupting her daughter. "She's earned it."

"Mother, you shouldn't interfere."

Lana smiled, holding Grandma's hand as she listened to the two older women. Reinforcements had arrived just in time. Lana didn't need to enter the battlefield by herself. This time, at least, she would be victorious.

Lana could use reason and logic to contend with Nancy's fantastical, bizarre conspiracy theories; her mother's theories concerning Lana's existence, however, were overpowering and devastating.

"Stay out of this, Mother! You've crossed the—"

"—*Nancy!*" yelled Grandma, sharply cutting her daughter short. "I will take her there myself."

Nancy harrumphed again and returned to the den, slamming the pocket door closed to sequester herself once more from the all-too-real world. Lana released Grandma's hand and looked into her loving yet troubled eyes.

"Thank you."

15

Hyde Park

Suyin Chen started off for her morning class at the University of Chicago just a few blocks south of her Hyde Park apartment. The sky was bright and sharp as she stepped onto her porch and debated whether to bring her light pink windbreaker. She unzipped it and tossed it onto a loveseat near the front door, revealing a cream-colored stretch T-shirt.

Intruding upon her thoughts was an ongoing contest she'd been having with her roommate about their lease. The battle lately was quite the distraction. But she had help if she needed it: a nice older lawyer she'd recently met. His name was Tom Edwards.

As she walked to campus, she took a moment to admire the open spaces and observe the lack of bustle in this neighborhood compared to her hometown of Beijing. Faces meeting hers nodded or smiled; one passerby wished her a good morning. Less a function of culture than of scale, she recognized that a place like New York would be much different than here. She didn't require a visit to that larger metropolis to confirm her assumption.

As usual, South Blackstone Avenue had light traffic. The coffee shop half a block ahead, however, was (as usual) quite congested.

Coffee wasn't a compulsive need of hers, though she enjoyed the occasional conversations with classmates as they consumed it. Also, she accepted the need to conduct business with some of her professors while a cup of it sat nearby. Ideally someone else would pay, as she found the drink rather impractical and certainly not inexpensive. More often than not, she would just have hot water.

"Hey Staci. Liking those shoes," an acquaintance said as he walked by her.

Oblivious and not expecting commentary on her wardrobe, Suyin (Staci to most she knew or met in America) ignored the compliment and continued toward 58th Street, setting her mind again on her biostatistics class.

* * *

Three long bursts followed by five quick pulses indicated a text from Lana. Tom started to reach inside his coat pocket for his smartphone, but instead resumed reviewing an associate's draft of a motion for summary judgment. Red marks on the screen indicated changes he had made to her handiwork—"suggested edits," he would invariably call them when returning the document to her. The phone on his desk rang; he pressed the speakerphone button.

"Marilyn asked about our motion. Have you had a chance to look—"

"—No worries. In a few seconds you'll have it," he replied.

"There's no rush, really. If you need—"

"—Relax, Lauren. I appreciate you staying on top of this case. And you really do a good job of managing the manager."

"I learned from you. Watching—"

"—watching me manage Marilyn, yes. Hmm, sometimes you are too good a learner." He paused a second or two. "I'm—"

"—joking, yes. I know," Lauren said, finishing his sentence for him.

Tom feigned a grimace then glanced at the image on his desk phone's video display, which featured a high-definition live shot of the drop ceiling in Lauren's office. As with more than half the people in the law firm's mothership location in downtown Chicago, she'd turned the small camera on her phone away from her chair. Another option was to twist the aperture shut; moving the camera, however, avoided the question, "Is something wrong with your phone?" Moreover, it signaled a deliberate opting-out.

He reached for his iPhone again and opened iMessages to see what Lana wanted, but no words appeared. Instead he saw a silver convertible, an image he'd seen earlier that day on her Facebook page, captioned as follows: "my favorite car—best part is me in it." Chuckling under his breath, he set the phone aside and walked toward the beverage center on his floor, ready for his morning coffee.

* * *

Somewhere else in the city, Lana was checking to see who had admired her latest Instagram post. Having attained twelve likes since she'd made the post earlier that morning, she counted five of the usual suspects, two hangers-on, three new fans she'd met in recent days, and two female acquaintances. Perhaps if he were more familiar with the app, she surmised, Tom would have been a thirteenth.

To be fair, Tom was one of over a dozen people who had liked a posting of the same photo on Facebook. *That sort of counts*, she reasoned. Also, she had only just signed him up for Instagram (and made him a follower of hers) a few days ago. *Definitely a late adopter,* she thought.

Returning her focus to her laptop, she lamented the intermittently functional spacebar. She still had a few hundred dollars remaining in the very modest educational trust fund her late grandfather had left her. A new computer technically would qualify for a disbursement. She could get by with this one for now, though.

Her travels over the winter break had consumed nearly all of the $2600 she'd raised on GoFundMe in late December—ostensibly to support the search for her father, but also an opportunity for her various admirers to help subsidize her lifestyle. She preferred to use what remained of the donations on incidental living expenses.

A text notification appeared on her phone and faded from the screen. It was a guy she knew in St. Louis named Ray, telling her how "fucking beautiful" she was. She briefly beamed as she stared into the black glass that reflected her image. Her head twisted slightly to the left and then re-centered itself, a nervous tic that was easy for all but the most observant to miss. (Even she seemed oblivious to it.)

"Lana, you using this?" asked a man named Stan, a regular patron of the establishment who—like her—enjoyed craft beers, the more obscure and local the better.

She removed her jean jacket from a nearby stool at the bar and read an old entry she'd written on a travel blog. She'd created the blog shortly before starting her winter break trip. Though she'd hoped to make regular additions to the blog during and after her journey, this one was the first and only entry.

> *My trip was everything I hoped it would be, and more. Going to Vegas with my friend Rudy and then touring the West Coast by*

myself was the relief I needed from a stressful time as I finish my last year of college. My friends—many of you reading this—made it possible.

I have an amazing life, which is something I keep reminding myself. And traveling through another part of the country made me appreciate living in Chicago. It's not perfect but we have it pretty good. Some of the people I met in Seattle, San Francisco, and L.A. were very…let's just say original. Which I thought was kind of refreshing. Chicago is still the Midwest, so we don't get that as much.

But, as much as I saw a lot of people who are very different, I realized they're also very similar, at least to me. I will definitely return there again after I graduate.

Satisfied, Lana clicked a button, closed her laptop, grasped a half-full beer glass, and decided to start up a conversation with Stan, who'd been checking her out from his lonely perch a few feet away.

16

Appeal

Standing above nearly every other structure in the City of St. Louis and every other judicial building in the country, the Thomas F. Eagleton US Courthouse was a source of pride for some, a target of derision for others. Almost thirty stories high and covering slightly less than a million square feet, the edifice was considered either a gleaming tower of justice or the most overbuilt courthouse in the nation.

Either way, it would be the arena in which third-year associate Scott Mason would argue his first appeal. Having the opportunity to argue before the Eighth Circuit was a special privilege, one his mentor certainly could have reserved for himself.

Scott's mentor, however, had already been the beneficiary of a firm culture in which newer attorneys received opportunities to do things their counterparts at firms of similar or larger size would not receive until working at least half a dozen years.

"You brought photo ID with you, right?" asked Scott's mentor as they entered the building.

"Yes, and my bar card just in case. And I put my belt and metal stuff in my bag. My phone's back at the office."

"You're like George Clooney in *Up in the Air*—but if there's some-body slow ahead of us, I doubt there'll be a second line."

"That's why we left early, though."

"Yes. Whereas I, being a bad influence and a worse example, would have barely made it on time."

"You're not a bad influence, Tom."

"Be sure to tell that to every one of my fellow partners you work with."

Scott smiled then handed his driver's license to the officer at the courthouse's security checkpoint.

I'm surprised they still let me around these kids, Tom thought, as they worked their way through the checkpoint.

Today's appeal would be argued in front of Judges Beamer, Dreyer, and Plimpton, a potpourri of jurists appointed by presidents who were (collectively) all over the political spectrum. Like many of their peers in the federal system, some of these judges' most distinguished qualifications for holding office were that they'd managed to avoid ever (1) posting or having anything posted on social media of an embarrassing or compromising or controversial nature; (2) writing anything of a similar nature; or (3) saying anything (or being quoted as having said anything) of a similar nature.

In many ways, reaching the federal bench was like being picked for a jury: You really weren't picked so much as left over after the ones some president or referring senator *really* wanted were dis-qualified or otherwise considered unpalatable despite having many redeeming and favorable qualities or traits.

Though he'd once dreamed of taking the bench at a state or (if he were really fortunate) federal court later in his career, Tom knew his political leanings and beliefs—some of which were published in his law school days—as well as other factors rendered him as likely to survive a confirmation hearing as Thomas Eagleton was to remain on the McGovern presidential ticket in 1972 after the country learned of Eagleton's previous treatment for depression.

"All right, thank you, counsel. We'll now hear the case of *Stearns Equipment v. Acme-Phoenix American Indemnity.*"

Scott immediately rose from his seat in the gallery and eagerly moved toward the first chair at the counsel table on the courtroom's right side. Tom meanwhile moseyed in that direction, happy to take the second chair so that he could observe his mentee in action.

Scott's opponent was a familiar one: Carmen Sanders, a much younger attorney who'd recently graduated from Northwestern University School of Law. Tom would be trying the *Nexfurnace* case against her at the beginning of August.

"Ms. Sanders, whenever you're ready," said Judge Dreyer, who as the presiding judge on the panel sat in the center of the bench.

"Thank you, Judge. And may it please the Court. This is a case about a greedy insurance company that—"

"Wait a minute. You're not arguing to a jury, counsel," remarked Judge Beamer.

"I'm sorry, Your Honor?"

"See these black robes? They signify we're more interested in the law than on how you characterize the facts—or the parties. Tell us about the law here, counsel, not what you think of the defendant."

"Very well, Your Honor," she replied, looking toward her opponents for a moment.

Tom nodded his head in amusement. The judge was right, of course; she'd made a rookie mistake. He expected to see more errors from her at the upcoming trial, though he knew her damn-the-torpedoes approach would have more resonance before a panel of laypeople.

Like a lot of lawyers who did reasonably well in law school in the late 2000s and early 2010s (even at a top-notch institution like Northwestern), she'd had to "hang a shingle" when employment at a decent-sized law firm became out of reach. Even classmates in the top ten percent of her class could not count on being hired by a large law firm, unlike their counterparts graduating before the Great Recession. For Carmen, finishing in "merely" the top fifty percent kept her from even being considered at an incredibly high number of places. It made her desperate and willing to take more risks to find success in the profession.

"Well, speaking of the facts, Your Honor, the district court shouldn't have granted summary judgment in this case. There were genuine issues of material fact. A jury should have decided those issues."

"Now you're talking our language, counsel," said Judge Beamer.

"Some very important facts, Judge," trying to craft an answer on the fly.

"Like what, the color of the pipe that was connected to the storage tank? You mentioned that in your brief, but how does that matter?" Judge Plimpton responded, still looking in the direction of Judge Beamer.

"Well, the fact that the district court couldn't even get the color of the pipe right in its judgment shows a basic misunderstanding of—"

"Hold on a second, counsel. Judge Nevins has been a district court judge for over ten years. You're not suggesting what I think you're suggesting, are you?" asked Judge Dreyer.

"No, Your Honor. My point was simply that—"

"Your point was that we need to take a closer look at the record," Judge Beamer stated, looking at both of his colleagues.

"That's right, Judge," Carmen noted.

"Continue please, Ms. Sanders," advised Judge Dreyer.

There was a long pause, and Carmen seemed unsure of herself for a few moments. The look on her face reminded Tom of a similar look Jill had during a recent conversation with him.

As the colloquy between Carmen and the judges resumed, Tom lost focus on the proceedings and began to think about the events of the last few weeks. He considered questions of space and time, not in a cosmological sense but in his relationships with others, particularly Jill. He recalled the thrown lamp and the smashed console, and reflected back on their first, seemingly random encounter more than two years ago. Were there hints of such intensity then?

* * *

A throng of people amassed near a large flat-screen monitor, eager to learn whether anything had changed since the airline's last announcement. Plows continued to push away the precipitation as planes circled above Lambert International Airport, their passengers keen to press down upon a tidy surface rather than be pointed elsewhere.

The blue, florescent glow from inside the terminal was harsh but preferable to the darkness outside. Jill questioned her chance of leaving St. Louis anytime soon. Ignoring the display, she stood and stared in the opposite direction, eyeing other portals she hoped could carry her where she wanted to be. *Why did I ever agree to an itinerary that routed me through this place?*

She'd welcomed the trip to China, a relief from work and a somewhat rare distraction. Walking along the Shanghai Bund had reminded her of strolling near the Navy Pier, a favorite destination in her adopted home of Chicago.

"Do you think we'll get out of here tonight?" she asked the person to her left.

"Not if we stay on this side of the terminal," the man replied.

For him, the trip was an end-of-year diversion neither planned nor even contemplated. His decision to hit Vegas had been impulsive, but an internet ad had promised a great deal, and to his surprise did not involve a bait-and-switch.

"Want to take a stroll to see if we can make some luck?" he asked.

"Why not?" Jill answered.

He grinned and nodded, gesturing for her to walk ahead of him through and past the gaggle. With a firm grasp on the extended handle of her undersized bag, she led the way.

For whatever reason, none of the waiting areas at any of the other gates looked like the one being abandoned. Groupthink or unfounded optimism or, more likely, a combination of the two may have explained the relative lack of movement away from the mob.

He noticed a 737 docked to his left, the hue of its skin and its flashing lights mostly obscured by falling flakes that were heavier now. Powered and prepared for use, its crew readied it for a flight north, the direction he needed to go; unfortunately, the display at the counter promised a journey twice the distance from where he needed to be—assuming the plane could even get clearance to fly.

Meanwhile, she maintained an unbroken pace ahead of him, expecting to find at least one means of reaching Chicago. Eyeing a tall, raven-haired agent in a royal blue uniform, Jill approached and smiled at the young woman.

"Do you have room for one more?"

"Do you have a boarding pass?" the agent asked.

"For my flight that you're about to cancel, down there on the other end, yes."

"I'm sorry, ma'am. You'll need to visit our customer service desk. Do you know where that is?"

"Actually, I do," her new companion announced, finally catching up.

"Your turn," Jill replied, motioning for him to take the lead.

In little time they encountered a queue that stretched at least 200 feet from a solitary desk staffed by two airline employees dressed like the gate agent. He and Jill looked at each other, sporting arched eyebrows and skeptical frowns.

"If we get stuck here tonight, we can grab a hotel room," he offered.

"The same room?"

"Why not?" he asked.

"Uh, first of all, we just met."

Unsurprised by (if not expecting) her response, the man observed, "That never stopped anyone. Give me your second reason."

At once confused and taken aback by his aplomb, for the moment she had nothing to say.

"Relax. Two beds. I'm really every bit the gentleman."

He looked the part, wearing a navy blue blazer with brass buttons, a blue pinstriped dress shirt, and a freshly pressed pair of gray slacks. She speculated he was thirty-three or thirty-four. A bit endearing with an outwardly innocent appearance, his pulled-back black hair—cropped notably shorter on the sides—evoked sophistication.

At this late hour, he likely took the prize as the best-dressed male in this part of the airport.

"Ha. Famous last words. Are you?" asked Jill.

"Yes. I'm just being practical."

"Practical? Again, I don't know you very well," she noted.

"I can say the same about you. It's a calculated risk on my part. You seem trustworthy," he declared.

"Calculated risk. Oh, I'm sure. But you kind of remind me of Patrick Bateman."

"Who?" he asked.

"You know, the guy from *American Psycho*. Played by Christian Bale."

"Oh, wow. Bruce Wayne. A fine-looking fellow. So that's essentially a compliment," he said.

"Not really."

"Fine. Well, on that note, I sense at least *one* of us will be getting out of town tonight. Hopefully *you* for sure."

"You would give up a seat for *me*?" she wondered.

Realizing the joke hadn't registered—or that she'd simply deflected it—he debated what to say next.

"I didn't *say* that," he emphasized. "You haven't even told me your name. Besides, you *do* realize I'm trying to get rid of you now, right?"

"You never asked my name. Or offered yours. And everything you're doing and saying tells me *I* should be the one ditching *you*," she noted.

"Fair enough. I'm Tom."

"Yeah, you definitely look like a Tom."

"What does that mean? And what's your name? I bet it's not as easy to pronounce as mine," he said.

"Wow, stereotype much? My name is Jill—a real tough one."

"Uh, OK you got me there. But I'm not really stereotyping. So, tell me what part of Southeast Asia you're from," he said, blatantly surveying her from head to toe while grasping his chin.

Donning a pair of 90s-style roundish eyeglasses, she wore a small gray sweatshirt, black tight-fitting jeans, and no makeup. He guessed she was in her upper twenties, and his eyebrows gave away that he'd noticed her shapeliness.

"Oh, you are really awful," she sighed, reaching for her iPhone and showing him her back, as if to suggest she was done with him. After quickly reading a couple of short texts from friends, she turned to face him again. "Enjoying the view? You must be, if—"

"—Excuse me, sir," someone interrupted. A few feet away from them, seated on the edge of a large planter, was a high-school-age girl wearing a hijab. Having noticed the pair chatting, she asked, "Are you in line to book a different flight to get home?"

"Yes," Tom said.

"You actually don't need to stand in this line. I can give you an 800 number you can call to handle it over the phone."

"Wonderful," he said, taking a piece of paper upon which the girl had just written something.

Stepping out of line, Tom walked toward a bench and pulled out his smartphone. "Here, let me call for you first," he told Jill.

"Huh, maybe you are a gentleman."

"Maybe," he replied with a wink.

The guy was charming and funny, and Jill sensed he was an old pro at it. She felt a bit uncertain about him, but certainly didn't mind his company.

* * *

Tom smiled, envisaging the matchless woman he'd been with since that chance meeting at Lambert. Jill had come to the US by herself at twenty-one for an advanced degree, with no relatives nearby to support her. She could be daring, decisive, and quite certain about some things—sometimes to Tom's chagrin.

At the same time, Jill had an uncertain, insecure side to her that Tom understood and accommodated, to a point. A few months after meeting Tom, she shared with him how she'd spent much of her youth in Ha Giang Province, Vietnam, far from her parents, her brother, and her hometown of Hanoi. She'd been sent there at the age of five to live with her grandparents so she could attend one of the best grade schools in the newly unified country. Though it was truly a great educational opportunity, being away from her parents and brother nearly year-round for eight years left her with a real fear of abandonment.

Tom was aware of Jill's heightened insecurity but wasn't willing to give up his connection to Lana. Jill, meanwhile, could not understand the relationship and could not really accept it...or Lana.

The tension produced a habit loop, he realized: His genuine affection and warmth made her feel special and loved; his time spent with Lana, however, pulled him away and reminded Jill she didn't have all of his attention. She felt she had most of Tom, but wanted all and felt she was entitled to it.

And it wasn't as though Jill had only Tom to choose from. She'd had younger types take interest in her too. Indeed, a few weeks before meeting Tom, and shortly after moving into her Gold Coast apartment, she literally bumped into a guy she could have wound up with in lieu of Tom.

* * *

"Oh my gosh, I am *soooo* sorry!" Jill exclaimed, reopening her apartment door and running into the kitchen to grab several paper towels, each of which she dabbed into a stream of water tapped from her sink.

As she returned to the hallway and started attacking the large coffee stain she'd just left on the front of the young man's pearl-white dress shirt, he calmly backed away for a moment, pulled out a handkerchief, wiped the bottom of his now-half-full coffee cup, and placed the cup on the floor against the wall. As she moved toward him again for a second attack, he lightly touched her shoulders.

The gesture didn't calm her; it seemed to do the opposite.

So he gently grabbed hold of her wrists, lowered his head toward hers, and said, "Hey, no worries. I've got plenty of other ones. I'm right down the hall. I'll take care of this." He paused. "Man, you were really in a hurry to get out of here!"

She laughed, relieved by his reaction to her clumsiness.

"Yeah, I was actually on my way to get…coffee."

"At midnight? Hard core. You working on something?"

"Yeah, we have a production issue at work. Anyway, will you at least let me take you for dinner? Like, not right now, but—later this week maybe? I would like to apologize and make it up to you somehow."

He flashed her a warm smile. "OK, I will let you do that. What are your feelings about Vietnamese food?"

"Well, I'm originally from there, so I heartily approve."

"Good. Well, nice meeting you, uh…"

"Oh, right…Jill!"

"Got it. So, again, I'm going to take care of this, no worries—really," he said, gesturing toward his chest. "Here's my card. Give me a call whenever."

She glanced at it, all the more impressed by him.

"I won't sue you," he said as he began walking toward the end of the hallway.

"Right, I'll hold you to that, Mr. Mason."

She watched him for a few more seconds as he walked away, then returned to her apartment. She'd skip the coffee and get some rest. Work could wait.

Well, it couldn't, but she needed some rest.

As for the young barrister, Jill no doubt looked forward to getting to know her new neighbor, but only as a neighbor. Scott was cute and smart and, as evidenced by his card, had a great job at a prominent law firm. And he wasn't exactly hiding that he liked her. Still, in her mind he was too young, which for her anyway meant too inexperienced in life—therefore, too risky. She preferred the steadiness that usually comes with age, after a sufficient number of hardships have tested and forged one's character.

* * *

"Thank you, Ms. Sanders, your time has expired," noted Judge Dreyer. "Mr. Mason, the Court will now hear from you."

Tom placed a hand on his mentee's shoulder and whispered, "You've got this."

Showing the poise of someone who belonged at the lectern, Scott lightly grasped it and looked at each judge for just a moment before he began to speak.

Just like we practiced, Tom thought. He then glanced in Carmen's direction, impressed with her ability to adapt during the oral argument. She was clearly a fast learner. Such skills were valuable to younger attorneys, particularly those who didn't have the advantage of working alongside other lawyers in the same firm.

He had a good sense now of what he'd face in the upcoming trial with her. The changing legal marketplace had forced Carmen to find her own way, seize opportunities, take chances, and gain experience working for herself she wouldn't have gotten so quickly working for others. She would take risks and be unpredictable. Not unlike Tom, particularly of late—and in some ways, not unlike Jill when she'd first arrived in the US.

He was unsure what to make of these realizations.

17

Invalid Hypothetical

"*Can you help me with something?*" read the text message from Suyin Chen.

Tom didn't mind the distraction. Off work but still wearing his navy blue sport coat over a white dress shirt and gray dress slacks, he stood out like a sore thumb in the two-story Edgewater coffee shop. Lana would be dropping by in about half an hour, and (like her) he enjoyed hanging out in this quirky area of town, a diverse neighborhood of artists, college students, and proud nonconformists. Though there were occasional looks of curiosity and brief stares in Tom's direction, the other patrons were accepting of his overdressed look.

"*I need your advice,*" Suyin said in a second text.

She and Tom had become Facebook friends about a week ago, after she was referred to him by the receptionist at his law firm. Suyin's roommate had recently abandoned the apartment they co-leased, leaving her high and dry. But she was asking about something else at the moment.

"*I hope you're not in jail. Criminal defense is not my specialty,*" he texted back to her.

"*Hahahaha,*" she responded.

"What can I do for you, Ms. Chen?"

"Trying to make sense of something. What does 'I am a single caring man' mean?"

"Need more context," he replied, sensing what was coming but wanting to give an honest opinion untainted by assumptions.

Suyin texted him a screenshot of a LinkedIn message she'd just received:

> *Hi, How are you? Sorry for disturbing you here, I didn't mean to bother you, I know its a networking site for business purpose and that is why i am here, But as I was browsing, I saw your profile with a beautiful smile that caught my attention so i decide to connect with you, I am a single caring man and I would like to know you more if you don't mind.*

"Let me call you. Easier to discuss over the phone," Tom replied.

Suyin answered on the second ring. "Hi. So what do you think?"

"It sounds suspicious, not to mention creepy. And I doubt he's single."

"Really? Why?" she asked.

"'Single caring man' means he's available…but why would he need to say 'single'? If he has to say the word, he probably is not what he says."

"Oh, that's the point! I see. What about 'caring'? Does that mean he has children?"

"I think 'caring' is used to cancel out the fact that he's married. He's emphasizing that he's 'caring,' and probably wants something he feels he currently doesn't have in his life…he wants someone who will care for him, and he will care back. Of course, this is all below the surface…you have to read between the lines. Also, he is being incon-sistent: He says he knows it's a business site and that he was there for that reason, yet he propositioned you."

"Thank you so much! I knew something was strange…but couldn't figure it out," she replied.

"You're welcome. Now I have a proposition for you."

"What?"

"When are we going to get coffee? It would be nice to chat in person. Don't you agree? And remember: It's just coffee. Don't read into it."

"Ha. You are too funny. What about next weekend?"

"Yes, next weekend is good," he confirmed.

"Daytime works for me. Somewhere public, please."

"Yeah, wouldn't want to go to your place at night. Who knows what might happen to me?"

"Oh, you think I would take advantage of you?" she teased.

"Next question."

"OK, fine. Where shall we meet, Mr. Lawyer?"

"Well, daytime actually is good, and I'll be downtown in the after-noon on Sunday. How about 1:00 and you pick where we go?"

"There is a place called Valois on 53rd Street in Hyde Park, not too far from where I live. Can we meet there rather than downtown?" she asked.

"Valois you say? Never heard of it."

"Really? How long have you lived here?"

"Just kidding. I know it well. In fact, I have a friend who lives close by that location," he noted.

"I have never been there before. What do you think of it?"

"You can't go wrong. True Americana," he said.

"What is 'Americana'? That's what you are, right?"

"No, Americana refers to a place or thing that really reminds you of being in America, as opposed to someplace else."

"Oh, I see. Well you definitely remind me of a typical American," she deadpanned.

"I'm not even going to ask," he replied. "Anyway, Valois is great."

"By the way, I don't have a car. Could you pick me up in front of Rockefeller Chapel? You know where that is on campus?"

"Sure, would be happy to."

"Thank you! See you then," she said.

Tom set his phone aside and resumed making time entries on his laptop. He'd been quite busy again this month, and had fallen markedly behind on tracking how he'd spent his time working for about a dozen clients on over fifteen different matters within the last couple of weeks. Notorious for being a "re-creator"—as opposed to an attorney who makes entries as he or she goes throughout the day—Tom had to skim or re-read items still in his Outlook inbox, appointments on his calendar, e-mails he'd sent, e-mails he'd saved in his personal folders, and documents he'd opened or saved on the firm's document management system or in Microsoft Word. Doing so enabled him to recall specific tasks he'd performed, and determine (or make a good faith estimate of) the amount of time he'd spent on each task.

The process was utterly inefficient and downright painful. Unfortunately for Tom, his tendency to jump around from one task to another (and often back) throughout the day made it very difficult to track his time as he went. He took solace, though, in knowing he certainly wasn't the only one who used this approach. About twenty-five percent of his colleagues were also re-creators. Or so he was told. By someone whose name he couldn't remember right now.

"Who were you talking with?" asked Lana, reaching the top of the stairs and emerging with a black mug of coffee.

"Oh, just some fascinating young woman I met in my office last week."

"In your office?" she asked, grabbing an open spot right next to him on the rainbow-colored, well-used sofa he'd sunk into.

"Yes," he responded.

"Is she pretty?"

"Beauty is in the eye of the beholder," he answered, involuntarily raising his eyebrows as he glimpsed a bit more of Lana than he was accustomed to seeing. Though her light-blue V-neck hanky hem camisole covered all but the last inch or two of her torn gray jean shorts, the rest of her consisted of long, thin, and pale arms and legs.

Lana shot him a grin. "And young, you say?"

"You know me."

"Oh, you are awful. How young is she?"

"Not as young as you, my dear. By the way, nice V-neck. Don't think I've ever seen you show this much skin before. Not that there's much to show up there."

She resisted the urge to respond to his dig—or to just slap him for once. She was, after all, rather enjoying his multiple failed attempts to subtly look at her.

When she couldn't resist any longer, she asked, "Do you have a picture of her, Mr. Creepy?"

"Hey, you're not the jealous type. Yet somehow I sense something here."

"Your sense is mistaken. It's pure curiosity. So, let me see."

She took hold of his phone and pulled up the latest photos in his sizeable cache.

"Asian. I should have known," she said.

"You know I have only the highest standards."

"Yep, a big reason you're so into me."

"First of all, who said I'm into you?" he asked.

"Oh, you can play coy all you want."

"I do like you, of course," he admitted. "A quarter Asian is still good enough for me to be interested."

"What about just *me*? Forget the demographics."

"What do you mean?" he asked.

"You know what I mean."

"Now *you're* being coy," he countered.

"Hey, I'm OK that you have female friends. I have a lot of guy friends; we've talked about this many times. But I'm just wondering, if we were dating and I made you be exclusive with me romantically, would I be enough for you?"

"It's an invalid hypothetical."

"Oh, don't throw me your legal objections. Answer the damn question."

"Well, you wouldn't 'make' me be exclusive, number one. You wouldn't 'make' me do anything. That's not your style, at all. I've always liked that about you."

Lana waited for him to continue. After a long pause she said, "Go on," motioning with her hand.

"And putting aside the whole exclusivity thing, some might mistakenly assume we're already a bit of an item."

"You make it too technical," she replied. "Clinical, even. And I hate to use labels. Regardless, I disagree that we're 'an item.'"

"Didn't say we are," he replied, briefly tapping the tip of her nose with his forefinger. "So what's this all about? Are you trying to make an honest man out of me or something?"

"No. But someday I would like to have a boyfriend. Someone who would treat me as being special enough that he wouldn't want to have anyone else."

Tom smirked and shook his head. "Someday, huh? What, when you're like thirty-five or something? Ahhhh, it was so much easier when I was your age. Your generation has made everything very vague and ambiguous."

"But we embrace the ambiguity. Labels just raise all kinds of expectations."

"Well, what's wrong with just the straightforward concept of dating? Let me ask you that."

"Dating implies romance. I'm not into that," she said.

"I understand. Romance implies a chase. And anyway, there's no chase involved with us, because I've already got you."

Lana pushed him backward a bit, pressing her palm into his chest. "*Do* you now? I think you are miscalculating."

"No, Lana. This whole conversation has actually been very enlightening. I'm rather flattered."

"What? How do you figure?"

"It's really relatively simple. You know I see you as a 'first among equals' when it comes to my female friends. You like that fact. So when someone new comes along in my life, you have your not-so-sly ways of getting the information you need to confirm—"

"—Confirm? Confirm what? You really think a lot of yourself, obviously. But I'll humor you for a moment. What information did I get this time?"

"That's easy. The photo."

"Oh, you think I'm that vain and shallow, comparing myself to another girl's picture?"

"Come on, Lana. Women compare each other all the time. It's what you do. To be fair, guys have their own ways of comparing with each other."

"What, do you all go to the shower and stare at each other's—"

Tom raised a hand and held it several inches away from her mouth. "Don't say it."

She reached out and slowly moved his hand away. And then, as was her custom when she had other places to be, other things to do, or other people to see, Lana declared, "Well, this has all been very interesting, but I need to go."

"Aw, don't walk away mad," Tom teased, as she went for the stairs.

"You wish," she replied, turning to face him. "I'm as no-drama as they come."

"Am I supposed to agree with that?"

"I'm not even going to say anything," she said, showing him her back. "Goodbye. I'll let you get back to overbilling your clients. And hey," she added, turning her head enough to make eye contact with him again. "I want to talk with you about something Grandma said to me before I left."

"Sure, looking forward. And hey, 'overbilling'? Don't you mean fighting for justice?"

Lana had already reached the top of stairs. He saw her raise a hand, shooing him away as she descended quickly and reached for something she'd left hanging on the wall. She disappeared within a couple of seconds as Tom shook his head in amusement and resumed the interminable struggle to account for his time.

18

The Beach

Lana's arms formed a "V" into the sky as the summer winds near Lake Michigan blew past her face from the southeast. She'd parked the Miata as close to the beach as she could get away with and was pleased to have some alone time. Coming to the shore at eight in the morning with nothing more than a black towel and a white bikini, she guaranteed herself an early and wide stake.

The rays of the morning sun bounced off the waves in front of her, sharply striking the front of her sunglasses before heading in countless other directions. She leaned backward and pressed her palms into the sharp granules of sand. She loved this urban oasis; the occasional, momentary chill that clambered along her skin only made her feel that much more alive. Few others were yet ready to brave the morning's feel.

Meanwhile, half-buried in the powdery grit was her phone, a silent reminder that Rudy was still ignoring her texts. Three missives in four weeks had gone unanswered. Unlike Rudy, she saw no point in playing games. After rubbing the sand off her phone, she began to type a new message.

"Hey, just let me know when you're ready to talk again. I'd be up for—"

Just then, her phone began to vibrate. An unknown number appeared on the screen. She swiped the screen and placed the device against her face.

"Hello?"

"Haló?"

Lana heard a deep, strongly accented voice and waited to hear something more.

"Is there a Lana there?"

"This is Lana."

A long pause followed, but no reply.

"This is Lana. Who is this?"

"Ah, very nice to talk to you, Lana. My name—"

Lana heard the man yell to someone else in the background in what may have been Czech.

"Oh, sorry. I tell some of my family to say I talk to you now."

"That's fine," Lana replied. "You were about to tell me your name?"

"Yes, sorry."

"You don't need to be sorry. I am actually very happy to talk with you, if this is who I think it is."

Lana suddenly felt overwhelmed; her emotions made thinking almost impossible. *What do I say? What should I say?* she asked herself.

"Yes, well, let me say my last name is Yilmaz. I think you maybe know this name."

"I think maybe too. Is this Duygu?"

"Duygu yes, this is."

Lana closed her eyes and for a moment held the phone against her chest. She could now stake her claim on something time hadn't erased.

"My mother is Nancy Truong. I think you met her in Paris in 1991."

"Yes, I remember Nancy in Paris then. But she said Nancy Roseland. Last name she always said was Roseland."

Duygu paused for a moment as Lana thought about what her mother's use of a different name meant and said, or may have said, about her mental state even at that time.

* * *

Nancy strolled along the quiet shore, looking west into the wide Atlantic as the sun faded on the horizon. She wore a pair of white cutoff jean shorts and an unbuttoned blue short-sleeved shirt atop a black one-piece swimsuit.

After finishing her first year as a teacher, she relished the opportunity to unwind and escape the pressures of family, work, and dealing with people in general. Having her first job after college—coupled with her mother's generous graduation gift—had granted her this freedom to explore, with centuries of history to see and feel.

The next morning's train would return her to Paris. She looked forward to walking through the narrow streets of the city. And if she could find a nightclub that wasn't too crowded, she just might check it out.

Crowds smade everything overwhelming and stressful for her. She hated the feeling of everyone's stares; she tired of shooing away the strange men who, drink in hand, would approach and ask her to dance, or for other things. She just wanted to listen to music and watch the band. She wished there were tables set aside for one, on a dark and secluded balcony affording a clear view from above.

Being at the beach alone at night, she could hear the waves as they came to the shore, feel the water at her feet, and see the lights of the city in the distance. No one questioned the way she dressed, gave her odd stares, or told her she needed to do something differently.

She'd experienced plenty of that treatment in the last nine months. Her students were fine; fellow faculty members, however, were an unwelcome challenge. She thought they were jealous of her and wanted to make her fail. Her students appreciated her unusual style in the classroom; her colleagues seemed threatened by it, in her mind.

Fortunately she was far away from them and from their judgment. Placing her on probation as the school year ended was their way of admitting they could not compete with her, she believed. They couldn't keep up with her and wanted to steal her students from her; she was sure of that conclusion.

It seemed nearly everyone back home either disliked her, questioned her wisdom, or envied her self-perceived brilliance.

So she'd be someone else on this trip.

Not an unfathomable, misunderstood teaching phenom, but a promising model from America visiting for the summer.

The tall, dark-haired and olive-skinned woman now setting her feet into the ocean would be Nancy Roseland. If the world couldn't appreciate her powerful mind, she would impose upon it her beauty and charm.

Scoring modeling gigs would be a breeze, she presumed—a way to earn extra spending money to do the things she wanted, like meeting local musicians, other artists, and like-minded travelers.

* * *

"So," Duygu continued. "Tell me more of what you know, Lana. I believe you but need to—how do you say—"

"I understand. You want to be sure I am who I say I am."

"Yes, just be sure—"

"—You want to be sure I am not trying to get something from you. Or claim to be—"

"—Ah, you know, Lana, my niece said you told her things; they are things very few people know of me. So I think you must be—what you call—the 'real deal,' maybe?"

Lana was confused: First he'd instructed her to tell more of the story she'd been told, as if to prove herself to him, but now—before she could offer what he seemed to want—he was suddenly reassuring her of his trust.

"Anyway, I know that Nancy stayed with you in Paris for several months in 1991, probably starting around May or June."

"This is right. You are right. But we are here to talk about you too, I would like. Tell me: I am interesting in knowing more about you. Tell me what you do now."

"I'm a student. I'm finishing college."

"Ah, a university student, you mean? Where do you study?"

"Yes. I'm at the University of Illinois at Chicago. I study finance and psychology."

"So, something to do with money and a person's head then?"

"Something like that."

Lana was determined to keep the focus on him and how he met her mother. Finally, she could hear some truth about the past untinged by mental instability, secretiveness, or manipulation.

"Now tell me more about you," she said. "I am very excited to be having this talk with you now."

"Yes, it is very good. I am happy we get to talk after so much time has been gone. Kind of hard to believe for me…that you found me, you know?"

"Hard for me, too. So you have a family business, I believe?"

"Yes, we sell jewelry. Do you know anything about jewelry? Ah, you are a young woman so, must be yes, right?"

Receiving gifts such as diamonds and similar "precious" rarities did not particularly appeal to Lana. If anything, she treasured the art at museums, for it was much rarer—one-of-a-kind actually—and was a gift to the world rather than to one person.

"I know a little but I've never worked in the business. Where is your business located?"

"We are in Prague. Do you know where this is?"

"Czech Republic, yes. Used to be Czechoslovakia. Bohemia some-time before then."

"Yes. Everyone know that, I think."

"Nancy told me you went to Paris on business. Were you there to buy diamonds?"

"Business some. Back in Turkey, I would be in military orders. So I go there, to Paris, and it was a difficult time. I needed to find a job soon. I asked the boss at discotheque I like to go to at night, if he could have a place for me there to help with something."

"A discotheque? You mean like a nightclub?"

"Yes, same thing. The boss said to me, '*Oui oui*,' you know."

"Then what happened?"

"I was going to say. Be patient. Not good to interrupt man when talking."

Lana sensed building a relationship with her father would prove difficult; he seemed to need one hand on the wheel and the other on the stick at all times. Perhaps not too unlike her, but still...*I'm a little more subtle about it*, she thought.

"Now here is the part you like, I think. I often give out papers on the street. To make traffic flow and help business for the boss."

He paused. "So I went outside with the papers or little cards, you see. I started to give them out. I remember this now. Then I looked up, and I remember..."

Lana waited patiently as she started to picture an evening scene in Paris on some narrow street lit by lanky restaurant signs and bright shop windows—a place enlivened with the energy and sophistication of the locals and worldly visitors strolling and frolicking.

She turned down her head and closed her eyes again, holding the phone tightly against her face as Duygu held his pause. A tear dropped onto the onyx fabric beneath her, splattering against a nearby thigh.

"Yes, I looked up, and then I saw her. Standing at a corner. She seemed to be looking for something, or someone maybe. Not sure. I decided to go up to her. Very, very nice. I was hooked, you say, like a fish maybe. She pulled hard."

"You got more than you bargained for, maybe?"

"Your mother—how do you say—she drove hard on the bargain? And you know, you came as a result of this connection."

He paused. "We were very young."

* * *

Nancy held one bare foot and both elbows against the cool stone wall of the ancient building as she stood near the street corner. Her black flats rested on their sides a few inches away as her sweat evaporated from them.

She wanted to enter the nightclub that stood catty-corner from her but was intimidated by the line of people waiting to enter. She considered just leaving and going back to the hostel where she'd been staying for the last few nights, but was keen on the music that was pumping from the place.

Near the head of the line and just outside the front door, Duygu stood proud and empty-handed, having given out his last promotional card for tonight's featured performers. He was earning his keep this evening and anticipated a nice reward from the boss. Unless the line showed any sign of slimming, there likely would be no need for him to canvass again anytime soon.

Standing 6'2" with crossed arms, he looked moderately muscular in his short-sleeved black T-shirt, and—if a bit taller and bulkier—could have passed as a bouncer. A hairline that started receding in his late teens led him to adopt, by his early twenties, a cue ball cut. The look actually worked for him when combined with his deep-set green eyes and light olive skin.

Taking note again of the more-than-sufficient queue of patrons, Duygu turned his head in the opposite direction.

Then he saw her, standing on the opposite side of the narrow street, looking broodingly at the sidewalk. He watched her for a time, marveling at what he perceived to be a feminine vulnerability amidst a radiant splendor. The woman was beyond gorgeous. It was only a matter of tactics now: determining how to approach her.

Without further consideration, he steered himself into the club and went straight for the maître d's station.

"Hey D, I think we're good for now—" the maître d' started to say.

"Just need one," he said, firmly but not forcefully moving the young woman's hand away from a short stack of cards and retrieving the top one. Just as quickly he departed her station, walked outside, jammed the card into a back pocket, and crossed the street.

Calling out in broken English as he approached the sidewalk, Duygu exclaimed, "You like the music, yes?"

Nancy looked up, at first seeming disturbed or annoyed.

"I *was* enjoying it," she replied.

The American sarcasm went right over him.

"Good. I like it too. Grabs you. Really makes your body move," he said, doing a very poor impression of John Travolta.

"Something like that. Who are you anyway? And how did you know I speak English?"

He was not accustomed to such directness from a woman.

"You are more beautiful to be from this part of world," he told her. "You must come from far, I am sure of this."

"*Too* beautiful, you mean. *Too* beautiful to be from here."

She looked him up and down.

"You obviously know how to flatter," she continued. "And I can tell you're not from this part of the planet either. Or maybe even from this planet."

"Is that because I'm *too* beautiful as well?" he asked, again missing her sarcasm.

She laughed. He was masculine but cute, confident yet aware of (and not at all self-conscious about) his lack of command of the English language.

"Or maybe…too sexy," she added, crossing her arms as she looked down again to put her flats back on. "My name is Nancy, by the way. Nancy—" she hesitated to say, extending her right hand toward his, "—Roseland. I'm from St. Louis."

"Yes, I thought maybe you could be American. From across the street, I think, 'That girl—she is too different for this place. Dance to tune of herself maybe.'"

She smiled and walked up to him, cupping her hand and briefly touching him on the cheek as she said, "I dance to my own tune, you mean. Well, you got me there. I do."

Stretching one leg then the other to take long but slow strides, she circled him in a tight radius as he stood transfixed. "You say 'maybe' a lot, but there's nothing 'maybe' about you when you look at me, is there, Mr. Travolta?"

He chuckled and tried to think of something to say.

"No, I am Duygu. Duygu Yilmaz. I come from Turkey."

She stopped her strutting, and from a position directly behind him reached into one of his back pockets.

"And what is this, Duygu from Turkey?"

He turned around to see her staring at the card he'd taken from the maître d'.

"So you want to take me dancing? Is that why you came over here?"

Astonished, he started to mutter something but stopped himself from sounding incoherent.

"You know, Nancy, you are a *lot*."

"A lot of *what*?" she asked. "A lot to handle, 'maybe'?"

He laughed and looked up into the night sky, placing his hands on his hips. When he looked back at her, she resumed her onslaught.

"And you want to find out," she asserted, grabbing hold of his hands, placing them against the small of her back, and pressing them firmly.

* * *

Duygu went silent for a few seconds. Lana detected a sudden change in his breathing and demeanor. He began coughing; it sounded forced.

She joined him in the silence, waiting for him to gather his thoughts.

"You know, Lana, after Nancy left…maybe a few months, you know, I heard she had a child. I heard that. But when she left, all I had was a fake last name, no phone number, nothing really…"

"I know. I don't blame you for anything. I don't want anything from you, except your time," Lana replied.

He paused again, overwhelmed by the memories from over twenty years ago. Lana heard someone in the background yell something in Czech again.

"Can we talk sometime more, maybe later, Lana? Someone needs me at the front door maybe."

"Sure. I actually should be going too."

"You call anytime. If I am not here, someone will try to find me or help you and say when to call back, OK?"

Lana smiled as she softly touched her towel against each of her eyes. "Yes, OK. Thank you. I really enjoyed talking with you."

"Me also, I think."

19

About My Father

Laptop open and hands typing furiously on the keyboard, Rudy sat on the L as he headed to his next demo of Cross-Doku-Crush. A potential investor at the recent conference had given him some compelling ideas about monetizing the game. Stage two was now far enough along to make him comfortable showing it off, and even if the investor was not ready to move forward, Rudy would happily accept more feedback.

Taking a break from his work, he looked up and watched the buildings pass by in the window across from him. Just then, he felt his phone vibrate and pulled it out of his back pocket.

"Hey, just let me know when you're ready to talk again. I'd be up for grabbing dinner with you tonight. I have some big news I want to share with you."

Rudy rolled his eyes and started to put the phone back into his pocket. Another vibration stopped him. He hesitated, and couldn't resist looking at the phone again.

"It's about my father."

Rudy now took firm hold of his phone with both hands and re-read the two texts. Whatever barrier he had built up over the last month concerning Lana, it quickly disappeared.

"*You found him???*" he replied.

A minute or so went by.

"*I hate texting. Tell me when you'll be back at your place tonight. We'll make dinner together and I'll tell you everything.*"

He wanted to see Lana again, but felt conflicted. On the one hand, despite his anger when she last visited his apartment and his later efforts to ignore her, she had reached out to him several times in the last few weeks. And at his apartment she insisted she cared about him. It sounded genuine; he didn't doubt that.

On the other hand, this latest request to meet him was about her and what was going on in her life. He was pretty sure that none of her recent efforts to contact him had anything to do with what was going on in his.

Nothing new there, he thought.

After going back and forth on what, if anything, he should say in response, he finally wrote, "*You can come over at 7:00. Grab some mostaccioli. I'm out. We can finish what we started last time.*"

* * *

By any measure, and he surmised by design, she looked stunning. He couldn't remember the last time he'd seen her in red. And it wasn't just red; the short, V-neck soft jersey dress was nearly fluorescent, with narrow shoulder straps and seams at the waist leading to a flared skirt and silver cork sandals. Light makeup and understated pink lipstick complemented the look.

"Is this your way of saying sorry?" Rudy asked, returning his attention to a large pot he was filling at the kitchen sink.

"Says the guy who ignored me for the last four weeks. Anyway, I don't see much value in rehashing things, Rudy. But I'll take the compliment. Can we have a no-drama evening, please?"

Lana placed a small bag of penne pasta on the kitchen counter, then hung her silver pleated clutch on the back of a chair near the kitchen table and promptly sat down. "I'm kind of tired. Do you mind being the lone chef tonight?"

"That's fine," Rudy said, setting the pot onto one of the burners he'd just started. "In the meantime, why don't you tell me what the big news is?"

Lana smiled and leaned back in her chair. "I talked to my father today."

Flabbergasted, Rudy stepped back from the stove and approached the table. "When?"

"This morning, while I was at the beach."

He took a seat opposite her. "Back up a second. How did you find him?"

She filled him in, leaving out no detail. "It was a surreal experience. When he described what it was like catching his first glimpse of my mother, I got teary-eyed."

He surveyed Lana's face; she looked as though she was about to tear up again.

"Was it like you'd pictured it?" he asked.

"Yeah. Like I was there, watching them meet," she replied. There was a brief pause. "When I was little, I always thought Nancy was very pretty. Growing up with all those Disney princesses, I couldn't understand why she would be alone."

"But you understood later."

"Yes. But my father didn't abandon her."

"And you respect him for that," Rudy said, crossing his arms.

"I do."

Rudy wanted to say something about his loyalty to Lana and how she didn't seem to respect that. But the conversation wasn't about him, and he'd agreed to the no-drama stipulation.

"Well, I'm happy for you, Lana."

"Thank you. You're the first person I told."

He uncrossed his arms. "So are you going to visit him soon?"

"Yes, early next month."

"How long are you going to stay?" he asked.

"I'm thinking I'll stay with him for a week, and I plan to go to some other places before and after."

Rudy paused, then stood up and walked back to the stove. "Could you use some company?"

"Don't you have to work?"

"I could take some time off," he replied, as he adjusted the burner. "Maybe join you for a few days of the trip?"

"I think I'd like to experience it by myself. I want to have a few days traveling alone before I meet him, and then some time to do other things afterward." She could see that Rudy was disappointed. "Maybe we could go somewhere after graduation?"

"That's not until December," he said, reaching for some basil and olive oil.

She got up and joined him by the stove. "Some things are worth waiting for," she said, giving the back of his neck a light squeeze.

At that moment, Chaz emerged from Rudy's bedroom. He trotted toward Lana and leapt onto the kitchen counter, right next to her. She took hold of him and began stroking his back, immediately causing him to purr.

"Want to visit your friend downstairs, Chaz?"

The cat responded with a meow as Lana approached the door.

"We'll be back in ten minutes, Rudy."

"Sure. But Lana—"

He couldn't finish what he wanted to say; she and Chaz had already left. *Upstaged by a cat*, he mused, returning his attention to the stove.

Though impressed with her achievement, he didn't feel as excited for her as he might have felt last summer or fall, when they were still dating. The search for her father—something he had always associated with her since they first met, when she revealed so much about herself so quickly—was apparently now over, and it felt anticlimactic. Moreover, despite her sharing of the big news, he didn't feel any closer to her.

If anything, though he could not immediately figure out why, he felt more distant.

20

All I Want

Suyin glared at the letter resting in her hands. She felt the thick bond paper and immediately pictured the stodgy old lawyer who must have written it.

He surely was working for Suyin's roommate *pro bono*, procured (no doubt) at the behest of her roommate's host family.

Everything seemed to come easily to Ning, who'd recently cast a spell upon the handsome doctor who headed that host family, and into whose home she'd recently moved. Suyin read the words again in disbelief.

Dear Ms. Chen,

Due to financial reasons, I am no longer able to reside at your apartment on South Blackstone Avenue (the "Apartment").

As you know, I never signed the Residential Lease Agreement dated August 26, 2013 (the "Agreement"), or the Addendum dated June 1, 2014 (the "Addendum"), and never had any direct dealings with the landlord. Instead, all of my dealings with respect to the Apartment before I occupied it were with you and your mother.

*The Agreement and Addendum, with all of their provisions, simply
do not concern or otherwise apply to me. You are free to keep my
personal property that I left in the Apartment, including my bed,
mattress, chair, and shelves.*

Best wishes,

Ning Li

What Ning had just done to her stung more than the words. With
about five months left on the lease extension, Suyin had few options,
and none that appealed to her. She'd planned out everything before
leaving for America, calculating her anticipated expenses, developing a budget, adding a ten percent premium for incidentals and
unanticipated expenses, and then going to each of her parents for
forty percent of the budget (and insisting upon covering the remaining twenty percent herself).

Suyin could not hold back the hate she felt as the first tear dropped
from her eyes. Though the tear mostly reflected this latest development, she couldn't help envisaging the pretty face of a different
young woman: someone who'd stolen Suyin's father away a dozen
years ago—someone who'd come into Suyin's home for tutoring,
which led to much more.

Foreseeing the same kind of disorder being wreaked upon the
American family her former roommate had begun living with, Suyin
felt dispirited. She then reached for her phone.

"I have a big problem with my roommate," she typed, hesitating
to press the send button as she unwittingly covered her mouth and
chin with her hand: For the first time, she realized she didn't know if
the intended recipient of her text was married. She hadn't asked; he

hadn't volunteered. She could not recall seeing him with a wedding band, but that was no assurance of bachelorhood.

Suyin didn't want to intrude or impose, and certainly didn't want to be entangled in any shape of polygon—triangular or otherwise. But she appreciated his giving spirit and kindheartedness. *Maybe he's just that way with everyone,* she hazarded to herself.

She considered waiting until the weekend, when she assumed he'd be less busy. She loathed putting things off, though. *Besides, he seems like a gentleman, and I could use a good lawyer right now,* she thought, firing off the text to Tom. She had reached a breaking point and was not so proud that she would refuse to seek help.

* * *

"You ready?" Lana asked, somewhat impatiently.

She'd just snapped a wide-angle shot of the luggage sitting outside her apartment, posting it on Facebook with the tagline, "Europe awaits!"

"Yep. I think you can lock up," Tom replied, as he felt his iPhone vibrate a couple of times.

"Oh, wait—I forgot one thing!" Lana exclaimed. "Here, I will need your help," she announced, lightly tugging at the front of Tom's sport coat as she walked past him toward the front door.

He followed her into her apartment. She snatched a bar stool and placed it in front of her wardrobe closet, then opened the right half. As the folding doors came open, Tom examined the contents: a distinctive mix of class and peculiarity that matched what he'd expected to see.

"Very nice. Classy but simple; elegant, yet unrefined," Tom observed.

"Thank you. And these are what I use for my job interviews."

Lana held up a German barmaid costume with her left arm and a Christmas minx outfit with the right.

"Hmm. All I want for Christmas is…"

She waited for the finish; none came.

"Is what? To see me in this dress?"

"I'm not going to say."

"What a cop out," she said. "Anyway, I need you to hold the back of the chair for me so I don't fall."

"You don't need to tell me why; I figured that out."

"A little testy, are we? I'm not used to that."

"I like to keep you on your toes."

"You mean like I am now?" Lana asked, reaching high for a small box on a shelf that must have been eight feet above the hardwood floor. The apartment's ceiling was nearly ten feet high.

As she reached for the box, stretching her upper torso, Tom had a hard time averting his eyes; her hip-hugging black jeans and cropped gray blouse now bore an additional inch of midriff. At the same time and quite unexpectedly, he spotted the slightest hint of love handles emerging from either side of her hips. He rather liked these minute imperfections, but wisely opted to keep that fact to himself.

Lana finally retrieved the box and tried to hand it to him. He seemed oblivious, or certainly distracted. She shook the box to reorient his attention.

"Enjoying the view?"

"Oh, sorry. You caught me looking."

He took the box, set it aside, and braced the stool again, enabling her to dismount. She lithely touched the tip of his nose with one of her fingers, then went to open the box.

"I was expecting a different answer to my question."

"Something more concrete, perhaps?"

"Something like that. Anyway, you better be on your best behavior if you're going to travel with me. I'm letting you know that now, for your own good."

"Have I ever been anything but wholesome?"

"I just don't want to find out you have a temper while we're on vacation."

"How quickly you forget: I scored like ninety-nine or something on 'agreeableness' on one of those Facebook personality tests. Whereas you blew up your phone when you took it."

"Wow, I'll pretend you didn't say that."

"Don't worry, Lana. I'll play nice, for the most part."

She feigned a serious stare. "What does that mean?"

"I know you like it when I keep you guessing," he said with a grin.

"I do like that side of you. It's good to know manic Tom will be joining me for part of this trip."

She removed a jade ring from its holder inside the small box and slid the ring on her left small finger.

"Cool ring. Where's it from?"

"My grandma in St. Louis gave it to me when I was fourteen. It always reminds me of her, back when she really knew who I was."

"What do you mean 'she really knew'?"

"She has Alzheimer's. She usually doesn't even know who I am when I visit."

"But you do visit."

"Yes. How did you—"

"—Look, she took care of you, raised you through what must have been a painful and very confusing time in your life—after seeing her own daughter arrested and hauled off to jail, then to a mental ward. She helped make you into who you are. I'm sure you feel you could never fully repay her."

"That's exactly how I feel."

Lana closed her eyes and tilted her head toward the floor, saying nothing more.

"Are you OK?" Tom asked, gently grasping Lana's left hand.

"Sorry, just remembering a nice day I had with Grandma the last time I visited her."

"I hope I get to meet her someday. I know she may not be able to understand or know who I am, but I'd like to tell her she did a great job. And that all the hard work was worth it…considering who she was dealing with."

Lana pushed away Tom's hand and turned to face him squarely. "Am I hard work, Tom?"

"You know the answer to that question, Lana."

"Well, thank you for putting up with me. And thank you again for your 'adventurous invitation.' You were right: I would have said yes last January. Now I've gotten you to say yes to mine."

"Yes. You have. You're welcome. Let's get you to the airport."

* * *

Jill reached for a switch above her to turn off the range hood, extinguished a burner, and poured stir-fried vegetables into a large bowl sitting on the nearby counter.

Tom reached around her waist from behind, and placed his face against hers.

"Looks almost as good as you," he said.

"Charming."

"You know it."

"Yes," she acknowledged.

"I'm a keeper."

"I agree," she said.

"So then, we're good?"

"For now," she said.

Tom grabbed two sets of utensils, a pair of large plates, and some napkins. Salads were already in their place, along with two glasses of water.

As Jill sat down, Tom prepared to discuss his upcoming plans. Transparency would be difficult this time, though everything he was about to say would be true. How much to say, and when to say it, was another matter.

"I have a great opportunity to tell you about."

"Really? What happened?" she asked.

"I think I'm going overseas."

"What for?"

"There's an international conference on appellate practice in Central Europe. We have some money in the firm's budget to cover this kind of outreach. The firm is willing to send me and pay half the expenses."

"Where will the conference be?"

"In Vienna, Austria."

Jill rose from the table to retrieve the salt and pepper shakers. "When's the conference?"

"Mid-August."

She sat back down. "Right after your trial. Isn't Lana in Europe in August?"

"Yes."

"Will she be going to Vienna?"

"I can't rule that out," Tom responded.

"How long will you be there?"

"About a week."

They ate the rest of their dinner in silence. Tom felt uncertain, concerned, and exposed. He was unable to think of anything to say to lighten the mood.

Under the circumstances, Jill wasn't about to help him out.

21

Both Sides

"Ladies and gentlemen, we are beginning our descent. Please return your tray table to its upright and locked position, and turn off all electronic devices," announced the flight attendant from a position far ahead of Lana, who was sitting near the window in an exit row. To pass the time, she'd been playing magnetic chess with her seatmate for hours.

Cottony masses below the 767's colossal wing obstructed any vision of the countryside over which the airliner now passed. At this high altitude, no hint of the weather below was evident. Similarly, she had no idea what was in store for her after touchdown.

As the plane descended below the clouds and rain began to strike the window beside her, she knew she'd seen both sides now: the highs and lows of an incredible life, the sunny and fluffy parts as much as the dark and ugly ones. She'd learned to appreciate her journey, even when it became frustrating and scary.

"Ma'am, you'll have to turn that off now," a young flight attendant said, leaning toward Lana and the passenger sitting next to her.

"Right, sorry," Lana responded, powering down her phone.

Her seat began to jiggle; a baby began to cry. A bell sounded, reminding occupants the fasten seat belts sign remained lit. A flight attendant sang her song again: "Ladies and gentlemen, please refrain…"

Lana eyed the wet wings of the aircraft and soon dozed off. She needed the rest and wanted to be at her best.

Less than half an hour later, a jolt caught her by surprise. She couldn't believe the plane had landed already. Outside, the rain pounded onto the tarmac as she turned on her phone. She was nervous, but also quite excited.

"*I think you are here maybe now?*" read a text from Duygu, one of seven from him that popped up as WhatsApp notification alerts. Lana didn't bother to read the other six, or the dozen or so new texts from a few other friends back in the US; she'd be at the gate and at the baggage carousel soon enough, and could catch up with her American friends after she settled in at her father's home.

"*Yes, just landed. I'll see you by the baggage claim in a few minutes*," she responded.

First she needed to deplane and visit the nearest restroom to compose herself. She felt more tense and anxious than she could remember feeling in a long time.

* * *

As Lana exited the secure area of Prague's international airport, a small girl approached holding five helium-filled balloons of various colors. The girl handed them to Lana, who was surprised, not expecting this kind of greeting. The girl then started running away as Lana lifted the balloons above her head and started walking toward the baggage carousels. No one looked familiar; she couldn't spot her father.

Eventually she saw him standing near one of the carousels, arms crossed, looking at the floor. The girl soon joined him, grabbed hold of his hand, and pointed in Lana's direction.

Lana stopped for a moment and appreciated the feeling of déjà vu—déjà vu times two, really.

She remembered a favorite photograph of herself at the age of five, holding the same number of balloons of various colors that her grandfather had just handed her as she entered his home. Taken by surprise, she had the same beaming smile on her face then that her father now had on his.

She also remembered someone she thought she'd lost a few months ago without knowing why or how or even exactly when. As the nearby carousel spun items around and a middle-aged man took hold of a light piece of luggage, she recalled the surprise of seeing Tom again at the Union League back home, looking at the floor much like her father had been a moment ago. She remembered Tom's warmth and the connection she'd restored with him that evening: a connection that—like the art surrounding them back then— was absolutely unique.

Lana now walked to where her father stood and embraced him, hard. Their heads rested against each other. Neither said anything. Twenty-two years of searching ended here, in this moment. Nancy's decision made long ago no longer held any power over either of the adults standing there; their connection was real, physical, and overwhelming.

Lana felt a tap on her leg. She stepped away from her father and looked down at the girl, who was still standing next to him. Lana bent down and extended a hand, but the girl refused it and shook her head.

"Ah, this is your part-sister, Alara."

Lana gave the girl a soft hug, which was reluctantly accepted, then looked to her father again.

"We would say, 'half-sister.'"

"I see."

"I'm so happy to meet you," Lana said to Alara.

The girl showed no sign of understanding what Lana was saying.

"She doesn't know any English," Duygu explained.

"Hopefully someday I can teach her."

"Maybe you stay the whole month, you can do it. Here, this is for you," he said, handing her a navy blue, velvety container.

Lana did not immediately respond. She slowly opened the box and inspected the shiny objects inside. The diamond bracelet and ring glimmered in the harsh airport lighting, and somehow felt out of place in her delicate hands.

"We can talk about how long you stay," Duygu continued. "Now come and we will go to my car outside."

* * *

The brick-and-stone façade of Duygu's townhome on the outskirts of Prague was larger than most of those she'd passed after leaving the airport. It looked like the kind of place where one could raise a family, and would be considered comfortably large (and quite expensive) if located in Rudy's downtown neighborhood back in Chicago.

As Duygu pulled his mid-size SUV into a narrow driveway that led to a reasonably sized one-car garage, Lana asked herself what it would have been like to grow up in Prague. What kind of person would she be today?

The SUV stopped a few feet short of the garage door. Duygu abruptly exited the vehicle and went to the back, ready to open the rear hatch. He nearly bowled over his newfound daughter, who (having somehow beaten him to the back end) now stood holding her carry-on bag as she prepared to retrieve the one she'd checked.

"Here, I take that for you," he said, reaching for the carry-on.

Lana pulled away instinctively. "That's OK, I've got it," she said.

"No, go inside."

Lana hesitated for a moment before muttering, "Sure."

"You must learn what I like and don't like. I will teach you. First step: Let go of the bag."

Lana smirked, appreciating the humor of the situation and the fact her father had a sense of it. Grudgingly, she unclutched what she really preferred to take inside herself.

"There, you see? Not too bad, right? Makes things easier for you, I think?"

As the rear hatch opened, Lana thought about reaching for her checked bag but decided to forestall another debate over who does what for whom where.

Easier for him, she thought, *and hard for me.*

"Come, you will like it here in my home, Lana. I am so happy that you can meet everyone."

Standing a few paces behind the two was Alara, who observed her father and half-sister talking to each other in a language she couldn't understand. Duygu said something to Alara in Czech, causing her to run inside the home.

"Lana, actually, wait here for a moment. I will take the bags inside then come to get you."

"I can help with—"

"No!" Duygu resolutely declared.

Lana was surprised and dismayed by her father's retort.

"Lana, wait here; I will get you. I will make things easy for you. Let me make things easy."

She nodded and said nothing more. Duygu walked away, appearing frustrated.

* * *

A continent away, an aluminum-alloy bird sliced through cirrus clouds at over 500 miles per hour, its nose pitched to climb another 15,000 feet as its engines delivered 14,500 pounds of thrust. The violence of sound and energy it produced on the outside went mostly unnoticed to the occupants inside.

One of them slept as an open laptop rested on a tray table ahead of him; the screen displayed a PowerPoint slide bearing a single word, white on a black background: "blame."

Tom had taken advantage of the opportunity to power-nap. He hoped the few minutes of rest would sharpen what he would deliver in less than two hours.

Beside him, an associate skimmed e-mails on a smartphone. As the "billing attorney" on the file, Lauren managed its day-to-day handling, freeing Tom to oversee this matter and others—ideally with minimal supervision.

Lauren made the ideal more of a reality when she worked with him on his cases. And her assistance freed him up to concentrate on other matters, like the *Nexfurnace* trial that was soon to begin.

As if to prove the point, she grabbed Tom's laptop to survey where he'd left things. "They're going to need to see the meat of the case, the good and bad elements, and we've got to make it simple," he'd told her when outlining the PowerPoint.

So far, Tom had twelve slides and barely twice as many words—captions or concepts, really—including "One-Armed Marine" with a photograph of the plaintiff in the Iraqi desert; "Redheaded Step-child" (an oft-used nickname coined by plaintiff's counsel) beneath the client's logo; and "If Only" next to the cover page of a safety pro-gram created by the "stepchild's" corporate parent, which had (in plaintiff's counsel's view) failed to ensure the safety program was handed down to the stepchild.

Lauren admired the way plaintiff's counsel could at once emo-tionalize and simplify a case for a jury. And Tim Keifer was no one's fool. He could crush your best witness on cross-examination with an "aw shucks," didn't-see-that-coming approach that mixed refer-ences to popular culture with a sharp wit and deadly sense of humor. Almost as easily could he overwhelm some of the best defense law-yers, holding them to the rules in plaintiff-friendly jurisdictions and in neutral territory alike.

On the "blame" slide that Tom had created before dozing off, Lauren inserted the image of a pointing hand and a smaller version of the client's logo. This part of the presentation would feature con-cepts and images she'd add illustrating the strengths of plaintiff's case.

"Lookin' good, kid."

"Someone's up," Lauren responded.

"Yep. How soon 'til touchdown? And how many more slides did you get done?"

"One. And we'll land in about an hour."

"Good," Tom replied. "By the way, I plan to have you give the entire presentation to the client. You're welcome."

Laura peered at Tom but said nothing.

"Now *that's* an icy stare," he said. "Relax, you're just shadowing, as advertised."

Tom's firm allotted fifty hours of "shadow time" to each associate per year. A client would not be charged for such time; nonetheless, the associate would receive "billable credit" (as if he or she had charged the client) while getting the chance to observe, assist, and learn from a more senior attorney at a hearing, mediation, deposition, client meeting, or other important event.

But Tom hadn't been kidding, at least not entirely. He definitely intended to use Lauren as more than an observer or assistant. Indeed, she would tag-team the effort, playing bad cop to Tom's good cop in discussing with the client the weaknesses and strengths, respectively, of the *Bordeaux v. Full-Tech* case. Doing so would better support and explain Tom's estimated chance of a defense verdict, as well as the client's potential exposure to a large plaintiff's verdict.

"As advertised?" Lauren asked, looking quite doubtful. "To whom? Did you get Marilyn's permission to have me co-present?"

"I'm a partner. Do I need permission?"

Lauren gave him the same stare as before.

"OK, maybe forgiveness. Don't worry, Lauren; we'll be fine! If you screw this up, I'll take the blame."

"It's not me I'm worried about."

"Wow! I see how it is. Anyway, since you're on a roll, why don't you knock out the next few slides while I get some more sleep."

"I can do that," she replied.

Just then, Tom felt his smartphone vibrate. The free Wi-Fi that came with the upgrade to business class was a nice perk.

It was a text from Suyin: *"Hey, thanks for all your help with my roommate and her lawyer. She's going to pay her half of the rent for the last three months of the lease extension. I can live with that. Good thing I had a lawyer of my own, or I'd be stuck paying all the rent."*

"You bet. Glad I could help. Good luck in your studies in the fall semester," he replied.

* * *

Several hundred miles to the northwest, strapped to another bird and reasonably awake, Jill Nguyen tapped away on her notebook computer.

"Anything for you, miss?" a flight attendant asked.

"Apple juice, please."

"What kind of program are you coding?"

The question was unexpected—*out of character for a flight attendant*, she thought—and she looked around the nearly empty plane for a moment.

"Guess nobody wants to go to Boise in early August," she remarked.

"*You* do!" the attendant cheerily replied. "So, you gonna tell me what you're programming?"

"Just a Java application for my agency's e-commerce platform. Do you code?"

"Used to. Retired from the Postal Service when I was fifty-five."

"How old are you now?"

"Fifty-six."

An awkward pause. He looked at least ten years older; her brain struggled for a moment with the disconnect.

"Yeah, I know," he went on. "Got a little restless sitting around at home. Drove the wife nuts. Now I bother young Asian ladies on empty planes."

She laughed, rather loudly, causing him to chuckle.

"How do you know I'm young?"

"No false modesty necessary, ma'am." He placed a hand on top of the seatback in front of her. "Now, please don't mind my asking—after all, you already know I'm taken—but I was just curious whether you're—"

"—still single? Yep. Thought I found The One a couple years ago. Now I'm not so sure."

He turned to look behind him in case one of the other flight attendants needed him. No one appeared to be in the rear of the plane.

"*Here* we go," he said, crossing his arms with a look of serious doubt.

"What?"

"Don't tell me there's just one guy out there you're supposed to be with."

"I believe in true love, if that's what you're asking," she replied.

"Wasn't asking. Was saying, 'don't tell me' that."

Now she crossed her arms and gave him an accusatory stare. "What about your wife?"

He pushed himself away from the seat, slowly but still enough to signal she'd struck a nerve.

"Oh, don't get me wrong—she's wonderful. I'm kind of *glad* she pushed me out of the house and back to work. Got to keep these old bones moving around. And the way I figure, if I'd waited for somebody perfect all through my twenties, I'd probably still be single."

He paused, thinking about what he'd just said. "No offense intended, ma'am."

She touched the base of her neck, holding three fingers there as if to check her pulse.

Noticing a slight grimace on Jill's face, he pointed to his bald head and asked, "See this?"

"What's that?"

"My cue ball. Had it since my mid-twenties. But not until after I snapped up the missus. Really fooled her, didn't I?"

"I don't expect perfection; most reasonable people don't either. I'm sure your wife didn't. And hey, some women dig older guys with bald heads. Anyway, back in my twenties, I wanted to focus on school and getting my career going."

"Ah, a serious girl. Good for you. Where'd you study?"

"As an undergrad, I actually went to China and studied at the Beijing College of Telecommunications and Posts. Then I got an assistantship at Southern Illinois University at Edwardsville."

"You working for anyone now? Or for yourself maybe?"

"Somebody else. Chicago's IT department for the last year or so. A rental car company for twelve years before that."

"Hmm, you must have started college at fourteen! Child prodigy, no doubt."

"Thanks, Mr. Flattery. I'm thirty-six. Came over to the US when I was twenty-one."

A colleague of the attendant touched his shoulder. "Marty, I need you in the galley."

"Sure," he acknowledged. "Well, Miss, a real pleasure talking with you. Good luck in your quest."

"My quest?"

"For The One."

"Oh, right," she replied. "Nice meeting you, Marty. I'm Jill."

He started walking away. Stopping for a moment, he turned back toward her. "And stay away from the older ones. Take it from me, kid."

Jill smiled, then reached under the seat in front of her to grab her purse. Somewhere in there she expected to find a pack of gum, perhaps tucked into one of the zippered compartments. She opened one of the compartments and found the gum, but also felt some thick paper next to it. Taking hold of the paper and leaving the gum, she pulled out what was actually a small, cream-colored envelope. On the front were the words "DO NOT OPEN 'TIL XMAS."

They were in Tom's handwriting.

22

Trial

Tom looked across the room at his counterpart, Carmen Sanders. Meanwhile, Judge Bolton continued to stare at a nearby computer screen, following along with the court reporter's transcribed stenography in real-time.

"Mr. Edwards?" the judge asked.

Tom's opponent calmly remained in her well-appointed executive chair, keeping both hands in her lap. She and each member of the jury were looking right at him. Judge Bolton continued to look at her screen.

"Present sense impression, Your Honor," he argued.

"I'm going to sustain Ms. Sanders' objection. Proceed, counsel."

The trial had reached its most critical phase. Tom was defending the design of (and warnings associated with) a consumer product: a high-end, stainless steel home furnace manufactured in Taiwan.

During a demonstration of the product by a corporate representative—the same Mr. Jeffries Tom now had on the stand—the furnace allegedly caused a massive fire, destroying a multimillion-dollar home but miraculously no lives, at least in a physical sense.

Carmen's clients were the couple who owned and had just built the place as their dream home, now more than two years ago. On their behalf, she filed a product liability lawsuit against Tom's client: the manufacturer, Nexfurnace.

Until the lawsuit was filed, the furnace model in question had a pristine track record. It was the company's most profitable product, and was powering a healthy rise in North American market share. The stakes were incredibly high; the facts and circumstances surrounding the incident were quite odd. It was just the kind of case Tom relished, and just the kind of lawsuit clients trusted him with as their go-to trial lawyer for one-off, high exposure cases.

Strictly speaking, Judge Bolton's ruling was inconsistent with the rules of evidence. Tom had laid the necessary foundation to "get in" or "admit" the testimony for the jury's full consideration.

But the standard of review in appealing most evidentiary rulings, called "abuse of discretion," left a lot of…discretion in a trial judge's hands. And no lawyer or judge could with a straight face claim to be one hundred percent right all the time when applying the medieval-era "rule against hearsay."

On the other hand, Tom knew this court, knew the judge's ways, and had gotten to know opposing counsel fairly well. He'd prepared meticulously for this trial, and was banking much of his case on this particular line of questioning, which wasn't controversial, prejudicial, or unfair to the plaintiffs.

So Tom wasn't ready to give up on the point yet. He looked again toward his client's corporate representative on the witness stand.

"Mr. Jeffries, don't tell me what you heard Mr. Coffey say," Tom instructed. "Let's break this down."

"OK," the witness responded.

"First, to be clear, tell the jury what was happening when the temperature inside the furnace reached 1000 degrees."

Tom's opponent composedly rose from her seat. "Judge, he's leading the witness, and he lacks foundation. Also, I move to instruct the jury to disregard counsel's reference to temperature."

"Agreed. The jury will disregard the reference to temperature. Either move on or find another way, counsel."

Tom made a fist with his left hand and touched it to his mouth. He took three steps toward Ms. Sanders, who remained emotionless, robotic even. She was almost detached, reacting as if programmed with nothing but cold logic. Definitely not the rookie he'd seen at the Eighth Circuit a few weeks ago.

"Mr. Jeffries, did Mr. Coffey speak? And I'm not asking what he may have said, if anything. My question to you is did he speak?"

"Yes."

"Where were you when he spoke?"

"I was in the same room, maybe from here to where the other attorney is."

"You're referring to Ms. Sanders, sitting at that table over there?"

"Yes."

"Let the record reflect the witness has referred to a distance of approximately twenty-five feet."

"Any objection to that estimate, Ms. Sanders?" the judge asked.

"No, Your Honor."

"Very well," Judge Bolton responded. "Proceed, counsel."

"After you heard Mr. Coffey speak, what happened next?"

"Well, there was an explosion."

"And Mr. Jeffries, if the explosion involved natural gas, do you know what external temperature would need to be applied—"

Tom's counterpart shot up from her seat.

"—Judge, we've already established that this witness has no independent knowledge on which to base an answer to the question."

"Yeah, this is what…the fourth time you're going at this, counsel?" the judge asked.

Tom didn't appreciate the question (comment, really) in front of the jury.

"Your Honor, I think a sidebar would be more appropriate—"

"No, we're not going to waste any more time on this issue. Mr. Jeffries, you may step down."

Though Judge Bolton's rulings were technically wrong, she was right about one thing. Tom had pretty much exhausted the conceivable means of getting in the critical evidence he needed regarding causation, at least through this witness: what caused the fire, and whether the furnace had "contributed to cause" it, under the standard the jury would consider at the end of the trial.

"Judge, I'm not finished with my questioning," Tom declared.

"I'm saying you are. Call your next witness."

"You can't do that, Judge. I've got other lines of questioning with him beyond the temperature of the furnace."

"Counsel, how many times are you going to try to hit on the temperature in front of our jury? You're beating them over the head with it."

"Judge, I don't appreciate your commentary on the evidence."

"What evidence? This witness seems to have nothing but hearsay and speculation to offer. That's why I'm pulling him off the stand."

"Judge, this is improper."

Tom's tone of voice was sharp; his self-control, noticeably absent.

"What's improper, counsel, is your attitude."

Turning toward Mr. Jeffries, the judge stated, "Step down, sir."

The witness started to get up but hesitated, looking to Tom for guidance.

For his part, Tom was incensed. The pointed colloquy with the judge had turned biting, much like the quarrel with Jill that began with a thrown lamp and a smashed console and ended with screeching tires.

"Mr. Jeffries, stay right where you are! I haven't finished my questioning," Tom exclaimed, pointing halfway between the witness and Judge Bolton.

"Mr. Edwards, you're going to force me to find you in contempt."

"Judge, I have to preserve my record! If I let you pull my witness off the stand—"

"I don't answer to you, Mr. Edwards, and you can make an offer of proof, as you well know," Judge Bolton calmly but firmly observed.

"You *do* answer to the Court of Appeals!" Tom yelled in response, seemingly not caring or perhaps unaware of how he appeared to those around him, including his own client.

"And *you* answer to *me*. I'm holding you in contempt. Bailiff, take Mr. Edwards into custody."

"Judge, this is highly prejudicial and you know it! I've been practicing over fifteen years and—"

"Keep it up and that'll be all you'll ever practice. I'm fining you $2,500 for that outburst, and ordering you held for twenty-four hours. Enjoy yourself, counsel."

* * *

"Thank you, sir," Roger Steele responded, noticing a button being pressed on a console behind a semicircular counter.

A loud buzzer sounded; a metal door opened slightly after a catch released.

"Last one on the right," said the officer behind the counter.

Roger approached the cell. Tom looked disheveled: His tie was loosened several inches, his hair was slightly unkempt, and he seemed to be missing his shoes for the moment. This was not the attorney Roger had nearly single-handedly helped promote to partner several years ago.

"Tom, what happened to you?"

Looking up from the floor he'd been staring at for the last minute, Tom recognized a familiar face.

"Roger."

"Tom, you've made a mess of things. We've lost the client on this case—well, our Chicago office has, anyway. Lucky for you, Carlton Blackmon down in St. Louis can take over the trial, and we haven't lost the client on any other matters…yet."

"That's good. I'll say this: I've had an interesting run with women lately," Tom commented, looking away from Roger and toward the cell's ceiling.

Roger could not understand the non-sequitur.

"With what women, Tom?"

"All of them—Carmen Sanders and Judge Bolton in the courtroom, Jill on the front porch, Lana off in Europe."

"Who's Lana?"

"Trouble, that's who she is. And a lot of work."

Roger ignored Tom's response, preparing to deliver the message the firm's executive committee had insisted upon.

"Tom, we're going to get you some help."

"Glad somebody's on my side."

"Judge Bolton's agreed to let you out early and to set aside her finding of contempt, with one condition: You have to visit a court-approved psychologist. We're sending you to St. Louis after you get back from Austria; the firm'll put you up at the Missouri Athletic Club."

"For how long?"

"The company line is you're temporarily taking Carlton's place in our St. Louis office while he'll be up here closing out the trial and handling the post-trial motions. So probably 'til late November. And Tom?"

"Yes?"

"This is also a condition of continuing as a partner. You need to attend four appointments with the doc. First one's set for you this Friday."

"Before I leave for Europe?"

"Yes. And after you get back from your junket, you need to behave yourself down in St. Louis."

"I get it."

"We'll look at things in November and go from there."

Tom looked at his friend, knowing without saying or asking anything that a lot of behind-the-scenes coaxing and cajoling must have taken place with the judge and many of the firm's partners. Once again, Roger was standing behind a friend in need, sticking his neck out when many others wouldn't have.

"So you think I'm crazy, Roger?"

"No. You just have some things to work out. We want to give you time and space to do that."

As Roger started to leave, Tom reached out and placed a hand on his friend's shoulder.

"Thank you, Roger."

"You're welcome. But Tom: You can't pull something like this, ever again. I mean it. The only one some of them think is actually crazy right now is me, for putting up with you."

PART THREE

DISCOVERY

23

The Maze

Thick mud clung to her shoes, slowing her down. A powerful wind struck her eyes with pollen, and she had to blink several times to regain clarity.

A voice echoed through the air, faint but piercing, awakening the child inside her. Lana smiled to herself, piecing together a plan. A flash of pink caught her eye. She was making up for lost time, literally. Within a few moments she was able to grab Alara's cotton shirt. Lana was no longer the captor, and it was her turn to hide.

Hide from the fact this was the first time she'd played with her sister. Hide from the reality she often denied: that parts of her childhood were stolen and never returned. She longed for this experience when she was Alara's age, playing in the maze within the Garden. But back then Lana never quite found what she wanted.

Alara twinkled with a huge grin and said something loudly in Czech.

Lana sensed what Alara wanted, knelt down to meet her at eye level, and traced a circle in the air with one finger. "Want to go again?" Lana asked, raising her eyebrows and opening her mouth widely to signal great excitement.

Alara nodded her head, intuitively understanding the offer. She turned around, covered her eyes, and began to count to ten in her native tongue.

* * *

"I see you!"

Lana ducked behind a row of well-manicured evergreen shrubbery and moved quickly to a corner as her mother smiled and resumed reading an inside page of the *Post-Dispatch*.

It was a school day, but Nancy had wanted to take her daughter to the Missouri Botanical Garden and didn't have to worry about arranging for a substitute teacher to fill in for her. In fact, Nancy didn't have anywhere else to be at the moment, having recently been advised her services at Metro High School were no longer needed. Regardless of what was happening in Nancy's life, though, it was Lana's special day and she wanted it to be remarkable.

Being at the Garden in the middle of the week was indeed special for Lana, who always counted the days until she, her mother, and Grandma would stroll through the place after Sunday Mass. Even in the present dead of winter, Lana could find somewhere to run, somewhere to hide, or somewhere to just be. It was another haven made so by routine and familiarity. No matter what else happened around her, Lana could count on the Garden for solace.

"Mom, try to find me!"

Nancy smiled again, refolded the newspaper, and slowly entered the Victorian Maze. She heard footsteps coming closer then moving away as she peered over the outer rows of hedges. Her soft, flat-heeled shoes deftly masked her approach.

"Where are you? You are so clever. I don't know if I will ever find you."

"Yes you can, Mom. I won't make it too hard for you."

Nancy grinned as she pretended to move one direction and with her peripheral vision spied Lana moving in the other. Concealing herself behind a corner for a moment, Nancy waited for Lana to reach a dead-end then soundlessly pranced straight toward the hiding place.

"Got you!" Nancy announced, as she grabbed Lana around the waist and pulled her in.

"You tricked me. I want another chance."

"We'll do it again on Sunday. For now we need to get home. Grandma's making something for you. Do you know what it is?"

Lana didn't miss a beat. "My birthday cake, of course!"

"Yes, you are so smart. And a good hider. And so pretty," Nancy added, as she stroked a thumb across her daughter's cheek.

"Just like you."

"You're a better hider than me, I think," Nancy said.

"Maybe. But you're a better finder."

"OK, we should get back. Let's go."

The pair walked from one corner of the Garden to another, taking several different pathways as they initially passed a turn-of-the-century brick building and then a domed greenhouse, eventually returning to the visitor center.

Lana was first to reach her mother's Mazda sedan, scraping onto the pavement a few remaining traces of mud from the sides of her shoes. Before entering the back seat, she pushed away several coats and a box of CDs. As usual, she didn't bother grabbing the seat belt.

In little time, the pair was on Highway 40, as a mounted police stable approached and passed on Lana's right. The trip home from the Garden was longer now, the result of yet another move—this one occasioned by Nancy's recent loss of employment.

Barely a year ago, the two could walk to Forest Park in a matter of minutes, dragging a sled through the snow. Lana missed being able to escape there with her friends from Clayton several times a week.

"Do you think it's going to snow?" Lana asked, as Nancy pulled into the driveway.

"Not sure. Want to go inside to let Grandma know we're home? I'll be there in a bit."

In the dining room, Grandma had everything ready to go: party favors, a couple of streamers, and the table set for four. She opened the door to the basement, calling for Grandpa to finish whatever he was doing and join everyone.

In little time, all were assembled at the table. Now in front of Lana and propped several inches above a satin, maroon tablecloth was a moderately sized cake whose chocolate frosting and caramel icing almost matched her long, dark brown hair. A lighted yellow candle shaped like an eight had begun to melt.

Lana stared at the candle for a moment. The birthday girl's face fused together multiple emotions and budding, unsettled traits: At once demure and poised, she seemed delighted yet troubled by something.

"What does the birthday girl wish for?" Grandpa asked.

"I told you what I wanted," Lana responded with a subtle grin.

"Hope I didn't forget."

With that, Grandpa left the table for a moment. Lana was beaming, rubbing her hands together in anticipation.

"It's too big to wrap, so you have to close your eyes," Grandpa advised as he was about to return to the dining room.

Lana pretended to close her eyes, straining to peek through her thick eyelashes. She knew right away what it was.

"Surprise!" Grandpa announced, as Lana fully eyed a wooden Radio Flyer sled held firmly in his proud hands. Lana left her chair and gave him a firm embrace.

"Thank you," Lana exclaimed. "Now if only it would snow."

"My turn," Grandma interjected, presenting Lana with a white box dressed with a red ribbon.

Lana immediately recognized the wrapping. *Another funky sweater*, she knew.

Sure enough, the garment when revealed was adorned with polka dots and lace; she wouldn't dare wear it more than once—and certainly not outside the house.

Nancy smiled, sensing what her daughter was thinking about Grandma's gift. As if to bail Lana out of having to say anything about the sweater, Nancy reached under her chair and took hold of a tarnished silver bracelet once forgotten but now recovered from many years in the basement. It featured a large, blue stone and old-fashioned chain, and was several sizes too large for Lana. Handing the bracelet to her daughter, Nancy explained, "This was given to me. It's your turn to have it."

"It's beautiful, Mom. Who gave it to you?"

"One of my friends, when I was younger."

"I've never seen anything like it before."

Grandma and Grandpa looked at each other at nearly the same moment. He nodded at her indistinctly, and silently excused himself from the table. Grandma followed after him a few seconds later.

"That's because it's from Turkey," Nancy noted.

"Isn't my dad from Turkey?"

Nancy paused, noticing the first few flakes of snow coating the nearby window sill.

"Isn't he? That's what Grandma said."

She deserves to know more, Nancy thought. "Yes."

"Well…can I see a photo or something?" Lana asked.

"I don't have any."

"Is the bracelet from him?"

Nancy instinctively clutched two nearby plates.

"Hello, Mom? Why can't you talk to me?"

"Yes, it's from your father," she said, and walked out of the room.

* * *

A fog slowly crept through the hedges, and Alara's sharp voice was subdued by the sound of the wind. Lana stood alone for a couple minutes, observing the pale clouds in the distance. She couldn't help imagining a life where this place was all she knew. It would have been a simple life, thousands of miles from her mother's demons. But was it the life she always wanted? Who would Lana Delacroix be without the bustling city streets, Grandma's sweet apple pie, and long bike rides at Forest Park?

Would she have been an outsider? Would she ever have been at home? Could she ever be at home?

24

Barbara

Tom stood at a window in the elderly woman's corner office. Prominently displayed atop the nearby building he spotted six enormous white letters arranged in a half-dome shape, spelling out the name of a comparatively large investment firm. Below him, cars whizzed by the Lumiere Place's massive electronic billboard that rose into the sky like a monolith next to the elevated interstate flanking the Mississippi River.

Barbara Peargreen sat at her desk and read the handwritten information and responses submitted by Tom on an intake form.

"This office looks familiar, Doctor."

"It should."

"And this building—it's changed its name, hasn't it?"

"Yes. This was TWA's headquarters when you were in law school here."

"Ah, yes. Memories of green at Wash U and Forest Park."

"Right, and the building used to be called One City Centre," she noted.

"I remember. There was a mall here too, wasn't there?"

"St. Louis Centre," she answered.

"It and TWA disappeared."

"Depends on how you look at it," she said. "The building is still here; there are still food places on the first floor, and offices on lots of the other floors. There's a movie house too; that wasn't here before. As for the airline, some of the planes are still there. They just say 'American' on them now."

"Yeah, but I'm not sold on the new look of those planes."

"Well, let's talk more about new looks, Tom."

"Are you suggesting I have one—a new look?"

"Not saying," she responded. "You brought it up. Tell me more about that."

"Perhaps I do have a new look, in some people's eyes. What do your eyes tell you, Doctor?"

"Well, this is only our first visit with each other. We have at least three left after today."

"Hold it, Doc. We have three left, period."

"Yes. Tell you what: Let's focus on the present, and we'll deal with the future when it comes. As to your earlier question, let me ask you: Do you think you care about how you look to others?"

"Well, my friend Roger tells me that as humans we need to care 'just enough' about what others think of us."

"Do you agree with that statement?" Barbara asked.

"Yes. Each of us needs to be their own person."

"Is that all it means? What about the 'just enough' part?"

Tom finally turned away from the window to face Barbara, looking her straight in the eyes.

"Well, there are social norms and expectations. Don't go out in public naked, unless you're at a nudist beach," he replied.

Barbara placed the intake forms on her desk in front of her then moved them to the side.

"Do you know why you're here, Tom?"

"Yes."

"You know my next question."

Tom walked to a chair in front of the desk and sat down.

"I'll say this, Doctor: You're not what I expected. I'm getting a lot more than I bargained for here."

"Well, your firm is picking up the tab."

"I'm a part-owner of my firm, though."

Barbara said nothing in response. She wanted him back on topic; he knew it.

"So, as for that question of yours: I'm here because I lost my cool in the courtroom and shouldn't have."

"And you know my next question, don't you?"

"Of course. The psychologist's favorite: 'And why is that?' or something similar. Am I right? Oh Barbara, we're going to have so much *fun* together!"

What is it with lawyers? she thought. *I'm going to have to talk with Judge Bolton. Could she send me some dentists or welders? Why does it always have to be lawyers?*

"Anyway, on the 'why' question: I'm not exactly sure why I lost my cool with Judge Bolton. Obviously, I was upset at the time. I thought she was clearly wrong to pull my witness off the stand when I had other lines of questioning to pursue with him. But I shouldn't have lost my cool, no matter how important the case, and no matter how you slice and dice it psychologically."

"Agreed. I'm here to help you avoid that happening again. Talking about what happened should help."

"Well, it can't hurt I guess. It really comes down to self-control, I suppose."

He turned his head to look out the window again, as Barbara waited patiently for him to expand upon his thoughts.

"We have these different layers in our brains, right? Some of my friends on the plaintiff's side of the bar like to talk about the reptile brain versus the ape brain. Others add in the mammalian brain. Again, lots of ways to slice and dice it. In whatever way you break it down, the prefrontal cortex is at the top of the totem pole, right?"

"Control over our emotions, exercising good judgment, among other things, yes," she said.

"We become more self-aware. Sometimes it takes a major event or shock to the system. There's a cathartic effect. We have the capacity to gain more awareness and control of lower-level, natural human tendencies that can become destructive if left unchecked. We become more resilient, or can. Some people are destroyed when the shock comes. But as the cliché goes, 'What doesn't kill you makes you stronger.'"

"Go on," she said.

"Losing my cool at the trial was like a wake-up call. That was my shock to the system. It reorganized my way of thinking: Who's in charge here—me or my hormones?"

"What else?"

"Well, there are those social norms we talked about."

"Do you see them as being too restrictive, Tom?"

"Society likes to put things in boxes, sort and categorize, label. But we need our own values. We have to appreciate life's opportunities and its beauty, which can come in many forms and surely in unexpected ways. Integrity is being authentic and true to ourselves, not society's definition of what's proper or who we can associate with."

"You live in this society. You're part of it, so can you ignore its norms?"

"No, not completely. Hence Roger's point about caring 'just enough.'"

Dr. Peargreen looked at the clock on her desk. She raised both eyebrows and smiled at her patient.

"Yes, well! Our time together is up today, Mr. Edwards. I trust you'll be back in two weeks?"

"I wouldn't miss it for the world, Doctor! But first, I'm off to Austria!"

25

The Salad

Trees passed by meters ahead of the passenger window as Lana grinned, comparing her reflection to those of Alara and Berker in the rear seat. She could see them both peeking over at her every few minutes, pretending they hadn't when she looked back at them, even for a split-second.

Grasping the seat back handle, she tilted herself rearward and closed her eyes, taking in the day's events. The quiet was oddly soothing.

"So, you like Prague," Duygu asserted.

"Yes, it's very beautiful," Lana affirmed. "I can't wait to see more of the city."

"Maybe you come back after graduation and stay for longer?"

"That might work out. I was actually hoping you'd come to my graduation. I would love to show you around and introduce you to my family."

"We will see. And, you know, *here* you have family, which is good. My door is open, Lana, for you."

"I hope you know how grateful I am for that. All of this is beyond what I could have imagined."

"Yes, very good. This is my life, our life here. Come back after graduation, see more."

"That would be great. But I also want to show you the life I know, and I think it would bring us closer. We both need to understand each other."

"We can understand. Tomorrow I will show you more of my life—you will meet my friend Yusef. He owns a shop also. And we will go to the mall. I think you will like."

"That's all great, really. But it feels like you don't have any desire to learn about my life."

"I am learning now," he replied. "Look, almost home," he added, pointing toward the family's townhome near the end of the street.

Lana surveyed the surrounding neighborhood and said nothing more. It lacked the density and bustling feel she was used to. Its serenity was appealing but foreign to her.

* * *

Just a few steps into the hallway, Lana was overtaken by the tang of paprika. She wasn't excited about another evening of traditional Czech food. Thus, on walking into the kitchen, and without a second thought, she began pulling lettuce and tomatoes out of the refrigerator.

"I'm going to make a salad. Do you want some?"

"No, sit down," Duygu insisted, taking the lettuce from her.

"You don't have to bother. I would rather make it myself anyway."

Duygu ignored her and continued placing items on the kitchen counter.

Lana stared at her father, frustrated and bewildered.

"Don't make that face at me," he snapped.

"What face?"

"What *face?* One that will look at me and say, 'I do not listen. I ignore you.'"

"Well, I do hear what you say, but I am an adult now, so I don't have to do what you want."

Duygu yelled something in Czech and threw a plate onto the counter. The plate shattered upon impact.

Lana headed for the staircase.

"You know nothing of respect!" he shouted, pursuing her but stopping at the foot of the stairs. By this point, Lana had already reached her room. She figured he'd be easier to talk to in fifteen minutes or so.

She fell into the bed, placing one hand behind her pillow as she stared at the fan blades churning above. Without thinking, she grabbed her phone and opened Facebook, noticing an unread message from Tom.

"Hey, hope you're doing well and enjoying your stay. Guess where I am?"

Lana typed a reply. *"Let me guess…this is your one text from jail."*

"Wow. Are you a psychic or something?"

"Yes, and I always knew you were hiding something. So they finally caught up with you."

"I hid nothing from anyone. But, I actually was in jail."

"Wait. You're not kidding?"

"No, I'm not. Blew my top in trial. At the judge. She wasn't amused. They call it 'contempt of court.'"

"So she threw you in jail? That's a bit harsh."

"I agree! Anyway, managing partner bailed me out. So again, guess where I am."

"Unemployed?"

"Not quite. More like exile. They sent me to St. Louis and have me seeing a psychologist, minimum of 4 times."

"You're in my old stomping grounds. Will you visit the Arch?"

"No. But enough about me. What's up with you?"

"Actually, had a great time with Alara and Berker this morning. Then just now my father and I argued about a salad."

"What? Don't tell me…you added too much cracked pepper on his lettuce and shortchanged him on the bacon bits?"

"Ha. Actually, I just wanted a salad for dinner because I'm so sick of Czech food. I don't think they know what vegetables are."

"What happened next?"

"This sounds really stupid. I didn't think anything of it when I told him I wanted to make it myself. But he insisted on making it for me. While I realize it was out of love, I felt like he was attacking my independence. I guess I should've been less blunt about it or at least hidden my facial expression, because he went off on me."

"Your dad actually sounds a little like mine when he was younger. My dad had a knack for just going off all the sudden on people—family, workers, you name it. Must be the Sicilian in him."

Lana laughed, as a pulsing ellipsis indicated Tom was writing another text.

"One of the reasons that I think I'm so agreeable and patient is that I grew up with a dad who could just fly off the handle sometimes. I really tried hard to avoid causing him to go off."

Lana smiled upon reading Tom's description of himself as "so agreeable." *He likes to say that about himself,* she thought.

"See, you're used to it because you had to adapt as a child," Lana wrote.

"*Yes, true…and one key thing in my case is that my dad—like myself—is a committed optimist.*"

"*The problem for me is my father has an Eastern European value system on top of a stubborn, type-A personality. It's funny, despite his somewhat shaky English, the other day he told me that I 'have an ego.'*"

"*Some things are just universal, Lana.*"

Lana grinned in response to Tom's dig.

"*He feels threatened when women are just as masculine as himself. I get it, he wants to feel like a provider. He wants others to change themselves for him.*"

"*Change is usually slow, and easier when not forced.*"

"*That's not how he sees it.*"

"*Hang in there. In the meantime, I need to get back to work—have to finish an appellate brief.*"

"*Looking forward to seeing you soon, Tom,*" she replied, finding herself in a better mood to reengage with her father.

* * *

Nancy paced barefoot in a tight circle on the floor of the small bathroom, bending up and down at the waist while holding her chin with one hand.

It was late July and quite warm in the tiny, air-conditionless Paris apartment. Compounding the problem, all the windows were closed—the better to protect her from the stares of the world she perceived to be closing in around her.

Duygu would not be back from the nightclub for about an hour. She had two modeling shoots left that week, and none again for two more. She'd been in demand for the first month or so after arriving in town, but her increasingly unusual requests—regarding (for

example) who could be nearby during a shoot, and at what times—
were wearing on the people she worked with. No matter how allur-
ing she could be in front of the camera, her peculiar behavior was
difficult to tolerate.

She'd greatly tested Duygu's patience as well. Tonight he would
be particularly upset about arriving home to an apartment that was
baking, though she was oblivious to the heat as well as the sweat
forming on the bathroom floor beneath her feet.

And now this. The device she'd placed on the sink next to her had
an unmistakable blue symbol on it. It was the second test she'd taken
in two days. And both results matched.

To be sure, Nancy sensed Duygu would be supportive. He would
not be angry at her for this.

But the news wouldn't stop him from fuming, smoldering, and
inevitably exploding at something else she would do in the future, or
something else that would happen. Even though his flare-ups were
usually short-lived, enduring his rage had become harder and harder
for her.

She loved Duygu. He still treated her at times like a princess, if
not a queen. He would probably treat the child like any proud father
would.

But she already faced a decision about whether to return to St.
Louis in mid-August for the coming school year. Her parents were
expecting her to return. The rest of her family was there; she had only
Duygu here, and though he was earning some decent bonuses from
his boss, she knew she couldn't keep modeling much longer. She'd
eventually start to show, and the number of callbacks had already
been dwindling: She hadn't landed a gig from anyone new in the last
three weeks or so.

And there was already enough fear from all the imagined terrors and growing paranoia inside her. Any remaining sense of freedom would only diminish if she continued her pregnancy in Paris with Duygu. And whatever pride he might take in the prospect of becoming a father, she wasn't sure how his family back in Turkey would receive the news.

Looking at the clock just outside the bathroom door, she recommitted to her choice. She walked into the kitchen, looked at the envelope and the keys she'd left on the small table there, and went into the hallway. She grabbed a large duffel bag, opened the door, walked outside, and hailed a cab.

* * *

Lana sat in the living room, drinking cold tea and playing with the case on her iPhone. Thirty minutes had passed since her father's eruption. The air felt heavy, clinging to her pale skin.

Duygu muted the sound on the television and looked down at his phone for a few seconds before giving Lana a cold stare.

"Now we talk about some things I like and don't like," he announced.

Lana stared into his eyes, making clear her intention to listen. She prepared herself for another long discussion about how to live her life.

"It's not nice to make faces and show attitude. That's not what daughters should do. That's not *normal*."

"Who are you to judge what is normal? It depends on your culture and how you are socialized. I've seen how you live, but you have no idea what I come from. I'm sure you would better understand me if you came to the US."

"What is this about culture? Daughters in *any* culture must respect fathers."

"I wasn't trying to be disrespectful. I was only trying to be direct. That's how I view respect."

Duygu did not immediately respond. He was unaccustomed to being challenged this bluntly by a family member—especially a woman.

"Children need to be there to listen and obey, not trying to 'have space.' You can have space later, after you go back to Chicago."

"Again, this has all happened so quickly, and it's going to take awhile to fully understand what it means to have a father in my life."

"You don't need time. I'm here now, but you make yourself distant. Look at Alara and Berker. They come up and hug me when I get home from work."

"They've known you longer than I have. It's different for me. Affection takes time to grow, and I'm not a child anymore."

"But I'm your father. We're the same blood."

"I know that. But having you in my life isn't as simple as flipping a switch."

"You have people just fine when we go out," he said.

"That's different. Talking about the weather at a coffee shop isn't the same as getting to know my—"

"You are *too* friendly when we go out in public. Like yesterday, when we sit at that shop, you talk to people you don't know. That's not what women do."

"*Again* with your assumptions and expectations. Why can't you simply be happy with who I am?"

"Happy, yes. But there are some things you must know and that I can teach you."

"And I appreciate that, but it goes both ways. There's a lot I can teach you as well, if you're open to it. I would love to show where I'm from and how I live."

"How you live is *stupid*. How people deal with you back home?"

"Wow, I don't even know what to say. Just because people live differently than you doesn't make them wrong."

Duygu shook his head, turned around abruptly, and walked toward the kitchen.

"Why can't you talk—"

"Talk talk talk. You stop talking and start acting like a lady!"

"Not all women have to be passive and tolerate men like you."

"You know, Lana, you now sound like your mother—crazy talk."

"What is so crazy about respecting your daughter, or any woman for that matter?"

"I love women. They must respect me."

"I'm done. I'm going to go outside for a few minutes. I need some fresh air."

"Yes, you go! You pack your stuff! You get out of my house! Get out of my life! You are just like your mother!"

* * *

The wooden beams of the A-frame roof paralleled each other, spaced evenly above Spartan beds that occupied over half the floor. Lana shared the room with one other female traveler; more people undoubtedly would arrive the following day, making the hostel less of a retreat. Leaving her father's house was not without regret. Still, she felt more awake and self-assured than she had for days.

The starlight protruded through the window directly facing her bed. She felt the sudden urge to get out and look around. There was a beautiful world out there, and she had nothing holding her back.

Lana threw down her bag. She only realized how heavy it was once she let it go. As the bag hit the floor, she heard the sound of wood striking wood and recalled the bracelet Nancy had given her, still in its original container.

Also still in its original container were the diamond bracelet and ring her father had given her at the airport. She'd left it sitting on his kitchen table, a striking reminder of the life she'd just left behind.

She didn't want money from him, or expensive things, or anything at all.

She wanted a father, but not at the expense of her dignity.

26

Trust

"The coffee is excellent," Lana said. "Everything here is, which is a relief after everything I experienced in the last few days."

"They have waffles!" Tom declared, peering into a display case whose glass reflected the black suit and light gray tie he still wore.

Flying to Vienna was pleasant, thanks in part to a free upgrade to business class. He'd gone directly to the airport from a court hearing downtown, without any time to change. The weather was agreeable as well, compared to St. Louis: less wind, more pleasant temperatures, more sun.

"You can have anything you want here," Lana said.

"Tempting; I'll stick with the waffles."

An olive-skinned, middle-aged man looked at Tom from behind the counter, smiled, and gestured in his direction.

"See something you like, sir?"

Yes, I'll have a half-plate of your waffles, a small serving of the Wiener Schnitzel on the other half, and a cappuccino, please."

Tom pulled out a Visa card, expecting to pay at the counter. The interior design of the place reminded him somewhat of a Starbucks back home, including the shop's forest-green-and-white, circle-shaped logo.

"We will bring it to you, sir. You can pay later."

"Ah, got it. Thank you," Tom replied, looking for a moment toward the rear of the shop. He noticed several patrons smoking behind a glass door that opened automatically as someone approached it.

"They're not Puritan here about nicotine, I see," Tom commented as he took a seat at Lana's table.

"They're not Puritan about anything here."

"Two days of advance scouting enough for you to draw that conclusion?" Tom asked.

"Not a conclusion. A fact. Which I knew before I arrived. Basic history, really." Lana amusedly grinned. She was unsurprised to see Tom still in his lawyer's uniform, even on vacation. Under the slicked-back hair, behind the coat and tie, and below the exterior, however, was that thoughtful, expressive soul who was a game companion.

There were very few others she'd feel comfortable traveling with. Lana resolved to make the most of the next four days with him.

"Hey, you can loosen your tie now. I won't tell anyone back at the firm," she said.

Black, loose-fitting jeans and a thin, dark-blue sweater with occasional streaks of silvery threading covered Lana's tall frame. Beside her feet were two black suede boots she'd removed. She lightly tapped the side of Tom's left knee with her right foot.

"Speaking of telling, Tom, what did you tell Jill about this trip? Doesn't really matter to me; I'm just curious."

"The truth, mostly: that I'm here for an appellate conference."

"Does she know I'm in Europe too?" Lana asked.

"Yes."

"What does she think about that?"

"As far as she knows, you're backpacking, couchsurfing, and hosteling your way across the continent."

"All true, with a pit stop in Vienna."

"Yes," he replied.

"I'm very happy you're here, Tom. You make my life more exciting. I don't want to make your life difficult, though."

"No, I chose to join you. The idea was originally mine in the first place."

"Yeah, a year ago. We'd known each other for like—a month?"

"Time-wise, yes. But I felt like I'd gotten to know you pretty well by that point. Have you read Arthur Aron?"

A young woman resembling the older gentleman behind the counter approached the table. Holding a stainless-steel tray in one hand and a ceramic plate in the other, she placed the plate on Tom's right and the tray to his left.

"Looks wonderful. Thank you," he said to the server.

"You're welcome. Anything else, sir?"

"Actually, yes. A question, if you don't mind. Are you related to the owner of this shop?"

"Yes. My father owns the shop. I'm Greta."

"Is that him over there?" Tom asked, moving his head in the direction of the counter.

"He is, yes."

She was a bit uncomfortable, or uncertain.

Tom noticed. "I'm sorry; I was just curious because you look like him. The resemblance is uncanny, really."

"I hope you enjoy your waffle, sir."

"You have your doubts on the Wiener Schnitzel?"

Greta seemed not to understand Tom, or his humor.

"Sorry Greta. I was joking. I'm sure everything will be wonderful."

"Yes, I *think* so. Well, let me know if you need something more."

Lana raised an eyebrow and flashed him a skeptical grin.

"Isn't she kind of young for you?"

"Oh, I don't know. She seems a simple lass. She's probably legal," he said.

"You're awful."

Tom paused, folding his hands as he placed both elbows on the table. "So, as far as getting around goes, I'm thinking we can use the subway in the city, and take a car to see some of the countryside," he said. "Four days is a long time; we should spend at least one away from town."

"Fine by me. Should I be the one to rent it? I look like less of a risk."

"Key phrase there is 'look like,'" he replied. "You never fooled me, though."

"Right. That's something you saw from day one. Anyway, getting back to Professor Aron."

"Ah, you know him," Tom said.

"We read from a study of his in one of my psychology classes."

"Have you heard of his thirty-six questions?"

"How to bring people closer together and create intimacy, yes."

"So what do you think?" Tom asked.

"I mean, yeah: It makes sense. You and I talked about a lot of things right from the start. I was comfortable with that. I connect with people who are open to me."

"Yeah, I like that about you."

"Anything you don't like?" she asked.

"Nobody's perfect."

"Agreed. But that's a cop out."

"I accept you as you are," he said. "You'll do."

Lana smiled then took another sip of coffee.

"Well, as I said, I don't want to make your life difficult. Jill is important to you. As she should be. You are blessed, in many ways. I don't want to interfere—"

"You're not. Look, I'm already here. I chose to come. No second guessing. Let's just enjoy ourselves."

* * *

Curved strokes of red, white, and blue were planted upon the green canvas that was the grassy area of the Schönbrunn Palace Gardens. Far in the distance on a hilltop behind Tom stood a triumphal arch adorned with a gilded eagle large enough to be seen even at this distance.

Lana snapped a shot of Tom, who'd turned his head to his left and toward her while the rest of his body remained in place. His olive dress slacks complemented his black sport coat and white dress shirt.

An older, gray-haired woman approached the two.

"Would you like one together?" she offered.

"Sure," said Tom.

"Go on, don't be shy," said the woman, gently pushing Lana in Tom's direction. Lana handed over her phone.

Turning the rest of his body in the woman's direction and sashaying to his left, Tom made room for Lana and held her around the waist.

"What a beautiful couple," the woman observed as she snapped two shots in quick succession.

"Thank you," said Tom as the woman returned Lana's phone.

"Enjoy the city, but not too much," she suggested to Tom, winking at him as she began to walk away.

"I think she was flirting with you," Lana remarked, nudging him with her elbow.

"No, she was counseling temperance."

"Does she need to?" Lana asked.

"No."

"How can you be sure? The opposite is possible, isn't it?"

"What is?"

"Intemperance. In your position, that is a risk," she said.

"What is my 'position'? What is the 'risk'?"

"Don't play coy," she replied, thrusting her palm toward Tom's shoulder.

He turned away just in time, causing her to miss the target. "Hmm, that doesn't happen often," he noted. "Helps when you have cat-like reflexes."

"Only because you're manic. Which is because you're with me."

"Am I? No, this is normal."

"You're looser; you let go of things with me," she said.

"I'd agree with that, but my reflexes are innate," he replied. "Say, you feel like getting something to eat?"

"Yes. Let's try that place near our flat. Then we can check in and dump off our bags."

* * *

According to the directions Tom had printed out, the oddly shaped key he'd received had to be turned counterclockwise in one lock, then clockwise in the one above it. Tom didn't quite have the sequence figured out.

Fortunately for him and Lana, their host was home and had heard familiar mechanical sounds at the opposite end of the hallway.

"It's OK. I will open it for you," Christoph announced from the other side of the door, taking hold of a knob.

Tom released the key in the upper lock and waited. Lana chuckled.

After opening the door to the flat, Christoph smiled and welcomed them inside. Lana placed her umbrella on a desk next to the front door.

Their host moved to his right, immediately seized the umbrella, and handed it back to Lana. She was confused. He rubbed his arm along the top of the desk. He then turned to Tom, ignoring Lana, and composed himself. "Please, the desk here does not have a coating—what do you call it?"

"Varnish," Tom responded.

"Yes, that's right."

"We apologize, Christoph. We'll be sure to keep any of our things away from the desk. I'm Tom. Pleased to meet you. This is Lana."

"And from the floor, please," Christoph added, pointing to his wood floor. "Please place your shoes on this carpet here, yes?"

"Yes. We will. Thank you. Sorry about the oversight," Tom said.

"Not a problem. Very nice to meet you, Lana. And you, Tom. Now, forgive me. I have someone waiting for me on the phone. Your room is at the end of the hall, on the right. I will knock on the door to tell you more later."

Christoph made a slight bow then went into an adjacent dining room that doubled as his office.

Tom had reserved the flat using Airbnb; it was his first time trying the service. At $112 per night, he and Lana had a comfortable place to stay in a charming, quiet part of the city. Within walking distance was a subway station; plenty of restaurants and shopping districts were also nearby.

In the guest room, Christoph had placed two pages of bulleted recommendations regarding places to visit, eat, and hang out to get a feel of the local scene. He had lots of tips a local would know, such as how to get a non-stop train ride back to the airport and which nearby train station had a place to check bags a day before a return flight.

The room was well furnished and appointed. Like the rest of the flat, it featured a twelve-foot ceiling with distinctive crown moldings. In addition to a king-size bed with separate comforters, there were touch-operated end table lamps, a single-serve coffee maker, two armoires, a decorative floor lamp, and two modern, adjustable radiators.

They also had use of a guest bathroom near the front door. It had its own adjustable radiator and ample room for one or two people to use it.

"I love it!" Lana declared as she jumped onto the bed, lying face-down and parallel to the two pillows at its head. "I'll pay you my half when we get back home."

"Don't worry about it. My firm is picking up half my travel expenses since I'm partially on business here."

"That's so cool. I hope I can get a job at a place like that someday."

"You'll eventually *own* a place like that someday," he said.

"You think so?"

"It's a safe bet."

"Thank you," she replied.

"I'm just stroking that huge ego of yours."

"Ha."

As Tom took a seat in a chair next to the bed, he looked at Lana for a moment.

"Something wrong?" she asked.

"No. Though I am having to work a little harder keeping my eyes focused on your face right now."

Lana looked down at her outfit and then back at Tom, smiling.

"See something you like?" she asked.

"Yeah, but it's not like I've never looked before."

"You have yet to touch, though. Why is that? Other guys I meet don't always have the willpower you have."

"They're younger," he noted.

"They don't give up, either. I have to fend them off."

"Well, to be fair, if I were their age—"

"If we were the same age, Tom…or, if you could go back in time and we met twenty years ago when you were thirty-three—"

"Ha. You mean twenty-three," Tom noted.

"Oh yeah. Anyway, what do you think would have happened?"

"I was a much different person then."

"What if you were the person you are now?" she asked.

"Ah, another one of your invalid hypotheticals."

"Fine. I won't make you answer. But I would like to get an answer to my other question."

"About willpower?"

"Yes," she responded.

"I answered it. Your other male friends are young. They can't help themselves."

"Being older doesn't make you any different, *per se*."

"I've had more time to figure out what I want. I want someone with more than an attractive face."

"But you're human," she said.

"Yes. How about you, Lana? You know something of restraint. You have all those young guys fawning over you. But you don't like fawning, do you? Turns you off, actually."

"Yes. I'm not physically attracted to them. That's one reason why I broke up with Rudy. They can start to bore me with their persistence. And I need my space."

"But you like to be pursued, don't you? By the more, the better?" Tom asked.

"I like having attention. I like being the center of attention; I admit it. But you've taught me something."

"What's that?"

"What it's like to share someone."

* * *

Several hours later, Lana walked into the guest room wrapped in a modestly sized white towel. Tom had been half-asleep, until hearing the door to the room close and its skeleton key being turned to lock it.

She dressed a few feet away from the bed, climbing into rainbow-striped fuzzy pajama bottoms and a red plaid shirt that didn't come close to matching.

As she climbed into bed, she turned off the lamp next to her and grabbed her phone.

"You asleep?" she wondered.

"I was."

"What woke you up?" she asked.

"You did."

"I tried to be quiet. I had to change."

"Yeah, that's what kind of woke me up," he said.

"You didn't see anything, did you?"

"Not much."

She pushed on his knee.

"What does that mean?" she asked.

"There wasn't much to see."

"Again, what does that mean?"

"My vision is kind of bad without my contacts," he noted.

"OK. Play dumb," Lana said matter-of-factly. She checked her phone and noticed it was down to only a five percent charge. Pushing her comforter away, she turned on the lamp again. "Hey, can you give me your plug adapter? I need to charge my phone."

"Sure," he replied. "I need to get out of bed to reach it over there."

"And speaking of bad vision, Tom, I'm pretty much legally blind. Like minus six or something with my prescription."

He stood up and unplugged his adapter from the outlet near his nightstand.

Looking to her right for a moment, Lana noted, "I'm not *that* blind."

Tom ignored her, handed her the adapter, and climbed back into bed. She turned off her lamp.

"Feeling awesome right now?" she asked.

"Yes, it's a nice feeling."

"OK, let's get some sleep now."

"Yes, let's," he said.

* * *

Sometime later—he wasn't sure when—he reached for her. Subtly, tentatively, and then determinedly, he stroked the middle of her spine with his first two fingers. Had he awoken already touching her? Was she awake now and did she sense his touch? Her body was so close to his; his skin could sense the heat of her. Did the answers matter?

Turned on her left side, she barely moved, her soft breaths masked. He assumed she was breathing. But she was like a statue, seemingly without life.

That couldn't be true, though: This was the same woman, not only within reach but right beside him.

He recalled the time he'd spent with Grace Ann during his time at the Academy. Theirs was a burning yet smothering liaison, over-flowing with youthful aching and a craving knowing few bounds. It was propelled and sustained by the thrill of secret meetings and precarious deeds, any one of which if discovered would have meant separation—the military's euphemism for expulsion.

Actually they were discovered, once. Only an officer's mercy saved them. Perhaps the officer was a graduate who'd engaged in similar activities as a cadet; they couldn't know, because upon entering the otherwise empty classroom the lovers then occupied, an overhead projection screen Tom had moved to block the door prevented the officer from seeing them.

"Please don't come in," he'd said to the officer at the time. She hesitated; Tom swore he'd heard a snicker. After a long, awkward pause, the officer turned off the light she'd just turned on and left quietly. Grace Ann and her companion thusly dodged a certain end to their early careers.

Now he felt the supple skin of a woman barely older than Grace Ann when he'd last dated her. Indeed, his last trip with Grace Ann—a weeklong tour of Oahu made possible in part through a "Space-A" flight back in 1992—happened just weeks after Lana was born.

He'd never touched Lana so lingeringly. He trembled slightly, sensing both ecstasy and compunction, as he kept stroking her spine in the same spot, with the same two fingers. He relished experiencing with her the kind of physical touch he'd until now neither sought nor obtained.

To Tom, the answer to his earlier question did matter. If she sensed his touch, was the experience welcomed or merely permitted? If she didn't, was his compunction an indicator he should stop? He couldn't stop, and didn't want to. Abnegation didn't suit him, especially not now.

Lana turned suddenly and faced Tom, startling him. He pulled his hand away, but she grabbed it and put it right back where he'd had it, pressing his forefinger and middle finger into her skin and forcing his arm to hold her at her side.

His movement unrelenting, his course fixed, he dared not deviate from it. Lana sighed impatiently then grabbed his hand again and directed it to a new location.

Here the territory became suppler yet retained a characteristic firmness. He instinctively extended his two fingers as before, but swiftly found himself corrected as she took hold of his wrist and pulled it away from her. She just as quickly gripped the back of his hand and slapped his palm against her right glute, hard. It was the kind of force she'd routinely used to strike his shoulder, either because she was too quick for him or he pretended he couldn't turn away from her in time.

The feel of her astonished him; he'd forgotten what youth meant in a physical sense. She was both taut and pliable, aided by a self-regard that made her treat herself, including her body, with the same level of respect she wanted others to show her.

He could now explore her body the way he'd always explored her mind. Her guiding hand encouraged him to touch her from a place of familiarity rather than longing. Feeling more comfortable, he ran his hand slowly down one thigh and over to the other, squeezing nearly every inch of muscle. Exploring her curves and other parts of her accented the known, confirming for him tangibly what he'd long recognized in her existentially.

As he reached her left hip, he felt the urge to squeeze it tightly, and did. With his other hand he gripped the back of her neck, and placed his mouth against her ear. "What happened to your clothes?" he whispered. "*Somebody* had a plan."

"I wouldn't be so sure," she said, turning onto her stomach.

He chuckled and sat up, got on top of her, and placed his knees to either side of her thighs.

"Wait. Let me get my soccer shorts," she said, laughing under her breath.

"Quiet, Lana," he said gently, slipping his hands under her and taking hold of her breasts. Though considerably smaller than her posterior, they had the same feel and tone, with perceptibly large nipples. *Say one thing for her*, he thought, *Lana can do more with an A-cup than nearly any man might think possible.*

After several slow and firm squeezes, Tom released Lana's breasts, slid his legs backward, and rested his entire body on her. She moved her arms from her side and placed her hands next to her head; Tom put his arms atop hers and took hold of her hands, interlocking their fingers and holding her for several minutes.

He then began kissing the back of her neck, leisurely working his way across each arm and hand and then down her back, massaging all the parts of her he'd just touched with his lips.

Without being asked, she turned onto her back and he worked his way up her body, still unhurried, starting from her feet, massaging each part before kissing it. When he finally reached the top of her right thigh, she opened her legs ever so slightly, hesitated, and tried to catch hold of his head. But he was too fast for her and was soon working on her left foot. She whimpered, causing him to stop.

"Was that a moment of utter vulnerability, Lana? Glad I could be here to witness it."

"Did I tell you to stop?" she retorted.

He let out a quiet, deep chuckle, then resumed kissing her ankle. Eventually he reached the top of her thigh and turned his head to the right, resting it there as she felt his warm breath pass over her, making her twitch.

He was making her wait. And surely liking it.

A short time later she cried out, "Oh—my—God!" as he began to savor her.

Upon hearing her outcry, Tom came up for air with a look of genuine concern on his face. "You OK, Lana?"

Now it was her turn to chuckle. "I'm peachy," she replied, touching the back of his head for a moment and encouraging him to continue.

He eagerly obliged.

Lana appreciated the fact that Tom knew exactly what he was doing. Sex was an uncommon experience for her, and he knew that too. He wanted to give her something she couldn't easily forget. After several minutes, he lifted his head, moved toward her chest, and licked one of her erect nipples, and then the other. Heading back to each breast for a return visit, he easily managed to place each of them into his mouth.

She placed her hands on his shoulders and with a twisting motion turned his body over. He didn't resist her. She sat atop his abdomen, touched the tip of his chin with her finger, then held it in front of his face to signal that he needed to wait for something.

"Should I close my eyes?" he asked, borrowing as much moonlight as he could to scan her supple frame.

She grinned. "If you want."

He decided that he wanted to, then sensed her moving and turning toward his groin. Her torso touched his, and before he knew it she was now down on him.

"Lana," he said, calling her name like he was making a statement. He turned his head toward the window and opened his eyes to see the moonlight. She had positioned herself over him; he touched the sides of her pelvis, recentered his head, and lightly pulled her in; she moaned as she continued to work on him. Stopping for a moment, she began to say, "Tom, that feels…"

They gave and received without possession; they shared without losing anything of themselves. A short time later, he lightly touched her side and guided her around; she knew they were ready. She sank into the bed, turning her head to stare into his big hazel eyes. Tom leaned over and kissed her lips several times. She placed a hand behind his head and opened her mouth, causing him to do the same. He slid one hand down her neck and to her abdomen, stopping there, fully aware she was eager for him. For once, their agendas were the same. Knowing that too, he slid the length of himself into her. Their bodies finally, fully merged as one.

Without tension or fear they made their connection felt, while recognizing and upholding the space each wanted the other to have— and more importantly, to keep.

The entire experience matched what he wanted and anticipated. He sensed the same was true for her. Each controlled while permitting the other control, the beauty of their connection inherent through the autonomy they expected each other to sustain. Though they managed to hold out for several minutes in this state, their minds and bodies had a moment of incredible release, after which Tom slowly slid down next to her.

Only then did he realize the experience was nothing more than a quite realistic dream.

27

The Meeting

Sunlight penetrated the thick curtains, whose cream hues permitted soft spears of luminosity to touch and silently bounce off the pale skin of the room's sole tenant.

A bright smile appeared on her face as she opened one green eye, then a second, slowly exposing both to the new day. She felt alive and uninhibited, once again in control of what happened to her.

Pushing the comforter toward her feet, she sat up and looked to her right.

"Tom?"

Hearing no response, she lightly touched the mound of fabric that was his separate comforter. Still no response.

She formed a tight "V" with her arms, pointing them toward the high ceiling; the right side of her face rested upon a bicep as she closed and reopened her eyes.

A small note on her nightstand grabbed her attention. She leaned over to read it.

*Hey Lana, I didn't want to disturb your beauty sleep so I snuck out
to grab a few things to bring back to the room. I'll probably look*

around a little at the Wien Mitte station mall while I'm out. Will try to get back by 9:30 or so.

Checking her phone, Lana observed the time: 7:52. *Might as well get some more sleep*, she thought. *Would be nice if he gets a bottle of red wine…and if he makes some coffee later.*

Feeling a bit warm, she slipped out of her pajama bottoms and put them under her pillow, then pulled the comforter back over her. Within a few minutes she was asleep again, alternatively walking or running through a green maze formed by shrubs and bushes of various sizes and shapes. Berker and Alara chased or hid from her; from a distance, Duygu snapped photos with his phone, which suddenly began ringing. Lana heard a door slam and the sound of footsteps, then saw Berker secreting himself within a dead-end of the maze.

"Lana," an unfamiliar voice called to her.

She made no response but held a content smile on her face, which felt warm as she turned away from the bright rays of the sun poking its way through a small cloud in a mostly clear sky.

"So beautiful, so young."

Struggling to stay asleep, Lana felt waves of consciousness coming upon her and heard the creaking of the box spring as someone sat down on the edge of the bed.

"Tom?"

"Hello, Sweetie," said the voice.

"Grandma?"

Lana opened an eye halfway then quickly awakened, springing out of bed and prancing around its nearest corner to squarely face the source of the voice.

"What the…What are you doing in my room?"

"That's an interesting question. Try this one: What are you doing in *Tom's* room?"

Lana couldn't believe what was happening. *Is this a cruel nightmare?* she thought.

"Oh my God! Jill!"

"You've got some nerve, I'll give you that. It wasn't enough to show off at the Union League Club. Or to go for a romantic stroll at the Garden at 2:00 in the morning. You upped your game and stole him away to Europe!"

Jill took two deep breaths in quick succession, briefly placing a hand against her chest to compose herself.

"He's taken, Lana! Don't you have any decency? I told you to back off from him!"

Lana grasped her shirt near its top button, then slowly took a couple of steps away from Jill and toward the desk in the corner of the room.

"Jill, calm down, it's not what it looks like!"

"No, it's exactly what it looks like."

"Again, it's not, but I don't have to have this conversation with you right now. We could have met in Chicago and talked, and you know that."

"We *did* talk in Chicago, at Rudy's expo booth. I said what I needed to say then."

Lana paused for a moment, spied the nearby chair, and took a seat, pulling her shirt down to cover her black lace hip-hugger panties.

"I still can't believe you would barge in on me like this. I wouldn't do that to anyone."

"Aren't you glad I didn't barge in on you last night while you were fucking my boyfriend? My, wouldn't *that* have been embarrassing?"

"I didn't *fuck* anyone. Please take your derogatory assumptions and get out of my room."

"You expect me to believe that? Do you think I'm an idiot? Look at you, holding your shirt down like you're ashamed of something. Did you forget to pack pajamas? Guess you figured you wouldn't need them."

"You can believe what you want, but I'm telling you nothing happened. We're just friends, and always have been."

Jill stood up and leaned in to face Lana.

"I'm sure you do this regularly, sleeping with different men around the world. You must feel very special. A man in every port, no doubt. How many of them are your father's age?"

"Wow, you don't even know me! You couldn't be any further from the truth."

Jill took two additional steps toward Lana, looming over her. Lana released the bottom of her shirt and crossed her wrists over her chest.

"The *truth*? The truth is you've been sleeping in the same bed as my boyfriend. Dressed like that," she said, pointing at Lana's crotch and taking two steps backward.

Lana looked at Jill for a moment then out the window next to the desk. Letting out a heavy sigh, she pulled her shirt over her panties again and gazed back at her unwelcome visitor.

"God, please give me a minute to get dressed and then we can talk, civilly. I understand why you're upset, but I'll say it again…nothing happened."

"Yeah, so innocent. Not the way it looked or sounded at the Club though, huh? I heard all about it. How do you think that makes me feel, to have friends and acquaintances tell me they saw Tom in the arms of another woman?"

Jill took another step back, crossing her arms and turning toward the window.

"They're exaggerating, Jill. Tom and I hadn't seen each other for like four months and I was happy to see him again. Maybe I got a little carried away and the hug lasted a couple seconds longer than usual."

"Longer than usual? Oh my gosh—what's the usual, honey?"

"Look, I get that you're jealous. What I want you to know is that you don't need to be."

"Who said you get to decide how I feel?"

"I didn't," Lana replied, fumbling for words. "I don't…and I'm not…I'm saying…based on the facts…there is no rational basis for you to feel jealous."

"Has Tom been teaching you how to talk like a lawyer? Special late-night tutoring sessions for you?"

Lana sighed, reached for a box sitting on the corner of the desk, and struggled to remove a piece of Belgian chocolate wrapped in gold foil. "Your insults aren't going to provoke me, if that's what you're hoping for," she said, unwrapping the piece of chocolate and almost dropping it. "You and I are obviously very different people."

"Yes. I'm Tom's girlfriend, and you're nothing. That's the biggest difference, right there!"

"Again, I'm fully aware he is dating you," Lana replied, holding the chocolate in her open hand and staring at it. "I haven't made a move on him; he hasn't made one on me. I have integrity."

"Integrity? What if I were a fly on the wall and took a picture of you and Tom sleeping in the same bed last night and posted it on Facebook? Do you think everyone would look at that picture and say, 'Oh, that Lana—so much integrity'?"

"Society likes to draw its own conclusions, usually without knowing the entire story."

"Well, you and Tom obviously have something special. Aren't you proud of yourself, Lana? You can capture middle-aged partners at big law firms and parade them around Europe. Meanwhile, back home you've got a whole *stable* of men after you! I've seen your Facebook page. Must make you feel really good about yourself. Well, here we are. I found your little nest; not as discreet as you thought, huh? I caught you and you're not getting away with it."

Lana looked up again, peered at Jill for a few moments, then popped the chocolate into her mouth. "I don't see myself getting away with anything. I'm having a good time, yes, but not doing anything wrong."

"If there's nothing wrong with what you're doing, why do you have to be discreet?"

"I'm being discreet out of respect for Tom, for myself, and for you, actually. I know that Tom is taking a risk by sticking his neck out to spend time with me, maybe risking his reputation. It's quite a compliment; I really appreciate the fact that Tom values me that much as a person, regardless of my age or what I do or don't do for a living, or how I look—"

"Oh, come on, Lana. Wake up and smell the coffee! Do you think for one second Tom would spend any time with you if you were ugly?"

"I can't say what Tom would do or not do, but I can tell you he's never tried to make a move on me. I'd call that loyalty, Jill. You're a very lucky woman."

Jill chuckled in disbelief then pointed to the door and in an even tone of voice said, "I want you out of this room and out of Tom's life."

"If Tom asks me to leave, I'll leave."

"I'm not leaving until you're out of here," Jill replied, recrossing her arms.

"Jill, that's not going to work. I'm not sure how you got in here but—"

"Tom gave me his itinerary. I met Christoph at the door and told him who I was. He seemed a bit surprised. I wonder why."

"We aren't getting anywhere. I've told you the truth. I'm not having sex with your boyfriend."

"Huh. You two obviously have emotional intimacy, regardless of whether there's any sex involved."

"You can describe it however you want," Lana responded, slumping in her chair.

"So are you telling me this is just some platonic friendship? There's no such thing! Not between a man and a woman, anyway, and *definitely* not with a man twice your age! Do you *really* think Tom likes you because of something other than your youth and your looks? You're delusional."

"No, you're just assuming things. A lot of things."

"Whether I am or not, sooner or later you're going to find someone more interesting. You'll have no use for Tom then. Bet you never told him that, huh? You're just using him for your own fun and entertainment while you bide your time for something better. You're both using each other, actually."

"Wow. You really don't know what you're talking about. You don't know *me*. You *think* you know me, but everything you're saying is just based on a bunch of assumptions."

"Well, whatever you have with him, it's not going to last much longer. I'm going to see him soon; I'm sure he's coming back anytime.

And when he does, I'm going to give him an ultimatum: Choose me or you." She smiled then added, "Of course, he'll choose me and dump you on the curb faster than you knew what hit you."

Lana rolled her eyes. "I don't think so, Jill. It's a false choice. Unless you and I can be civil, it's only going to hurt Tom in the end."

"What? Are you thinking we'll share him or something? Do you really think you're ever going to be my equal?"

"That's not the calculus. It's not that simple, Jill. And wow, you obviously think a lot of yourself."

"That's interesting to hear, coming from you. And yes, it actually *is* simple."

"Jill, I was actually just telling Tom yesterday that I know you are important to him, as you should be. I accept that. I'm not threatened by that. Actually, I'm happy that Tom recognizes that fact."

Jill laughed. "This isn't a negotiation, Lana. Tom has to choose between keeping me and having his young, tasty treat."

"Again, it's a false choice," Lana responded, taking another piece of chocolate.

"No, you've just made him *think* he doesn't *have* to make a choice."

Jill's tone changed suddenly, in mid-sentence. She stepped backward again, bumping into the bed. She began crying, profusely. Lana was shocked to see Jill's frontal assault vanish in an instant.

"You've changed him, Lana. You realize that, don't you? He isn't the man I met three years ago, and it's your fault. You've corrupted him. It hurts me. I don't think you understand, at all. Well, I hope this happens to you when you're my age. That will be your just deserts."

"Whatever he is now is who he is," Lana replied. "He's living an authentic life. If I helped him toss out some filters, I've done a good thing. Any changes that happened came from a pure place."

Jill was spent and stayed silent. Lana stood and moved toward her, briefly touching her shoulder.

"Don't touch me," Jill snapped, slapping Lana's hand away.

"I'm sorry," Lana said, returning to her chair. "I didn't mean to cause you any pain, Jill, now or before. I don't want to upset you, but I have to say: I don't think you can dictate who someone associates with." She paused, waiting to see whether Jill had anything more to say. "Well, I can see you need space, so I'm going to grab some clothes, take a shower down the hall, and leave the flat for a few hours. Tom said he'd be coming back around 9:30. I'm going to take one of the keys with me; Tom has the other one. I plan to return around noon, unless Tom tells me otherwise. I'm not expecting you to agree with my plan or my intentions; I'm just telling you what they are."

"Just fucking leave," Jill said.

* * *

"*Heads up. We have company,*" read the text from Lana.

Rudy was puzzled, and annoyed. *She forgets, I'm seven hours behind her*, he thought, setting his phone down next to his alarm clock, which read 1:57 a.m.

Seconds later, another text arrived. Rudy rolled over in his bed and reached for his phone again.

"*And by company, I mean Jill. She just waltzed into the flat and right into our room, while I was sleeping!!!*"

Rudy rubbed his eyes. *What is she talking about?* he wondered. He was accustomed to getting an occasional text from Lana with little to no context, but he could usually get the gist of what she meant. He found himself stumped this time, however. *And what's Jill got to do with anything?* he asked himself.

"I may need to get a restraining order when I get back to Chicago. I'm serious, Tom."

Now it all clicked. *Unbelievable*, Rudy thought. *Fucking unbelievable.* There were so many things he wanted to do or say at that moment, though not all options were simultaneously available to him. Among other things, he considered throwing the phone against the wall, writing back to Lana as if he were Tom, writing back as himself, deleting her from his phone, deleting her from his life…

As he contemplated his next move, he received another text, but this time from his Facebook Messenger app. Curiously, it was from Lana.

"Had a great time with my sister and brother the other day. Then my father and I argued about a salad."

Though still incensed, Rudy decided to play along—at least for now. But he certainly wasn't in a mood to play fair.

"What did you do this time, Lana?"

"Why would you think I did anything? Anyway, I just decided to make a salad for dinner because I was so sick of Czech food. I don't think they know what vegetables are."

"Poor Lana. Got to keep eating those veggies, even if you have to demand them from your gracious hosts. Wouldn't want to mess up that stick figure of yours."

"What the fuck, Rudy? Body shaming and making fun of me now? This isn't like you."

He didn't feel like giving her the courtesy of a response, but was curious to know more. *"Perhaps not. Anyway, what happened next?"*

"OK, so, I know this sounds really stupid," she continued. *"I didn't think anything of it when I told him I wanted to make it myself. But he insisted on making it for me. While I realize it was out of love, I felt*

like he was attacking my independence. I guess I should've been less blunt about it or at least hidden my facial expression, because he went off on me."

"*Yeah, I guess so too, Lana. The nerve of your newly-found father to attack your independence! Surely he just disqualified himself for Dad of the Year.*"

Rudy was now grinning from ear to ear. He let out an extended, boisterous laugh.

"*Anyway, here's what I know, Lana. You say you hate drama, but conflict surrounds you. It follows you. Did you ever think or has it ever occurred to you that the instigator of so much of the drama…is you?*"

He paused in thought then continued texting. "*I swear, you can be your own worst enemy.*"

And with that, after confirming that his messages went through, he promptly powered down his phone and soon went back to sleep.

28

Getting Tight

With a grocery bag cradled in one arm and his smartphone held out in front of him with the other, Tom pressed the power button to reveal the time: 9:41. As the elevator reached the third floor, he noticed that the door to the flat was opening.

"Ah, you did some shopping?" Christoph asked.

"Yes."

"Here you are, go right in. I am off to the furniture store."

"Thank you. How were your sales yesterday?"

"I sold one piece: an armoire. Maybe I should sell one to you now. Things are probably getting tight in there very recently?" he inquired, motioning with his head toward the guest room at the end of the hall.

Tom blinked his eyes twice deliberately, showed a tentative grin, and replied, "How do you mean?"

"Oh, just a little Austrian humor."

"Ah, I see. Well, hopefully you'll have many customers today eager to spend their money," Tom said as he used the back of his hand to press the button on the elevator for Christoph.

"Let us hope."

Tom set the bag on the desk next to the front door, which he closed and locked. He reclaimed the bag and walked down the hall. As he looked into the guest room, he saw that Lana was still sleeping and, not wanting to wake her, placed the bag on the floor and against the wall. He then disrobed, grabbing a set of new clothes for himself and walking to the guest bathroom for a shower.

Hot water came out of the ceiling-mounted fixture almost instantly. Extending his hands above him as if worshiping, he rested them against the front wall of the shower and lowered his head, enjoying the thick and heavy stream of water as it massaged his neck and upper back and ran down to his legs.

"Hey, what's going on there?" Tom asked, as he felt his ankles and the top of his feet being rubbed.

"Shhhh."

Hands gripped his lower leg and caressed his calves, releasing some tension. Tom slightly lifted his right foot, probably no more than an inch, but felt a sharp pull that caused it to pound back onto the ceramic tile beneath him.

"OK, feet stay on the ground, I get it," he observed.

A hand slapped his right buttock, hard.

"What the *fuck!*" he exclaimed, opening his eyes but continuing to face forward and hold his hands in place.

Again a finger came to his lips, as did a hand to his neck, squeezing it gently. He chuckled and said nothing more. Hands returned to his calves and soon grasped him at the knees. He adjusted the temperature to make the water a bit warmer.

Minutes later, the hands swept around to his hips then pressed deeply into the front of his thighs, returning for a moment to the tops of his knees. Fingers slowly crept upward from there: two spiders dazedly crawling on masses of flesh.

Summoning more willpower than he'd had to muster in years, he immediately grabbed hold of and removed the hands from his body the moment they attached themselves to—

"Sweetie, I'm flattered, but—"

"—but what, Tom?"

He wondered if he was dreaming again, and squeezed the back of his neck to confirm he was not. Something about her voice—

"Afraid lightning won't strike twice so soon? Stamina not what it was when you were her age, *huh*?"

Oh my God! he thought, turning around and fully opening his eyes.

It really *was* her, standing before him wearing a soaked black cocktail dress, no less. He turned off the water in a flash, rotating the controls sharply to the right with one hand behind his back as he placed the other hand on her shoulder.

"Jill! How did you…what are you doing here?"

He swept the shower curtain to one side and reached for a towel hanging on a nearby rack.

"More like, what are *you* doing here, *with her*?"

"Jill, it's not what you might think."

"Not what I *might* think? What else *could* I think? What else *should* I think?"

She walked out of the shower and stood on the floor just outside the bathroom as tears began to form in her eyes.

Frightful of what Christoph would do or say if he saw what was happening just then to his hardwood floor, Tom removed the towel from his waist and wrapped it around Jill's legs, desperately trying to soak up as much water as he could. He reached for one of her hands and placed it against the towel so that it wouldn't fall, then grabbed another towel and placed it on the floor next to her feet.

"Come on, let's get you out of these wet clothes," he urged, putting a hand on her left hip and taking hold of her right hand to steer her toward the guest room. As she started to cry softly and placed a hand over her face, he gently removed her dress, yanked a robe from a nearby coat rack, and wrapped the robe around her while easing her down to the bed and into a sitting position.

Jill looked up at him, showed a very slight smile, and regained her composure.

"Tom, I've asked you this before and I'm going to ask you again. I want a straight answer this time. What are you hoping to accomplish with her?"

An uncomfortable silence endured for nearly a dozen seconds.

"I don't know, Jill. It's the worst answer I can give, but there it is."

"I *know* you don't know. This time you've actually told me the truth. And that scares me. Not that you told the truth, but what the truth is."

"Look, I haven't gotten intimate with her. I was kind of uncomfortable back there in the shower, actually."

Jill shook her head. She wasn't sure whether to feel anger or pity. Uncertain what to sense, she laughed—not at Tom, not at herself, but at the situation, particularly in light of the news she soon needed to deliver.

"Like you said, you really don't know. Neither does she, probably. I think you both don't know what you want, and you have that in common, which somehow tightens your bond."

"Jill, you may not want to hear this, but I'm sure that if you two met—"

"Oh, we have. Twice actually, including just this morning."

Now it was Tom's head that shook.

"Wow. Would I have *loved* to have been a fly on the wall…"

"You're not taking this seriously, Tom. And neither is she. This fantasy here in Vienna is far from reality. And your reality is about to get all the more real."

He looked at her briefly then turned to face the window. Something about her demeanor was peculiar; at that moment she had a confidence and calmness that was dampening powerful emotions he knew should otherwise be evident, if not exploding out of her, under the circumstances.

"What do you mean?"

"Tom, I'm pregnant."

29

Traveling Alone

The steak's seasoning and preparation removed the need for any sauce. As she held her glass of cabernet, she appreciated the warm smile of the approaching attendant, whose light-blue scarf distinctly complemented the all-red outfit below it.

On the screen in front of her seat, *Midnight in Paris* played; she clearly heard the dialogue of its characters, thanks to the noise-canceling headphones supplied by her host, Austrian Airlines. She noticed that the service on the plane easily outclassed what she typically received on domestic flights in the US.

On the seat to her left were a blanket and extra pillow. She tried to focus on the film, but everything in the movie seemed to take on peculiar meanings in light of what had happened recently in real life. The movie's protagonist had found himself almost one hundred years in the past; she wished she could go back just two days.

The same attendant approached from the opposite direction.

"Is everything prepared to your liking, Miss?"

"Yes. Excellent. My best to the chef."

"He's here if you'd like to tell him personally."

"Oh, that's OK."

But the attendant was already motioning to present the decked-out-in-white gentleman responsible for the meal. Meanwhile, someone several rows ahead pressed a call button, triggering a familiar chime in the cabin.

"Excuse me," said the attendant, pausing for a moment and offering another smile before walking away.

"Traveling alone this evening?" asked the chef.

Slightly annoyed at the interruption, she paused the film and turned her head and body all but squarely to her left.

"Tell you what. You sit here and the answer becomes 'no.'"

She picked up the pillow and blanket and stuffed them between the edge of her seat and the lower sidewall.

"How can I refuse?" he responded, welcoming the opportunity to get off his feet. Though he still had a few more passengers to greet—or at least walk past or be seen by—he could spare a few minutes before the crew would need him again.

"It's OK if you did. It's not like it hasn't happened before."

"Now who would refuse the likes of you, Madam?"

Ignoring the question, which she took as rhetorical, she asked him, "Are you Italian?"

"From Sicily. Do you know where Palermo is?"

She grinned, looked at the floor, and back at his face.

"*Oh* yes. I have a—"

A couple of seconds went by.

"A husband who is?"

"Ha. No."

"Of course not. You are too young to be married. Boyfriend maybe? Sicilian boyfriend?"

"You are asking some really personal questions, you know? But you *are* cheering me up a little, so I won't lodge a complaint this time."

"Forgive me. So what is the answer?"

A brief smirk quickly became a grimace as she ruminated on the question.

"I'm—not sure what—or who I have."

The chef looked toward the front of the plane. The attendant who'd introduced him was looking right at him and pointing in the direction of someone sitting approximately five rows ahead.

"Well, just remember, Miss: You always have yourself."

* * *

Three hundred miles to the east, a gray Mercedes made its way around one hairpin turn and then another, at times climbing several hundred feet per minute as it traversed a narrow roadway through the Austrian Alps.

Her forehead crumpled as she squinted her eyes. High beams ahead signaled for her companion to regain his side of the pavement. He kept drifting though, triggering the oncoming driver's horn.

She turned slightly toward her companion. He was a blend of predictability and wildness, somewhat complementing her spontaneity. And like him, she too could trigger one's attention.

"We're going kind of far from our home base," he declared.

"What does that even mean?" she asked, pushing his shoulder.

Ignoring the question, he picked a favorite song to play and cranked up the volume.

She heard the opening line and rolled her eyes.

"Of course," she muttered.

Again they heard the tale of a starlet singing in a garden for a man whose soul was both sweet and blood red, as the starlet wondered whether anyone else could put up with her—and her ways.

Right now she'd had about enough of *his* ways, at least when it came to his driving.

"Would you please stay on the correct side? I don't like being honked at."

"Do I need to play some Toby Keith? Quiet, woman."

"First of all, you hate country, and so do I."

"I wouldn't say I hate it. It's just one of my least favorite forms of music."

"Second of all—"

"—second of all, easy on the sass."

"You like it, and you should enjoy it while it you can."

"Wait, what does *that* mean?"

Tom smirked and gave Lana a doubtful stare. Holding the same smirk, he slowly turned his head toward the windshield, saying nothing, while Lana looked at the floorboard for what seemed a couple of minutes.

"So what *is* my home base, Tom?"

"Nope, you can't answer with a question. Also, you mean *our* home base, right?"

Lana looked ahead as the car crested a steep hill and reached a plateau. To the left was a sprawling valley; in the distance appeared a hitchhiker making his own way forward, steadily climbing the next hill.

"There's something I want to get off my chest, and you're the first person I want to tell."

"Let me guess…you're pregnant. At least I know it can't be me."

"Wow, it's impossible to talk to you sometimes."

"Hey, why are you—"

"Can you be quiet for once?"

"Fine. Go ahead," he said.

"As difficult as this month has been, I've learned so much about myself from it. I finally have a better sense of clarity and direction."

"How so?"

"My whole life, I feel like I've been running away from something. I wasn't entirely sure what it was, but I began to think it was normal."

Tom nodded, intrigued.

"I moved away for college because I wanted to distance myself emotionally and physically from everything that happened."

"You made a good decision, Lana. Chicago's not a bad place to end up."

"No, it's not. But lately I've been thinking about my mother a lot, and my childhood back in St. Louis. Projecting a light from 10,000 feet, I think she saved me from an even worse set of circumstances."

"Seems like she did, yeah."

"I had nothing to run away from. I've been in Chicago four years, and it feels less like a home than St. Louis. Now I realize the problem wasn't the city—it was me."

"But you have people in Chicago who care about you, a lot."

"Yes, and I'm grateful for that. But I can't keep running away."

"So what does that make me? An escape?"

"Well, in some ways, we're both escapes for each other. And that's not necessarily a bad thing."

"So then, what? We're using each other?"

"You won't let me finish. This isn't just about you."

"I get that, Lana. I do. But I don't like where this is going."

She turned away from him and looked into the sky through the window to her right.

"I'm starting to regret even bringing this up. I expected better from you," she said.

"Nice. So anyway, good for you and all that you're at peace with your past. But that doesn't mean you have to move back to it."

"I haven't found any opportunities that interest me in Chicago. I've visited St. Louis a couple times this summer, and a friend wants me to help launch a startup."

"What's so special about this friend? Surely you'll have a better chance launching a startup in Chicago."

"I feel so insignificant there. I need to be somewhere I can really make a difference."

"You're not thinking this through! Other than this 'friend,' what connections can you rely on? Isn't this just as much an escape? You're still running, Lana."

She turned to face him again. "Wow, I thought you would be at least *a little* happy for me!"

He abruptly swung the vehicle off the road, sharply brought it to a stop, and turned his head toward her with a scowl.

"What the hell, Tom? You're the one not thinking. Why are you so emotional about this?"

"Is there something wrong with showing a little emotion every now and then?"

"No. I've had a very emotional week myself, as you know."

Tom knew. He also knew the drive, the music, and the present company either were or had become escapes from something—someone—unavoidable.

In traveling to Europe, he hadn't meant to upset anyone or damage his relationships with Jill or Lana. He wanted to believe having both women in his life was necessary, even healthy.

But after revealing she was pregnant, Jill made clear that Tom had a choice to make. And he hated ultimatums. Unwilling to respond to her "it's-me-or-her" demand, he left her feeling betrayed, and she decided to get on the next plane headed to Chicago.

More aware now of the circumstances and the stakes— and of an uncertain future—he was unable to focus on the present moment. Though being with Lana was enjoyable and offered stimulation, inspiration, and some thrills, her need for new adventures and intellectual challenges was something he knew he could not consistently supply. Crossing the middle line was daring and had its fun, but was not without effect on or risk to others.

"When is your flight again?" Tom asked.

"Trying to get rid of me now?"

"No, just trying to figure when we'll need to get back to Vienna tomorrow so I can drop you off at the station."

"So you can get rid of me," she replied, lowering her chin and blinking her eyes at him several times.

"Hollywood, here she comes."

"Actually, I think that with the right script and role, and matched with the right director, I'd nail it."

Tom sighed and looked at his phone to see if he had any messages. Lana noticed he'd done it several times since picking up the rental car.

"Jill didn't leave on the best of terms, did she? Have you heard from her?"

"No. She's still in the air."

"But I mean after she left—"

"—after I practically made her leave, no!" Tom growled, slamming both hands on the steering wheel. "What would you expect? I can't *blame* her for ignoring me!"

"Whoa. Do you want *me* to drive? I'm not used to seeing you like—"

Violently turning his head toward her, he interjected at nearly a shout, "—like *what*? We can't all be cool and aloof all the time like you, Lana. And we can't always do whatever the hell we want, whenever we want it. Some of us have to be adults sometimes."

She maintained her composure, but the lines on her forehead showed surprise as well as anger.

"What is up with you? Yelling, now insults…I didn't sign up for this. Is there something you're not telling me?"

"You want me to stop at that hotel down the road there and drop you off, Lana? Give you some time for yourself? Some precious space? Maybe you could meet a few new people there and send me a text when you're ready to be picked up."

"If you're going to be boorish, Mr. Agreeable, maybe I should do just that. Of all the times and places to find out you have a temper, you do it to me on vacation."

Tom nodded his head, as if he'd made a discovery or convinced himself of something.

"Fuck *you*, Lana. No wonder your dad can't stand you."

30

Desire and Love

"What does Tom want?"

Tom kept his hands behind his head and continued to look at the ceiling.

"A lot of things."

"You really like that chair, don't you?" asked Dr. Peargreen.

"I do. I can see why Sigmund thought having his patients lie back on one of these could encourage them to spill their guts."

"That's nice. Now back to my question."

"Well, we were talking about desire versus love. But it's a false dichotomy, Doctor."

"Why do you say that?"

"Well, it doesn't allow for platonic friendship between a man and a woman, which happens all the time."

"Oh, I never said that kind of friendship doesn't exist."

"But it seems like you're saying desire or love will exist or develop at some point, creating some sort of irreconcilable tension when one or both of the friends are in a committed relationship with another person."

"No, what I'm suggesting is that emotional intimacy is perhaps inevitable with these kinds of relationships."

"And I'll grant you emotional intimacy is a *sine qua non* when it comes to platonic friendships of any kind. I'll even grant you that when you throw a man and woman into the mix, a lot of those friendships will evolve into something more."

"And you see your relationship with Lana as not involving something more."

"Right."

Barbara made a note on a legal pad. "What would Jill have to say about that?"

"A lot. And she did…say a lot. Many times. Really, I thought transparency about Lana would put Jill at ease. It seemed to do the opposite."

"You are genuinely surprised about that."

"Yes. I truly believe I kept it platonic. That *we* did: Lana and I. The only romance was between me and Jill," he stated, looking to Barbara for validation.

She did not look up during what became a long pause, instead making additional notes.

"I don't know," Tom continued. "Perhaps we're getting into semantics, Doc. What is romance? And why do we need to categorize or try to put 'Lana and Tom' into some box and then draw conclusions once we feel the satisfaction of having created the box and then having put them into it?"

"Tell you what: Let's look at it from Jill's perspective."

"Sure."

"She's been with you almost three years, and now she's pregnant. She's really vulnerable now, Tom. Her security was threatened all along by 'Lana and Tom,' no matter how one may characterize or describe that relationship. Let's assume your relationship was platonic. There was no guarantee it would stay that way. Something could have happened to change the dynamic, and not just for Jill, but also her child—your child, too, Tom. In Jill's eyes, all along you were playing with fire."

"Barbara, if something were going to happen between Lana and me—"

"—it would have happened already, yes yes. And past results don't guarantee future ones."

Tom sat up in the chair and turned to face Barbara.

"Nothing did happen. Anyway, she's leaving Chicago anyway, and I haven't heard from her since that ill-fated Austrian road trip."

Barbara nodded her head and made another note. The sound of traffic on Washington Avenue and a crackle of thunder interrupted another long pause.

"Have you tried to contact her since then?"

"No," Tom replied, looking at the floor for several seconds.

"What about Jill?"

"What about her?"

"Have you reached out to her?"

"Yes, several times. I'm getting the silent treatment. She's upset—I get it."

"How far along is she with the pregnancy?"

"I'm guessing about four months now. Say, Doc…I appreciate your concern, but can we get back to whether I'm fit to return to duty?"

"You were fit the first time you walked into my office."

"No wonder you've been enjoying yourself so much when I've been here! For once you get to deal with a 'normal' person."

"Normal or not, hopefully by now you see that what happened at your trial and what happened with Lana and Jill has caused a lot of confusion and trauma, not just with them but with some of your partners and others who work with you or know you fairly well."

"I understand. And like Roger said, I do need to care 'just enough' about what other people think."

"Right. You have the capacity to be empathetic, Tom. Use that empathy to help understand what it's like for them."

"I can do that, and can be more sensitive to that, and can even compromise on things—like I've always been willing to do—but if I believe in something strongly, I'm not going to give up on it if it costs me my integrity."

"Meaning what?"

"Meaning who I am."

Dr. Peargreen made a few more notes on her legal pad, circling the word "integrity."

"But on occasion, you may have to make a costly choice. Also, who you are isn't fixed, is it?"

Tom placed a thumb under his chin, carefully contemplating the question. "I suppose not. My personality has changed; we've discussed that a lot during these sessions. I'm not saying I'm not willing to change."

"So what is Tom saying? What does Tom want? What is Tom willing to do?"

"I guess it's like this, Doctor: When it comes to change, it's going to happen on my time, and in my way. I will choose when, where, and how. Now, don't get me wrong: I'm going to be sensitive about it; I'm going to consider other people's perspectives. But in the end, it's my decision."

"And what if the person you're dealing with takes the exact same approach?"

"If the other person takes the same approach, there will be mutual respect, self-respect, acceptance."

"Ideally, yes. In practice, maybe not so simple."

"Life's not simple. Embrace the complexity."

"Some people aren't comfortable with complexity. They prefer black and white."

"I agree; some do. You treat them with the same respect and sensitivity and try to understand their perspective. It doesn't mean you have to agree, though. You can offer to agree to disagree, and hopefully they accept your offer."

"What if they don't?"

"You accept that they don't."

Dr. Peargreen jotted down a few more notes, scribbling away with her left hand.

"One more question, Tom."

Tom stood up and walked toward the window sill, looking down at short-sleeved office workers crossing Sixth Street. Mid-September in St. Louis still felt mostly like summer, though some evenings could bring a slight chill.

"Shoot."

"Are you ready to go back to work?"

"I was ready the first time I walked into your office, Barbara. But I do appreciate our time together. You've made me think, which was needed. Hey, it could be a lot worse…unlike Lana's mom, I'm not being committed or thrown in jail or anything. Other than my recent few hours in the Cook County klink. So I think I can handle two more meetings with *you*."

Dr. Peargreen stopped writing and looked straight ahead for a moment.

"Lana's mom…what happened to her?" she asked.

"She was a paranoid schizophrenic. It got to a point where she was emotionally abusing Lana. When Lana was in eighth grade, she locked herself in a room when her mom was chasing her around the house."

"Then what happened?"

"Lana called the cops on her. They came and took her mom away. A judge eventually stripped her of her parental rights, and the grandparents got custody."

"What about the father?"

"Lana didn't have a father—at least, not then."

Barbara again looked at the wall straight across from her desk.

"Wait a minute…what is Lana's mother's name?"

"Nancy. Nancy Truong, I believe. Why do you ask?"

Debating what to say in response, Barbara reached behind her desk and opened the bottom drawer of a file cabinet. She scanned the labels of at least two dozen folders, then settled her eyes upon one in particular. Grabbing it, she turned around and placed it on her desk without opening it.

Again she debated what to say.

"She was my patient."

* * *

A few minutes' drive away, Lana took in the warm September day. The light passed widely and freely through the windows of St. Louis Attitude, an eccentric's paradise full of original if occasionally kitschy mementos and souvenirs. It was a business, yes, but also an anchor and perhaps even a landmark in this particular quarter of South City.

At the front desk were identical twins Ray and Jeremy Branch, proprietors. At thirty-five, they looked at least a few years older—mostly a function of male pattern baldness—but had the heart of teenagers and the spirit of preschoolers, in every good (and bad) way.

Ray spotted a familiar shape approaching from the corner of an eye, and instantly sprang to sensory attention. Her walking pattern, a combination of bouncy verve and model-like poise, garnered one thing: notice. And to the amazement of many—man and woman alike—Lana could do it in understated, no-brand attire that tended to hide more than show.

"Liking the flannel today, Ray," she announced, opening her arms for him as he embraced her like a child would his mother, even resting his head for a moment on her shoulder. And just like that she pulled away, leaving her quarry breathless and unsated.

"*God* you look gorgeous," he proclaimed, as a couple nearby raised their eyebrows at the public display of affection. *Definitely out-of-towners,* he thought. "How are you, Babe?"

"You always call me that," she replied.

"But you are. And all mine. Mmmm, I love how that sounds. And soon you'll be living here! How's the apartment hunting going?"

"The only one I belong to is myself. I like you Ray, but—"

As he raised a hand to cut her off, she moved the appendage aside and continued. "No really, we've talked about this."

Sensing a brief stare or two, he lowered his voice and approached her ear. "Sorry, but after I've made love to someone I—"

Now it was Lana's turn to raise one hand, and her voice. "We *fucked* a couple times, Ray. It's called friends with benefits." Actually, it had been more like mercy sex, to get him to stop talking about his ex-wife and all the drama that went along with his divorce and trying to raise a nine-year-old.

Upon overhearing Lana's F-bomb, the nearby couple vanished from the shop, lost to Ray and Jeremy as customers. As the front door was closing, one could overhear the woman muttering something about millennials and asking her husband why they "were even in this part of town to begin with." The proprietors and Lana wondered the same thing.

"Screw them," Jeremy said.

"Yeah, we don't need their Gold Coast money," Ray added. "Go back to Chicago and root for the Cubs!" he yelled, not loudly enough for the former customers to hear outside but certainly at a sufficient volume for folks still shopping to pick up.

"Hey, high-five," Lana offered. The brothers speedily slapped her palm in succession.

"So how was Vienna?" Ray asked her, firing up a small coffee-maker and grabbing some locally branded coffee beans from a small nook behind the front desk.

"Started well, ended kind of crappy. The Summer Palace was cool, and I liked how easy it was to get around the city. My Airbnb host freaked out about his furniture getting a drop of water on it. Other stuff happened that I'd rather forget about."

"Too bad I couldn't be there with you. Did you hook up with any locals or guy-friends while you were taking it all in?"

She pushed him in the chest. "Jealous much? You always ask me things like that. No," she lied. "I didn't see and definitely didn't stay with anyone I knew—or anyone new—during the like forty-eight hours I was there."

"Easy, Babe. Just teasing," he asserted, as his voice and tone rose to match hers.

Lana paused a few seconds, lowering the tension in the room. "Can we talk about something else? How's business?"

Ray gazed at the orange molding atop the front door. He struggled to conceal a dead-giveaway pout.

31

The E-Mail

Lana finished reading the e-mail, then read it again. She was clear on what she thought, but not sure how she felt.

Lana,

I wanted to discuss my thoughts with you in person or at least on the phone, but wasn't able to reach you. I don't want to put it off any longer.

Our relationship has never been well-defined. There's been some avoiding of labels, I know. To some degree that was fine, because we didn't care and it didn't matter (at least to us) what impression we gave other people. I liked that about us. At the same time, recent events have made me understand that this ambiguity has made it difficult to be clearly committed to a relationship that should be important to me.

I value our friendship and care for you greatly, but I simply have to accept that our friendship cannot continue.

There are some things I need to tell you, not so much to get them off my chest but truly to help you in relationships going forward. These are some difficult thoughts to share, but they've been on my mind for the past few months, and more so recently.

I don't see much value in rehashing a bunch of old topics we've talked circles around. I know now that the only thing important to you…is you.

Though I enjoyed the time we spent together, I struggled with the lack of affection, communication, intimacy, and, above all, commitment. Lana, when I think of the things that are important in your life right now, I realize I'm a sidenote. A healthy relationship would have overlap and would see things from the perspective of "us" rather than the perspective of you, or what's best for you.

Thinking of what is best for you, I just do not find myself enduring the expectation of an "us." We are really on separate pages there.

I no longer want to hope for an "us." It's not healthy for me. In fact, it's toxic. The level of interest and effort isn't mutual. I refuse to continue ignoring the weight of my own misplaced expectations. The fact is that a year after you broke up with me, our interactions are still as lopsided as ever.

It's time I put some proper focus back on my own needs.

Best Wishes,

Rudy

The second reading was harder than the first, as the meaning of his words truly began to register. Tears flowed freely and fell weightily, creating puddles on several keys in front of her laptop screen.

She and Rudy had known each other almost since her arrival at UIC. She'd rarely been out of touch with him for more than a week or so. Now she might never see or talk with him again.

His reasoning was, well, reasonable. Though she believed she'd made her intentions clear, she knew he wanted something more. But she couldn't change his desires. She accepted him as he was. Now, and perhaps truly for the first time since meeting her, he was conscious of his own needs. She understood that he wanted to reclaim his space. With this realization, she felt a loss. She didn't like the feeling.

But Rudy was right: So much was going on right now. She could use some focus. Maybe he was doing her a favor.

She would be going to Europe again a couple of weeks after graduation, and this time for almost a month. She needed time to plan for the trip, and to prepare herself mentally and emotionally for a reunion with her father, who wanted to try to patch things up with her.

Duygu was a lot more than Lana had bargained for. But then how could any adult really set any expectations when meeting a parent for the first time, as she had back in August?

Truthfully, he was like her in many ways; she knew the similarities caused tension. They both sought control. A key difference, though, was that Lana simply wanted control of herself.

Duygu, however, wanted to make decisions to control others. He also felt a strong need to show his masculinity. Lana was not the kind of woman he was accustomed to dealing with—far from it.

Lana was not afraid to assert her freedom. Back in August, before the salad incident, she'd insisted upon going into Prague on her own to spend time with people her own age. In response, Duygu blew a gasket, unable to comprehend how someone he'd waited twenty-two years to meet would want to do anything other than maximize her time with him. His dramatic, over-the-top response (complete with thrown objects directed at walls or countertops or even ceilings) had nearly caused Lana to go home earlier than she eventually did. She'd stopped herself from leaving, though—at least that time.

Soon she would be returning to him, despite the arguments in Prague and her early, forced departure. She could not stand the thought of doing what her mother had done to him twenty-two years earlier: leaving and abandoning him. She would be better than her mother. Lana's choice would be different. Lana would control the circumstances this time, while being selfless—or at least something other than self-centered.

She looked at the laptop screen again. Intuitively, she knew what Rudy was doing. After all, she'd been doing it for years: putting herself first, becoming self-centered and feeling good about it, treating selfishness almost as a virtue.

She had no regrets, and believed she was a better person than the one she had been as recently as high school. And she wouldn't have wished what had happened to her as a child, teenager, and young adult—those circumstances—upon anyone else.

Circumstances had forced her to make important decisions for herself earlier in life, and over time those decisions made her powerful. The social influence, the magnetism—those were all functions of having transcended her circumstances.

And yet, she needed balance. Rudy was right: Her self-centeredness could make her relationships with others lopsided. Having everything, or at least most things, on her terms felt good. But how did it make others feel? That was a question she rarely considered.

She didn't want to push others away. She wanted to remain close to those she cared about.

One thing was for sure: There would be no easy solutions. She would start by working on her relationship with her father. She wouldn't give up. She would try to understand him better, even if he didn't seem to be trying to understand her.

Things with her father were lopsided, and not in her favor. But she would accept that fact, at least for now.

She felt her phone vibrate and looked at its screen.

"Hi, how are you, Lana?"

"I'm fine. How are you?"

"I miss you."

Lana smiled and thought about how to respond.

"I am looking forward to seeing you at the end of December."

"Good. And maybe I can show you Turkey also. We could see Istanbul."

"That would be great. I think I would enjoy it."

"You will, I know this."

"You are probably right."

"I am right."

Lana smiled again. *My father's a little bit too much like me sometimes,* she thought.

32

Ones That Give

Accompanied by a desktop computer and occupying less than fifty square feet of space in a world of cubicles, Jill cried silently, knowing the machine wouldn't mind. Her computer screen, lifeless and spent, ignored the alternating current that attempted to power it.

Parth, her neighbor at Chicago's Department of Innovation and Technology, was anything but silent.

"What was the mutual fund's performance last year? We have been putting in money for the last ten years! I expect the amount to be more than what I see on the statement," he explained to someone on the phone.

About a minute later, he declared, "No, I can't come in tomorrow. My daughter just delivered a baby. My wife and I are leaving tonight to visit. I'll call you next week after I'm back to Chicago. I want to go over the *whole* portfolio."

Parth's allusion to his new grandchild touched a nerve for Jill. She wondered what she would do without a commitment from Tom concerning times ahead. At that same moment she felt a life growing inside her. If born, the life would become her foremost concern. The child could consume her, demanding a level of attention impossible to satisfy absent a father.

She was aware of the impact any future absence—Tom's absence—would have in the child's life. Who would or should bear the blame for any such absence? Jill, for bringing the new life into the world? Tom, for his betrayal in refusing to respond to her ultimatum back in Vienna? Both of them, for their stubbornness?

Undoubtedly, the child would resemble Tom in some way, becoming a daily reminder of his absence. Should she have an abortion and start all over again? Regardless of what she might do in the future, she promised herself to marry first the next time around—if there were a next time around.

For now, she just needed to try to get through this "time around." At least she had a job that could support her and a baby. Resolving to focus on programming and take her mind off the future, at least for now, she reached for her phone, turned on some music, and put on her headphones.

She submerged herself in a world of logic based on zeros and ones, endeavoring to forget her pain. In the digital world, if something went wrong, she could tap development tools to identify any problems with the program, and then fix it and run it again. She could take satisfaction in watching a program run flawlessly based on what she, as the programmer, told it to do.

She wished the non-digital world could be as logical and turn out the way she wanted it to function. She knew, however, and tried to accept that some things can be fixed while others can't.

Unable to focus on her work for more than a few minutes at a time, Jill thought again of boarding the plane back to Chicago over two months ago and flying home without Tom. Her emotions were raw then; she recalled how tears had streamed uncontrollably down her cheeks.

Now, as she cried softly and thought about her situation, she resolved to focus on the future rather than the past. She pushed her laptop away from her, opened a spiral-bound journal, and took a pen in her right hand to start a new entry:

People don't appreciate having everything, or nearly everything. They want something they can't have, and don't even know what they want.

Skillful people play hard-to-get with multiple pursuers. The harder someone is to get, the more her pursuers want her. Meanwhile, the ones that give their whole hearts get heartbroken in return.

Learn the game, play it with a cold heart, and you won't get hurt. Suffering makes you harder; the more you suffer, the less sympathy you have for others. Don't believe that happiness lasts. Just live in the moment, having a great time in exotic places with people who offer moments of excitement, without promises or expectations concerning the future.

If others have true love and true happiness, think nothing of destroying such feelings. Take and feel no blame, for who is to blame? After all, life is not fair. We are merely along for the ride, making the most of our journey, seizing the good times we can get today, not knowing where tomorrow will take us and who we will be with next.

Our natural instinct is to support and boost our ego, our existence. But who have we become? Is it who we want to become? Is the self-made image real?

What are our values and beliefs? What do we want? Such things are shaped by our experiences and those we connect with. Such things reflect our view of the world. They reflect who and what we hold close to our hearts. Such things, such people drive our behavior, our response to the world.

We can be young at heart, but do we really want to do what the youthful do? To get confused about relationships that they can throw away, starting new ones easily?

I know the energy of youth is attractive. The unattached free spirit rubs off on people, encouraging us to let go of who and what we are. Do we really want to do what they do, figuring things out as they go? The most daring of them often have nothing to lose: no jobs, no family, no responsibilities. They can live anywhere in the world. They can live here for a few months, and then across the country or even somewhere else on the planet for another few months. They want to make friends around the world. They want to "find out who they are."

Let them. There is no anchor, no commitment. Do we really envy their lifestyle? Do we really want to lose what we have and become them?

Life is hard. Work can be hard. Can we ever appreciate what we have and make the best of it? Some say and feel that because life is not fair, we need to do what is best for ourselves, and only for ourselves. Is that what we want to become? Will it serve us well?

What we have is not perfect. Do we really want to damage it, throw it away, and start anew? Are we sure the new thing will be better and will last? Do we have the mental agility to cycle through relationships in this way?

As for me, I know who and what I want.

"Ready for a new monitor?"

A short, inconspicuous young man held a slim cardboard box in both hands and stood at the entrance to Jill's cubicle.

Still distraught, she reminded herself to be strong again, for not only herself but also the new life inside her. She removed her headphones and turned off the music that was still playing through her phone. Noticing the time while pressing the phone's power button, she realized two hours had passed.

"I'm ready," she said, standing up and reaching for a sealed business envelope that was addressed, stamped, and about to be dropped into the mail bin on her floor. Inside the envelope was a smaller one, still unopened: the way it would be returned to Tom.

* * *

Rudy popped open his laptop, eager to take another stab at fixing some code for stage two of Cross-Doku-Crush. Some subroutines were still preventing it from functioning well enough to demo it again for the investor he'd met with a few months ago.

After several minutes, he was gaining good momentum. And he needed it; the demo was just two days away.

Just then a notification popped up in the bottom-right of his screen. It was an e-mail from Jill. He clicked on the notification box before it faded away.

Hey Rudy, hope you are well. Things are good here. The baby is coming along fine. Thanks again for your being there for me at the last doctor visit. You're a good man, and deserve someone who can be there for you as well.

Tom has been trying to contact me, but I'm done chasing him, and I'm not going to tell him things he should already know.

I did talk with his friend Roger the other day, who I happened to run into during lunch in the West Loop. Interestingly, he said Tom and Lana haven't seen each other since he left Austria. Apparently she said or did something that really pissed him off. Roger said they may be ghosting each other. Actually, I was kind of surprised Roger knew what ghosting meant.

Well, good luck with phase two and the next demo. I'm sure you'll kill it.

Jill

P.S. I hope the code I sent you was helpful. Happy to help more.

33

Pats on the Back

Docked and secured to his desk by a steel umbilical cord, Tom's laptop displayed nearly seventy e-mails, all received after yesterday's lunch with Richard Michaels, head of Cavo Braun's appellate team.

Three of the newest e-mails were from Richard, who had a knack for reaching out and readily finding Tom during the lunch hour, as he'd managed to do yet again. A fellow perfectionist, Tom was less the taskmaster now than in younger years. Richard obviously had not changed in this regard, though that fact was one of many personality ticks Tom liked about his friend (with some irony perhaps).

Richard had the deep, nasally voice of Elliott Gould and at one time the looks to match, perhaps channeling Trapper John from the film version of *M*A*S*H*. While in St. Louis earlier in the week on client visits before heading back to Chicago, Tom was sure to include a stop for sushi with Richard. The quarterback on a team of several attorneys defending multiple putative class actions, Richard provided the steady and determined leadership needed to protect the interests of a prominent client whose business model depended on its attorneys' ability to defeat what was a frontal legal assault.

Tom appreciated the connection and mutual respect he had with his colleague, who treated him as an equal and essentially as co-counsel, even though Tom and his firm were in the role of local counsel for Cavo Braun. Indeed, after Tom assisted in getting at first one and soon thereafter a second case transferred from the US District Court for the Northern District of Illinois to the Eastern District of Missouri, Richard lobbied the client to have Tom remain in both cases—in Cavo Braun's own backyard. Tom could think of very few equally meaningful signs of appreciation.

Pressing "Reply All" to Richard's most recent e-mail, thus roping in the other three members of the Cavo Braun team, Tom began to write a response but stopped after typing just a few words.

He leaned back in his tall leather office chair and surveyed the confines of his Chicago office. The place was within his customary domain; his exile had ended.

Since pulling into the firm's parking garage earlier that blustery December morning, he'd received at least a dozen hearty welcomes from colleagues: enthusiastic waves from inside a car or two, pats on the back while walking to the lobby, grasps of the shoulder from people entering or leaving the elevator, and brief visits to his office.

Another visitor was a few steps away.

"Hey, guy," the visitor said.

"Roger! Thanks for dropping by," Tom replied, immediately standing and extending a hand.

Roger gave a firmer-than-usual handshake. "Great to have you back, Tom."

"Great to *be*!"

"Looks like you haven't missed a beat. Most of the real estate on your desk already has no vacancies."

"You're assuming I left it empty before going to St. Louis."

"Ah."

"And actually, I did," Tom said, returning to his chair.

"So what's your excuse then? Not that being visibly occupied is necessarily a *bad* thing."

"It's what you make of it, Roger."

"And what does Tom make of it?"

"The most I can, for the clients *and* for me."

Roger nodded his head and crossed his arms. "Explain."

"I function best when busy, with occasional bursts of surprise and deadline-driven puzzles thrown into the mix."

"Being busy can be good, yes."

"Broken up by healthy distractions, of course. Emphasis on healthy. It's why we take vacations, right?"

"How often? At least for you, anyway?" Roger asked.

"About once every three months seems to work best for me. And you have to prepare yourself to unplug before actually unplugging—and then commit to it, as much as you can."

"What if something comes up all the sudden and you can't prepare yourself?"

"Like my trip to Vienna back in August?"

Tom looked past Roger at the small bookshelf against the opposite wall. On top of the bookshelf was a shrine of sorts, comprised, among other things, of souvenirs and other reminders of previous trips and vacations. Tom fixed his eyes on a cream-colored, untorn admission ticket lodged beneath an empty Czech beer bottle. The bottle was harbored atop a book of illustrations entitled *Auf der Couch*, a gift from Dr. Peargreen. She'd acquired it during a visit to Vienna's Sigmund Freud Museum much earlier in the year.

"I wasn't thinking of that in particular, but OK."

"That was spur-of-the-moment, impulsive," Tom said. "A distraction, for sure, and something that maybe started healthy but definitely ended up unhealthy."

Roger uncrossed his arms, formed an uneasy grin, and turned toward one of the windows in Tom's office. "Yeah, you went from having one woman who adored you and another who respected you to—"

"Don't remind me, Roger," Tom replied, mirroring the expression on Roger's face.

"Sorry, guy," Roger said, walking toward Tom and extending a hand. "Something will work out."

Accepting Roger's right hand for a closing handshake, Tom briefly cupped another hand on Roger's shoulder and removed it. Roger gave a wink and began to walk away.

"*Something*, yes," Tom acknowledged. "As for what that will *be*—"

At the threshold of the door, Roger turned around and interjected, "—what that will be is what Tom makes of it. Hang in there, my friend."

After a pause, during which Roger reached the corner of a short hallway, Tom called out, "Thanks. I intend to!"

From around the corner, Roger yelled back over his shoulder, "Good! We need you."

34

Commencement

The gymnasium had everything one would expect: hung banners proclaiming historic sports victories, the hum of dozens of lamps overhead, bleachers full of family members and friends, and a buffed basketball court full of hundreds of men and women clad in blue. Appearing atop a few mortarboards in various colors were Greek letters, heartfelt messages, earnest appeals, or weighty questions such as "Now What?" or "Thanks to My Fam" or "I Need a Job." Most of the soon-to-be graduates wore black shoes, though some preferred sneakers, heels, or even boots in distinctive (or at least different) colors.

From her seat somewhere toward the front of the assembled host of students, Lana turned to her left and right, trying to find any audience members she could recognize. She'd invited her aunt and uncle—Nancy's siblings—along with a foster mother and three other people who'd figured in some way in her life. The university had allotted each student only six tickets; at that moment, Lana wasn't sure if any of them would be used.

* * *

Sitting alone somewhere, Tom Edwards held one of the cream-colored tickets. He, too, was looking to his left and right, but not for

Lana—or for anyone else in particular. *What am I doing here?* he wanted desperately to know. The ticket had unexpectedly arrived in the mail a week earlier, along with a handwritten note:

Dear Tom,

I hope you will come to my graduation. I'd like you to meet my Uncle Charles and my Aunt Vanessa. You and Vanessa would get along well, I'm sure. We'll probably grab something to eat afterward, and it would be great if you'd join us.

I debated whether to reach out to you. It's been over three months. Maybe you're depressed, and if so I respect that. This isn't the first time we've had radio silence for several months. Maybe you're still upset at the way things blew up in Austria.

Maybe you don't want to have anything to do with me—I don't know. Believe me, I would like to know, but if you need space to figure things out, I'll continue to give it to you.

But I don't feel like I have to be the one to try to sustain something. It's a two-way street. I suppose in this game of chicken, I pulled off the road first.

Anyway, this is me, reaching my arms out again. Decide what you want to do. Just don't expect me to reach out again like this.

Really hope to see you,

Lana

Tom crumpled the ticket, looked down at his shoes, and continued to ruminate on the last several months.

* * *

Somewhere else in the gym, Rudy Santana had a ticket in his left pocket. That ticket, too, had arrived in the mail with a handwritten note, and, like Tom, Rudy was surprised to receive the invitation:

Rudy,

You know I'm not big on receiving gifts, but having you at my graduation would be one of the best gifts you could ever give. You probably think I don't deserve such a gift, or anything, from you. But no matter how you feel now, you know you made such a difference in my life at UIC. And I know I made a difference in yours. Come be with me at our old stomping grounds.

Uncle Charles and Aunt Vanessa should be there, and I'm sure would be happy to see you again. You can have lunch with us and then be on your way. It's all I ask.

Really hope to see you,

Lana

Typical Lana, he'd thought after first reading the letter.

* * *

In yet another location, Jill Nguyen sat with a notebook computer on her lap and worked on a subroutine that required a few more lines of code to enable a program to function more efficiently.

She placed a hand over her belly. She'd begun to show a bump, which today was covered with a sleek black dress that accented her ample curves, including this latest one. She felt good—and that she deserved to. Her destiny was in her hands, the way it should be. Beside her was her journal, in which she'd written numerous entries in recent months. It was her therapy and had given her strength and courage she would continue to need.

Most of all, writing—along with the passage of time—had helped Jill see that the desperate woman she'd been on Tom's front porch, throwing lamps and man-toys around in the pounding rain, or in Vienna confronting another man-toy, was not who she wanted to be.

* * *

"Lana Marie Delacroix!" announced the charismatic dean of the business school.

On the massive screen mounted high on the wall behind the stage full of administrators and faculty was the image of a young woman who'd just stood and begun walking toward the middle aisle. She no longer looked to her left or right, but only straight ahead.

She quickly reached and ascended a short staircase, turned to her left, and stepped toward center stage to accept a metal cylinder in her left hand and the dean's hand in her right. She released his hand, turned again to her left for the obligatory photograph, then extended both arms skyward and launched herself into the air. The sprightly leap revealed her long legs and silky white high-hemmed dress, and sent skyward her mortarboard and a gold honor cord signifying highest praise—*summa cum laude*.

Several faculty members noticeably frowned. The dean reacted differently, giving her a thumbs-up as she retrieved her mortarboard and jogged away toward another set of stairs.

For a split-second, as the photographer's shutter rapidly opened and closed, she didn't care who was in the audience, or wasn't. She had something no one could take away from her.

* * *

A half hour later, a cluster of audience members congregated in a large grassy area outside the gymnasium. The majority of them looked intently at smartphones, texting or reading texts from graduates who'd begun exiting the building.

Many of the technology-free grandparents and great-grandparents looked around bewildered, recalling an earlier time not that long ago when people could manage to find each other in crowds or public places without the aid of cellphones or a global positioning system.

For mid-December, the weather was quite unusual. A light breeze off Lake Michigan, a clear sky, and a temperature approaching seventy amazed everyone present.

Two people now recognized each other, though not without some difficulty at first. They quickly closed the distance between them, meeting somewhere in the middle of the horde.

"You made it!"

"Not sure what I'm doing here."

"That's OK. You won't regret it—I promise. Now don't say anything more. I need to find a few more people. Do you mind?"

"No, go ahead. I've got some e-mails to catch up on."

Within the next ten minutes, four more people approached the *ad hoc* meeting place, all led there by the same person. Confused looks met the glowing smile of the ringleader, while the sixth person (who had been there first) continued to catch up on e-mail.

Almost simultaneously, someone in the group asked the person checking e-mail, "What are *you* doing here?"

Charles briefly spied his watch and stared at the sky for several seconds. Vanessa showed a slight grin but said nothing, looking down and lightly kicking at the grass beneath her.

Finally, the person checking e-mail looked up and calmly asked, "Yeah, what's going on here?"

Stepping into the middle of the group, still smiling, was the ring-leader, Rudy. He stretched out each arm to hold everyone in place, then dropped his head for a moment. He was either gathering his thoughts, protecting himself from attack, or keeping some of those assembled from attacking each other—perhaps all of the above.

"OK, OK. Now the *reason* I've brought you all together—"

"Wait. Who invited *her*?" asked Lana, pointing at Jill. Lana began to pace inside the hastily assembled circle. "I gave *you* a ticket," she said, placing a finger on Charles' chest, "*you* a ticket," touching Vanessa's shoulder, "*you* a ticket," punching at Tom's shoulder (and missing, possibly on purpose), "and *you* a ticket," punching at Rudy's chest—and connecting. "Obviously a big mistake by me, Rudy."

Jill said nothing. Vanessa raised an eyebrow and watched with curiosity. Charles looked at his watch again. Tom crossed his arms and turned away for a moment, mimicking the slight grin Vanessa had shown earlier. He then looked at Jill and her baby bump, and his grin soon became a beaming smile.

"Lana, step back and hear me out," Rudy replied, extending one arm in her direction and another in Jill's.

Lana's breathing was elevated; her stare into Rudy's eyes was deadly. Rudy dropped the arm pointed in Jill's direction but kept the other in place, trying to keep things under control. Lana looked around the circle and caught the eye of Vanessa, who gave her an encouraging, calming nod. Very reluctantly, Lana stepped back. She didn't like not being in control, and particularly didn't like being ignorant of what was happening, or why.

"OK. Let's start with this: Jill, nice to see you again. Of course you know Lana," he said, gesturing in her direction, "and I'd like you to meet her Uncle Charles and Aunt Vanessa. We'll dispense with the customary handshakes at this time."

Hands on her hips, Lana looked down and kicked at the grass a couple of times.

"Uncle Charles and Aunt Vanessa, of course you know me and your niece. Tom Edwards here is a lawyer who has become a friend of Lana's over the last year. Jill Nguyen, over there, has been Tom's girlfriend for almost three years. To avoid upsetting anyone, I won't try to characterize the geometry of this particular triangle."

"Smart move," said Lana.

"Yes," added Tom.

"Correction: *had* been," said Jill.

"Is anyone hungry?" asked Charles.

"I could do lunch. Does anyone have any ideas on venue?" asked his sister Vanessa.

No one responded.

After a few additional awkward moments passed, Jill said, "Rudy, doesn't it seem more like a square rather than a triangle?"

Rudy smirked and responded, "Fair enough."

Lana placed her hands on her hips and cocked her head at least thirty degrees to the right, her green eyes piercing like laser beams into Rudy's skull.

"Now, I have some things I want to say," Rudy announced. "This is for the good of everyone, except Vanessa and Charles. You're here to encourage civility."

"Wow, you thought of everything, Rudy," Lana sneered.

"You'll get your turn, Lana."

"*My* turn? I'm not really sure what's going on here but I know one thing: This is my graduation and I don't appreciate you hijacking it, Rudy. But let's get on with it, I suppose. I must say I'm astonished at your boldness—"

"Thank you." He turned to face Jill. "So, I'm going to start with you."

Jill had been watching Lana's and Tom's faces and was clearly enjoying herself. Like Lana, Jill had no idea what was happening, but that fact had a much different effect on her. Tom seemed to have no idea either, and appeared to be very curious about the proceedings.

"Thank you, Jill, for accepting my invitation," said Rudy.

"So you invited *her* without asking me," Lana realized. "What gives you the right—"

"I actually invited her to this spot, where we are standing now. Not to your graduation. Stop interrupting."

"I'm not *trying* to be rude, but this is *my* moment," Lana snapped, looking from face to face. "Not yours," she added, staring at Rudy.

"As I was saying…Jill, you surely didn't have to agree to be here today. So thanks again. I'll come back to you later."

"You're welcome," Jill replied, offering him a genuine smile.

"Tom, you're next. You see that woman over there?"

Rudy saw where Tom looked and said, "No, not that one."

Tom turned his head away from Vanessa and fixed his eyes on another person in the group.

"Not her either, Tom."

Moving his eyes from Lana to Jill, Tom crossed his arms again and grinned.

"Don't play dumb," Jill said.

"Tom, that woman over there loves you. As I've gotten to know her over the last few months, I'm come to see how much that is true. She came here because I told her someone important in her life would be here."

"That would be *me*?" Tom asked.

"*Was* you," Jill replied.

"Jill, please," said Rudy.

"Oh, alright. It's just the whole playing dumb thing—"

"Jill?"

She smirked and became quiet.

"Tom, now take a look at that woman over there," Rudy instructed. Two seconds later, he had to add, "No, the younger one, Tom. Sorry, Vanessa."

"It's OK, Rudy. I'm comfortable in this skin of mine," Vanessa said.

"Tom, I love that woman over there. And I know you once cared about her too. But, as I'm sure you figured out during your European adventure, she's not the one you want; the other one is," he said, pointing at Jill. "Tom, the choice is clear: Ask Jill to take you back, while you still can. Hopefully she'll hear you out."

Tom looked at Jill, hoping for some kind of reaction to Rudy's statement. She remained focused on Rudy, however, as he then turned to face Lana.

"Lana—"

"*Here* we go," she responded, removing hands from hips and leaning back as she crossed her arms. "*This* should be good."

"Lana, you see this man standing in front of you and looking at you right now?"

"*Are* you standing?"

"Ha. Well, you heard me say it to Tom: I love you. You've heard me say it to you before. And I'm going to say something now that you've never said for yourself: You love me too."

"*Do* I now? *Someone's* having a great day."

"And we're not talking about loving *knowing* me. The fact is you're in love with me and just can't get yourself to admit it. It's obvious, yet you deny it."

Rudy paused. Everyone in the circle was listening intently.

"I know you better than you know yourself sometimes, and no one else is going to put up with your crap the way I can. I know you can see it, and there's a part of you that wants someone you can hold onto. But you're afraid of holding on too tight—afraid of losing another person close to you."

For a moment, Lana looked as though she wanted to interject something. But she remained quiet and kept looking at Rudy, waiting to hear more.

"You know, Lana, you like to pride yourself on how logical and rational you are. How *you're* going to pick the time, and *you're* going to pick the place, and the way, and the man. Well *I'm* that man, *this* is the time and the place, and *you* need to finally let go and let *me* show you the way to your own heart."

"Did you rehearse that line? What makes you—"

But before Lana could deliver another line of her own, Rudy approached her with the intention to seal with a kiss whatever deal he'd envisioned.

At that moment, something inside Lana swelled; she felt a desperate desire to retake command and thrust her hand in front of her before Rudy could come any closer.

"Rudy, I care about you in my own way, but this *isn't* the place and now's *not* the time I want to talk about it with you. I'm actually meeting someone," she said, pointing to a young man in a stylish suit who had been standing on the periphery.

Rudy waved his hand dismissively.

"Is there a problem here?" the young man asked. The question was more out of curiosity and did not sound like a challenge.

"Yes, there is!" Lana exclaimed. "This has turned into the graduation from *hell*. I can't *believe* you people!"

"Scott! What are you doing here?" Tom asked, extending a hand toward his mentee, who was carrying a laptop bag over one shoulder.

"I *was* meeting up with Lana," Scott noted, shaking Tom's hand.

"Not for like another hour though…unless Rudy invited you here too!" Lana groused.

Grinning, Jill waved at Scott. "Hey neighbor!"

Tom turned toward Jill. "Wait—you know him too?"

"We live down the hall from each other, actually," Scott said.

"Oh, *perfect*!" Lana snarled.

"Listen, Lana…we can catch up next week," Scott said. "You're right, I'm early."

"That's OK, Scott. Please stay. The rest of us were *supposed* to be at lunch right now, but Rudy—"

"Actually, speaking of that, Lana," Vanessa said. "I think Charles and I will just meet you at the restaurant—"

"Wait, no. You can stay, Aunt Vanessa," Lana replied.

But Vanessa had already started walking away, with Charles just a pace or so behind her.

Then, noticing that Scott had left as well and was now already at the parking lot, Lana yelled, "Hey, Scott…don't go!"

Tom raised an eyebrow in Lana's direction then turned to face Jill. "OK, OK. Before this situation gets any further out of hand, Ms. Nguyen and I are going to take a little stroll."

Putting her hands on her hips, Lana took a step in Tom's direction and started to say something more, but stopped herself and looked down at the grass for a moment. She then slowly turned around and began walking away from the now-empty circle. When she looked up again, she saw Rudy in front of her, offering—then giving—the hug he knew she needed.

The spectacle had sparked something in Tom. Witnessing Rudy's audacity—irrespective of Lana's initial response—caused Tom to gain a newfound respect toward someone he'd never seen as a rival, and whose persistence in pursuing Lana he'd pitied.

But now, rather than pity, Tom felt inspired. He wouldn't have expected Rudy, of all people, to be the organizer and instigator of this spectacle. After all the complaints Tom had heard Lana make about Rudy—and about so many other men that were part of her life, including her father—Rudy had managed to summon from somewhere the gumption to go for broke with her while trying to prove her wrong about him.

Lana's response was to try to reassert control. *Typical Lana*, Tom thought. *Control might be what she wants, but it's certainly not what she needs.* He looked over to Jill, who had her own thoughts about the whole situation.

"Lana and your own mentee. Bet you didn't see that coming, did you, Tom?" Jill taunted, patting his shoulder like she might a small puppy.

"Frankly, my dear—"

"Don't say it," Jill interjected.

"What I was going to *say*," he continued, taking her hand in his, "is I'm *very* happy to see you."

"*Really* now?" she replied, looking skeptical as she released his hand and stepped away from him.

"Yes, really. I've been trying to contact you, and figured you'd respond…eventually. Walk with me a little bit?"

He stepped toward her and tentatively extended his right arm. She paused.

"Eventually, huh?" She looked at him then took his hand. It felt comfortable, familiar.

"Yes. I wanted to say I'm sorry for the way I treated you in Vienna."

He then escorted her away from the remaining crowd, whose size had dwindled as most graduates by then had left with their family members and friends.

They soon reached his car. Tom started to open the passenger door; she placed a hand on his chest.

"I've got my own ride, Tom."

"I don't plan on taking you home," he replied.

"Good. So we're on the same page for once."

"I have something else in mind," he continued, as he reached into the car.

Jill looked at her watch and then away from the sedan, observing various graduates and their entourages walking together on the sprawling campus.

"A peace offering," Tom announced, handing her a familiar-looking envelope. "I'd like a second chance, Jill. I didn't know when I'd see you again, and I'd been holding onto this for whenever I did."

A car's horn caused them both to look toward another part of the parking lot, where they spotted Lana and Rudy next to a sliver Miata with the top down. They were arguing with each other…in the way a couple would. Tom raised an eyebrow and nodded in Rudy's direction. He subtly nodded back.

Tom then returned his attention to Jill, who felt a kick in her belly, offered him a knowing smile, and took the envelope.

About the Author

Timothy C. Sansone

Tim is a St. Louis attorney blessed to count many women of courage, strength, dignity, intelligence, and independence as colleagues, friends, and family. These are women who reject expectations of who does what for whom, recognizing that life's unique opportunities and beauty can come in many forms and in unexpected ways. Some of these women have inspired his writing, and their unique voices sometimes echo in his protagonists' words and deeds.

As a lawyer who focuses on complex litigation, Tim regularly works on cases in which the stakes are high, the facts of the situation are nuanced, and both sides have dug in. Relationships often have the same characteristics, whether they involve work, family, or romance. Their success or failure rides on both logic and emotion, as well as how different personalities and life experiences intertwine or diverge. In the end, both cases and relationships are about people's stories. And Tim enjoys telling those stories to judges and juries in the "real world" as much as he enjoys creating those stories for his readers in the fiction he writes.

In particular, Tim has developed a unique passion for telling stories about worldly women—and the men they encounter and work with—who when cast together will aim to make the most (if not a mess) of it … and perhaps both. These are people of influence who have a knack for earning our respect while occasionally driving us crazy, in no particular order.

Tim credits his wife Sherrie, his son Charles, and his daughter Victoria for giving meaning and purpose to his life, as well as his parents, extended family, and friends. He accepts that forming deep relationships with others can be hard and risky, and appreciates how much they can make life worth living.

Through his storytelling and blogging, his support of the women in his life, and his advocacy for women's advancement in the professional workplace, Tim promotes women's success through their own agency. He enjoys writing stories about this kind of success to inspire readers of all generations to better understand the complex dynamics of relationships and give women both the space and support to achieve and grow.

For more information about Tim and his writing, visit timothycsansone.com

Suggested Questions
for Book Clubs

- When Jill writes at the end of her journal entry, "As for me, I know who and what I want," does she have someone and something specific in mind? If so, who and what?

- Lana has waited her whole life to meet the mysterious man who is her father. When she meets him, she finds the relationship frustrating. Is she more frustrated because of the ways she and her father are alike, or because of the ways they are different?

- Jill tries a number of tactics to convince Tom that the relationship he has with Lana is ill-conceived. What are the ways that she tries to convince him? Do any of them work? Do any of them make matters worse? Is Tom right to push back?

- The four main characters experience change in the novel, and (to a lesser or greater extent) growth. Reflecting on the words and deeds of Lana, Tom, Jill, and Rudy, who experiences the most growth and in what ways?

- Though Lana is described as asexual, she repeatedly comes on to and inevitably pushes men away. Why? Regardless, what reasons might Tom have to resist her advances? Is it reasonable (or credible) that he does? Is the dream sequence in which Tom consummates his relationship with Lana authentic? Explain your answer.

- Lana is portrayed as confident, assertive ... almost dangerous. Is this portrayal (or self-portrayal) the real Lana? If so, where does it come from? If not, what is she covering up or compensating for?

- Lana has many conversations with Rudy about their relationship. She is sometimes brutally honest with him in denying him what he wants, yet he rarely gives up. Is Lana being fair (or, at least upfront) in how she deals with Rudy?

- Early in the book, Jill and Tom discuss what makes a man "better." Does being married to a good woman make for a better man, or is being with a good woman enough?

- Both Tom and Lana have personal experience with mental illness: Tom with what appears to be a form of bipolar disorder, and Lana with her mother's paranoid schizophrenia. Is mental illness (to the extent it's shown or discussed) fairly and accurately depicted in the book? How have Tom's and Lana's experiences with mental illness directed their choices in their lives?

- Tom has unusual introductions to both Lana and Jill: Lana at the Southside Ballroom in Chicago, and Jill at the airport in St. Louis. Regarding the nature of these introductions, and the way they play out, do they reflect more of Tom's personality ... or Lana's and Jill's? How are the outcomes similar or different?

- Jill confronts Lana in Vienna upon finding Lana alone in Tom's room. After a heated argument, Jill collapses into tears. Why would she show this side of herself to Lana? Later that morning, was Tom right to feel cornered by Jill when she surprised him in the shower and disclosed her pregnancy? And later still, was Tom right to confront Lana during their ride through the Alps, and what were they really arguing about?

- Lana gets very angry with the truck driver who blocks her way into the senior community where her grandmother resides. Is there any symbolism in the scene that relates to (or reflects upon) her relationship with her grandmother? How is Lana different with her grandmother than she is with everyone else, and why?

- Tension builds throughout the book for Tom as he dives deeper into his relationship with Lana, even as he tries to maintain his relationship with Jill. What signs are there that he is not handling the situation as well as he perhaps could?

- After arriving at Tom's room in Vienna, Lana tells him he's taught her something: what it's like to "share someone." What does she mean, and what are your thoughts about that meaning (or concept)?